This is a Collection of previously released works:
Love For All Seasons
Medusa's Secret
Athena's Challenge
Web Of Lies

ISBN 979-8-9875917-1-0

Publication of Saray Books LLC - D.A. Henneman, Author
Book & Cover Design: Sumo Design
Editor: Alexa Nussio

Manufactured in the United States of America

GODDESSES *in* LOVE

GODDESSES
in LOVE
COLLECTION

D.A. HENNEMAN

To Rachel & Jarah

May you never grow too old to wish upon
the stars and follow your dreams.

Thank you for your support and love
while I did the same.

Love you more than you will ever know. XO

LOVE FOR ALL SEASONS

A STORY ABOUT HOW
PERSEPHONE AND HADES
REALLY MET...

1

On the Island of Crete where she made her home, Hecate, the Goddess of Witchcraft, tended her garden. There were countless things to prepare for the upcoming Samhain celebration, and she worried she wouldn't have time for them all. It was especially true since a number of her potions would require substitutions, and when she did mess with the ingredients, they weren't nearly as potent. While she had endless supplies of magick at her disposal, she didn't use it for her spells and ceremonies. There was something pleasing about doing things as the humans did, and she felt more connected to the earth because of it.

She spent most of her time on the island; it was the place she thought of as home. Lately though, it had been a great deal harder for her to do the things she once enjoyed. The seasons had stopped changing decades before, and her crops had been growing less potent ever since. She loved Demeter and her daughter, Persephone, but having everlasting spring was affecting more than her potions—it wasn't good for the planet as a whole. Nothing ever had a chance to properly rest and rejuvenate, even the humans she cared for. Her workload had increased because of it.

If things didn't correct themselves soon, she would have no other option but to take matters into her magical hands. That would be a last resort as stepping on godly toes always had consequences. If she dabbled with the seasons, Demeter would be impossible to live with.

As she pushed her hands into the soft soil, she pulled out a small tuber and felt the sides for rot. It seemed to be fine, but only by cutting into it later would she know for sure. She had barely enough rosemary from the prior season to complete the recipe, since her herbs had been spindly and almost unusable. If she didn't find a way for her rosemary plants to produce, she wasn't sure what she was going to use to signify remembrance in future celebrations. In her opinion, there wasn't an adequate substitute on the planet that would work for that.

"Impressive carrot."

A masculine voice laced with a playful tone interrupted her solitude. The visit from Hermes wasn't entirely unexpected, but it had been some time since he last came to chat. Perhaps her thoughts from the night before had prompted his arrival.

Hecate shook her head and shot him a wry glance over her shoulder. As suspected, his eyes weren't anywhere near the pile of carrots she had at the end of the row.

"You aren't even looking at the carrots."

"Perhaps it was my carrot I was thinking of."

Hecate snorted and shook her head. "It usually is. And I wouldn't know if it was impressive."

"A fact we can easily rectify." The smoldering look stopped her breath momentarily, then she came to her senses.

Hecate finished plucking the last few potatoes as she responded. "We've already decided that wouldn't be a good idea."

"More like you decided," he mumbled.

She ignored the comment. He had always made his intentions clear, and she was the one who had always stopped his advances. Hecate didn't miss the intrigue on Mount Olympus and knew that an affair with Hermes would have tongues wagging. It wasn't anyone's business who she spent her time with, but it was always best to avoid gossip. Other than Demeter and her daughter Persephone, there weren't many that preferred the Earth realm to the heavens. Hermes shared her connection to the Earth realm and Underworld, so they had a lot in common.

"You haven't been coming around as much." She tried not to let her tone reflect her disappointment. "I thought perhaps you'd grown tired of my company."

He didn't respond immediately, causing her to look back and take in his thoughtful expression. When he caught her eyes, he pasted on a smile. "I've been busy," he said with a knowing grin.

"There hasn't been anything going on in weeks. That seems hard to believe."

His grin widened. She felt her cheeks flush, but thankfully, he didn't say anything about her comment. He didn't need any encouragement from her, what had she been thinking?

With a shrug of his shoulders and a wink, he confessed. "You're right as usual, you can see right through me."

"If that were the case, I would have known you were coming."

"True," he said. And then in true Hermes form, he bounced to another topic. "I'm pleased I'm one of the few who can still surprise you. By the way, those trousers I gave you look amazing on you. Barbarians or not, they have the right idea when it comes to clothing."

Hecate stood and turned, watching his eyes move from ass to chest height. When his eyes finally made it to hers, her unamused expression made him blush. "While I'm sure they don't mean to have women wearing them, they are easier to work in than a dress. I'm actually glad you thought of it."

"Me too."

Hecate laughed at his tone; he never did stop trying. She imagined that she gave quite a show in his newly acquired clothing, especially since she had sized them for a better fit. They really didn't leave much to the imagination now. The thought of what it did to his "carrot" flustered her.

It was safest to keep the conversation on track. "What brings you here today, Hermes?"

"Can't a god just stop by and chat with a beautiful goddess?"

"In your case, not really." She wiped her hands on her thighs, taking a bit of female pride in Hermes's attention. He was a beautiful man. There was no denying her attraction, even though she chose not to act on it. "As the Messenger of the Gods, you aren't generally the bearer of good tidings."

"True," he laughed. "But today, I'm not here on official business, at least not from Zeus."

"Okay, I'll bite." Hecate walked closer, intrigued by his appearance and the hint of the dimple she had always admired on his masculine face.

"If only I were so lucky," he muttered with a sigh. She was close enough now to see the bob of his Adam's apple. She had always made him nervous, and that suited her. Much more than him knowing she was attracted to him as well. He cleared his throat and pretended his last comment wasn't vocalized. "I'm actually here to ask for your help."

That got her attention. After she had helped in the war against the Titans, the gods had pretty much left her alone. She thought it was because Zeus didn't want to be anymore indebted to her than he already was. Her power tapped into the old magick, and most of the Olympians didn't trust her, even though Zeus owed her his life. Although they were friends of a sort, it was strange to her that Hermes would seek her aid, especially considering that Zeus was his father.

Another step and she was close enough to see the flecks of gold in his crystal blue eyes. She was one of the only goddesses without the tell-tale sign of godhood; her eyes were a rich brown like the other Titans. She had always thought that Hermes's eyes were slightly more compelling than the others, especially when combined with his dark curly hair and muscular build.

"Help with what?"

"Well, I noticed that you haven't been traveling to the Underworld of late."

"Hades doesn't need me to help guide the souls of the departed, he has you."

"Yes, except that's the thing. There aren't many arrivals. I got to thinking about the frustrations you've had with your crops and saw a common thread. It's like there's a whole lot of sowing without much reaping, in all things."

"Lots of births, but not a whole lot of deaths." With as busy as she was with her preparations, she hadn't thought about it until now. He was right.

"Precisely," he said. "I'm sure it's Demeter's fault. Persephone's as well. Her perpetual happiness is tiresome."

"She can be rather much," Hecate agreed. "But she is a sweet girl and doesn't mean any harm. You are right though; the celebrations have been harder with the lack of seasons. Not having rosemary alone makes celebrating local traditions nearly impossible, especially this time of year."

"Yes well, I believe that their happiness is harming the planet more than we realize. There needs to be a cycle to all things. The fact that Demeter has things stuck in spring mode is wreaking havoc. You have to agree it was much better before Persephone came along."

Hecate didn't like the direction the conversation was heading. She loved Persephone, almost as much as she would her own daughter.

"What are you saying, Hermes? That you want to get rid of her?"

His eyes widened; she was relieved to see he was horrified. "Of course not! I would never suggest such a thing! However, I do have a proposal that I believe will work in both our favors."

Hecate was desperate enough to listen. Hermes had a unique way of finding his way through things. It was one of his gifts. If he had a solution to her produce and herb problems, she would listen. "Go on."

"It's common knowledge that Hades needs a girlfriend. If for no other reason that it would get him off my back. Since things have slowed down, and there is no longer a need to help ferry souls to him, he has me doing all kinds of other odd jobs."

"Like what?" Hecate laughed.

Hermes rolled his eyes and shook his head in disbelief. "Does it really matter?"

"Not unless he has you playing tricks on your father again. The last time you messed with him it almost started a war."

"I told him Zeus was off limits. He decided messing with my step-mother would be just as much fun."

Hecate shook her head. "That is entirely worse." Hera was not someone any of the gods wanted to cross. Her temper was vile. "In that case, I agree that a woman in his life would do him some good. Now that I think of it, he has been pretty grumpy."

"Grumpy? Is that what you call it?" His exasperated expression made her laugh. "It isn't funny, Hecate. Do you have any idea how many tedious jobs he can come up with to spend eternity on? He really needs to find something else to focus on."

"What are you proposing?"

"I am proposing that you and I set Hades up with Persephone. They are both single and overdue to fall in love. If they hit it off, then we'll get rid of both of our problems at once."

ecate imagined the rant she would have to listen to if they followed through with Hermes's proposal. It wouldn't be pretty. "Demeter would never go for that," she said finally. It wasn't that Hades was a bad guy, on the contrary, he was sexy, powerful, and an amazing cook. His chicken marsala was to die for. At one point, Hecate had even considered giving him a go, but they ended up being better friends.

"I'm not sure we will ever be able to get Persephone alone." Honestly, the fact that it was Hades wasn't the problem. It was more that Demeter didn't think anyone was good enough for her daughter.

"That's where you come in."

"I'm not sure I like the sound of that," she countered. She picked up the basket of carrots and potatoes and started up the path to her cottage. "I'm Persephone's goddessmother, so I don't want to do anything that causes issues."

Hermes took the basket from her arm and hurried ahead to open the door for her. She noticed a small bundle of fresh flowers he had placed on top of the vegetables. It wasn't the first time he had brought a gift for her, and she smiled at the fact. He always remembered that narcissus were her favorite.

"That's the beauty of it." He placed the basket on her kitchen table and sat on the bench nearby. "I have it from a really good source that Persephone is looking for some excitement."

"Well Hades is exciting alright," she murmured. She put the flowers in a glass filled with water then turned back to the sink to rinse the potatoes. "And who did you hear this from, anyway?" She was more than a little curious about who he was spending his time with.

His pause caused her to turn and look at him. His smug expression had her turning back. Deep breaths. It wasn't good to give him too much encouragement.

She could swear she heard a little chuckle before he cleared his throat. "Just a friend." His tone was deep and knowing. "She spends quite a bit of time with Persephone."

Hecate tried not to let the news bother her. It wasn't like they had an understanding. Neither had acted on any of the previous flirtations.

"If you continue to scrub, there won't be anything left of that potato."

His breath moved the small hairs on her neck. She hated that he could move so silently. She shot a comment over her shoulder. "You don't need to worry about my potatoes."

His eyes filled with mirth. Just as quickly as he came, he was back in his seat. The conversation started anew as if he never paused it. "It seems that Persephone is tired of spending all of her time with her mother. She wants what the Oceanids have."

"Which is what?" Hecate tried not to let him get to her. She had always had the upper hand in their relationship and wanted that to continue. She placed the last of the vegetables on the towel to dry and wiped her hands.

"Company of the masculine sort. It seems that her handmaidens have had quite a few secret rendezvous with some of the randier gods."

"They aren't so secret," Hecate mumbled. "I've heard all about the so-called parties. And the fact that you are the one to deliver the invitations."

His smile grew wider, and a wicked gleam lit his eyes. What was wrong with her? Why was she encouraging him?

"I do deliver the invitations," he said softly. "But, if you must know, I never stay after the message is received."

"It is none of my concern what you do with your time, Hermes." Hecate blew a stray curl from her face in exasperation. His chuckle prompted her to trounce up the stairs to her bedroom. "I need to get out of these clothes."

"I am happy to help," he called after her.

His laughter followed her as she stomped up the stairs. When she was out of sight, she couldn't help the smile that came to her face.

After changing into a toga and sandals, Hecate took one last look in the mirror. She wiped the smudge of dirt on her cheek she had missed earlier. Since there was no time for a shower, she dabbed some essential oils on her neck and wrists then joined her guest downstairs.

Hermes was waiting for her in the small room off the kitchen, looking very much at home in her favorite chair. He closed the book she had been reading and placed it back on the small table where he had found it. It was late, and the room was growing dark, so she lit a few candles and sat in the chair across from him.

"Thank you for the flowers, by the way."

"You're most welcome."

Swallowing the lump that rose in her throat, she dismissed the attraction between them and redirected the conversation.

"I've thought about it, and I do see some benefit in making introductions between the two of them." Her next comment squelched his grin. "However, we both know how Hades is, so the meeting must be chaperoned."

"That's probably a good idea. Who did you have in mind?"

"The two of us, of course." She was having a hard time reading his expression in the dimming room. "I will make sure that Persephone remains as she is, and you will ensure that Hades keeps his hands to himself."

"It isn't his hands you need to worry about."

"Precisely," she agreed.

Hermes laughed. It caused a reaction so fierce she had to shift in her seat. "I will agree on one condition."

His tone caused another squirm. She watched his expression; the way the candlelight flickered in his amused eyes caught her breath. Standing at a crossroad, very much like the one she was guardian of, she awaited his demands. The choice would be hers to fulfill or deny, but she already knew what choice she'd be making. Keeping her voice even, she replied. "And what would that be?"

"You spend one full day and night with me. Twenty-four hours of your undivided attention, doing anything I desire, and I will help rid you of eternal spring and bring the seasons back."

"You're mad," Hecate snorted. "I am not having sex with you, Hermes."

"Who said anything about sex?" The words he said were in direct conflict with his expression. There was no mistaking his tone.

"You have. Practically each and every time we see each other."

"Can't blame a god for trying."

Hecate stood and paced the room. She thought better on her feet. Not to mention her feelings were starting to manifest as reactions to parts of her body that had no right reacting that way. Why did he have to look at her like he wanted to lather her with honey and lick off every...

"Are you alright?"

He watched as she fanned herself then lifted her hair from the back of her neck. Hermes shifted in his seat and crossed his ankle over his knee. When he cleared his throat, she lowered her arm and resumed pacing. The flying pheromones were affecting them both, but why?

She caught a scent and put her wrist to her nose, the fragrance confirming her suspicions. Yohimbe and musk. What were the chances? She had used entirely the wrong oil blend. Shaking her head, she laughed at her predicament, one that would affect them both until dawn.

"I will be fine," she said in exasperation. "I just don't understand why you can't ask for something normal, like a spell to bring someone back from the dead."

"What's the fun in that? Besides, I already have an in with the god of death so that would be the last thing I would ask for." He leaned forward, tipping his head in observance. The playfulness in his voice was gone, his tone thoughtful. "Is what I ask for truly appalling?"

Hecate looked into his sincere blue eyes and soaked in his beauty. What he asked for wasn't appalling, but it frightened her. He let out a relieved sigh when she shook her head. "No. It isn't. Okay, Hermes, I will agree to your condition, but I have one of my own."

The look on his face almost made her laugh. He looked truly nervous. "Which is?"

"That Hades and Persephone meet before we spend the day together so we can see if they are well-suited. After, we can spend our twenty-four hours together, but at no time will either of us be unclothed."

Hermes smiled. He was happier with the terms than she thought he would be. It made her wonder what he was up to.

"Agreed."

Too easy. Why was it that she felt she had made a deal with Hades instead of with the Messenger of the Gods? What had she done?

3

The Samhain celebration was on the weekend, so they only had two days to prepare for the clandestine meeting. It hadn't been agreed what each of them would say, only that they would each get their god or goddess to attend a luncheon at a predetermined place and time.

It gave Hecate much more to prepare ahead, since she wouldn't be able to keep her normal schedule. The hope that this would be a solution to their problems had her moving forward. She found Persephone in the narcissus fields near her cottage. The same flower patch she suspected Hermes stopped at on the way to her house. Hecate kept herself tucked behind a tree and watched Persephone from the shadows.

Persephone's nymphs were nearby. Their twittering banter made Hecate miss her youth.

"You should've seen him!"

"Well, I would have been able to had you not rushed me out of the cove," said the pretty blonde.

Persephone added to the conversation. "Poseidon is going to have a problem with you entertaining guests."

"He isn't our father, so what do we care? Besides, he has better things to do." The nymph that spoke had beautiful skin the color of a new spring leaf.

"I heard he's been hanging around a priestess at Athena's temple. I think her name is Medusa. Anyway, it's highly unlikely he'll worry about what we are doing."

"I wouldn't be so sure," Persephone warned. "He takes his duties pretty seriously. I suppose the excitement of entertaining those men makes it worth it for you."

The blonde handed Persephone the chain of narcissus blooms she had fashioned. It was added to the large basket near the goddesses' feet. "You are always welcome to come with us. There were more than a few disappointed men last time when you didn't show."

"I appreciate the invitation, Acaste. But I'm not sure I'd be comfortable. I'm happy reading and working on my paintings."

"You won't meet anyone by spending so much time alone," Acaste said. "Perhaps if you joined us, you would meet someone with the same interests?"

"Perhaps. Or I could wait until Fate plays her hand. I don't think it is her plan for me to live my life alone. I will find love one day."

Hecate strolled out of the woods and announced her presence. "Well, if it were up to your mother, you would spend all of eternity alone."

Persephone smiled and rose to her feet. "Goddessmother, it is so good to see you!" She looked around her to make introductions, but the Oceanids had scattered. Hecate had always made them feel uncomfortable. She supposed it was the rumor Hermes started about her turning Nymphs into decorative shrubbery surrounding her house.

"I couldn't help but overhear you. It seems my goddessdaughter is getting older, and young men are starting to be of interest."

Persephone flushed. Her smile pinkening her cheeks. "The interest has been there for some time but not enough to pursue it. I'm content with my life so far."

"Ah yes, but I can tell you from experience, eternal solitude can be very lonely. Even as much as I like being alone, I still have the occasional visitor."

"I'm aware Hermes is sweet on you," Persephone said knowingly.

Hecate tried not to flush. It was one thing if it was known he liked her. It was something else entirely if it was known she liked him back. Gods and goddesses had a way of using that sort of information to their benefit.

"Well, too bad for him it won't ever get him anywhere," Hecate laughed. "But I do adore the flowers."

Persephone smiled. Holding a bloom to her nose, she closed her eyes and inhaled. Hecate could see the visible signs of her relaxation. The trees and flowers all bent slightly toward her, as if paying homage. "They do smell like heaven," Persephone said softly.

"That they do," Hecate agreed. "There are those who have never enjoyed their sweet fragrance. It seems a crime they are kept from it."

That piqued Persephone's interest. "Do you know of someone? Perhaps I could show them around the meadow."

"I am sure he would like that."

"He?" Persephone's voice was light and feathery. If Hecate wasn't mistaken, she detected interest. "Is this young man someone who has never been here?"

"He has been here but has kept his distance. He's a bit shy."

She contemplated the information then posed another question. "So, he doesn't attend parties?"

"He has, but he doesn't enjoy them. He prefers his solitude."

"I know how he feels," Persephone said. She stepped closer to Hecate so her words couldn't be overheard. "Do you know if he likes to read?"

"He has one of the largest libraries I've ever seen. He is very well read. As a matter of fact, I am just finishing a tragedy he recommended."

Persephone's eyes lit up. She was clearly intrigued. "Does he have any other hobbies?"

Hecate shrugged. "I'm not sure, but I do know he's a great cook. Oh, I believe he likes to draw as well."

"Seems too good to be true," Persephone murmured.

"I assure you, he's not. Too good, that is." Hecate watched the young goddess's interest grow. As timid as she acted, perhaps the naughty boys intrigued her. She knew how she felt.

"What do you mean by that? Is he trouble?"

"Oh, I am entirely sure he has been. But I also believe that the love of the right woman is just what he needs. He is extremely loyal to those who call him friend, and he has called me that for some time."

"He sounds like someone I should meet," Persephone whispered. "But we can't tell my mother."

Hecate pulled Persephone into a hug and whispered back. "I wouldn't dream of it. This will be our little secret."

Hecate had only been home for ten minutes before Hermes fluttered down into her yard. She was sitting on her garden bench contemplating her decision to bring Hades into Persephone's life. She was glad Hermes was there so they could compare notes.

"So, how did it go?" Hermes took the final few steps to the bench and plopped himself beside her. He smelled of sulfur and sage, and she closed her eyes to draw in a lungful. How she missed that scent. Perhaps having Persephone to visit in the Underworld wouldn't be so bad after all. "Hecate?"

She opened her eyes and glanced over. Smiling, she responded to his question. "It went as well as expected. She seems interested and has agreed to meet him as we discussed. How about your meeting?"

"Not as problem-free as yours it seems. He thought I was lying the entire conversation, so I had to repeat everything twice."

"Well, you have to admit, you do tend to be a trickster."

He chuckled and nodded. "I suppose you're right. But never with you."

She looked into his eyes and gauged his sincerity. If she had to decide right then and there based on his expression, she would have to agree that he had never deceived her. That warmed her in places she would examine in the calm of night.

"I appreciate that, Hermes."

"Oh, I almost forgot." He reached into his satchel and pulled out two pomegranates. "I brought you these." He looked for a reaction. "I thought it had probably been a while since you had one."

Hecate surprised him with a kiss on his cheek. It had been a while, and his thoughtfulness touched her. "Thank you, Hermes. It was sweet of you to remember my fondness for them." She stood and held her hand out for him. "Let's go inside, I think I have some yogurt that would go nicely with this."

"I would like that," he said. "I can fill you in on the rest of my conversation with Hades."

"Perfect."

Later, when Hecate was alone in bed with her thoughts, her mind wandered back to her visit with Hermes. The fruit dabbled yogurt had been delicious as was the company. It was increasingly harder, as the moments ticked by, to ignore the facts.

First, that she was lonely and tired of her self-imposed solitude and, secondly, that she was extremely attracted to him. He made her feel young, as if she were the only woman in the world who caught his eye. She knew that wasn't the case, she'd heard about the other lovers, both godly and mortal, that he'd had in his centuries of life. But his attentiveness was addicting, and resisting his charm had become futile. So why did she resist? At the end of it all, she was a woman with needs, and he was a man willing to cater to them. What was it about opening herself to him that scared her?

It seemed that the day together would provide her with the answers her heart needed. She would either see that her fears were founded, and they would remain friends, or they would investigate their growing attraction and see where it led.

Either way, Hecate knew one thing for sure. Things between her and Hermes weren't ever going to be the same, and somehow, she was okay with that.

4

Hecate spent most of the next day preparing her home for company. It was agreed that the date would take place there, in order to keep it from the nosy nymphs. Persephone's "friends" would be the first to report Hades's visit to Demeter, especially since it was their job to keep an eye on her. Hecate didn't want to start any trouble at this stage, but she knew there would be a price to pay if the couple hit it off.

Hermes had showed up first thing, with a bouquet and two more pomegranates for her fruit bowl. He insisted on being put to work, so she gave him a list of repairs she hadn't had time for. He kept himself busy all morning working on the storage shed at the back of her property. She was nearby tending the garden and trying not to be distracted by his shirtless body.

"I finished replacing the tiles on the roof, so you shouldn't have any more leaking."

"I don't know how to thank you, Hermes."

"No need. I like working with my hands." He shot her a boyish grin. "I've noticed that you don't have a good place to split bulbs and thought it would be nice for you to have a workbench. I'd be happy to build one, and you seem to have enough material over there."

Hecate looked into his eager face and found herself nodding in agreement. "I've wanted one for the longest time. Are you sure it isn't any trouble?"

"Not at all. It should only take me a few hours. Unless there is something else you need done."

"I think I have most of the outside finished, so the inside is all I have left. How about I go make us some lunch and I'll call you in when its ready?"

"Sounds great. You'll know where to find me."

Her pulse fluttered and heat rose to her cheeks as she watched him saunter away. The attraction was deepening by the minute, and his easy nature was compelling. She found herself wondering about the twenty-four hours they would be spending together and what he would have in store. Glancing over once more before heading in the house, she watched his muscular back as he chopped wood to size. Perhaps she had been too hasty in demanding they remain dressed the entire time they would be together.

Hecate was inside the kitchen and had just finished making the salad when she heard Hermes knock.

"You can come in. Lunch is almost done."

"I thought I had better wash up." He walked toward the hand pump in the kitchen, and she shook her head.

"You can use my washroom."

"Thanks. I'll be quick."

True to his word, he was back by the time she had the table set. He took the seat closest to the door, the one she thought of as his since he was the only one that ever sat in it. He popped a pepper in his mouth then added a few more to his salad.

"This looks fantastic."

"Thanks. The bread was made yesterday. It's a gift from a woman in town who I helped out." His look of concern had her explaining. "She wasn't feeling well, so I gave her something to settle her stomach."

"It really is a problem if you can't grow your herbs, isn't it?"

Hecate nodded. "I've been making do. But yes, if I'm not able to create my potions, many will suffer. I have quite a few people relying on them. Rosemary is especially hard to come by."

"At first, my motivation was purely selfish. I wanted Hades off my back, if I'm being honest. But now I see that this could be a really good thing."

"I'm starting to think that as well," she said. "Although, I am a little concerned."

"About what?"

"Well, that I haven't been completely honest with Persephone about who she'd be meeting."

There was caution in his tone. "Do you think that will be a problem?"

Hecate shook her head. "Ultimately, no. She asked me all sorts of questions about him, what his likes and dislikes were, what he liked to do in his free time, whether or not he was handsome, but never his name."

Hermes's eyes met hers, and his voice cracked. "What did you tell her?" He cleared his throat and took another sip of wine.

"I was honest. I'm pretty familiar with what Hades likes to do." Hecate watched Hermes over her wine glass, and it occurred to her that her comments could be misconstrued. His head tilted, and his jaw clenched slightly.

"And his looks?"

"I told her he was handsome."

"And?"

Hecate rose from her seat and paced the room. Was he really questioning her? "What do you want to hear, Hermes? That I told her when he walks into a room he commands it? That he is one of the most intelligent, sexy, and engaging men I know?" She watched as his grip on his glass tightened. He was upset, but she needed to make her point. "That his charisma could make any woman, or man for that matter, swoon? Yes, Hermes, I told her all those things, but you know what else I told her?"

He looked up, and the hope in his eyes nearly stopped her breath. His comment came out as a whisper. "What?"

She knelt beside his chair and placed her hand on his arm, causing him to turn in his seat and give her his full attention. "I told her that while I felt that this particular gentleman wasn't necessarily someone I would want to be with, that I believed she could be quite happy with him. They share many of the same interests."

Hermes lifted his hand and caressed her cheek. There was relief in his eyes and perhaps something more. Her heart screamed the truth, but she kept it from passing her lips. It would have to be enough that he knew her heart didn't belong to another.

His thumb paused on her lower lip in the softest of touches. "I am really glad to hear that," he whispered then pulled his hand back.

She stood and walked back to her seat. The conversation started anew but, this time, without the jealousy that had dampened the mood. "So, did he ask about her at all?"

Hermes looked as though he had gotten caught with his hand in the sweets jar. "About that."

"What do you mean? Hermes, does he know who he'll be meeting?" Hecate took a nervous sip of her wine. It helped her to swallow the lump of fear in her throat. "It was supposed to be a blind date. If word gets out ahead…"

"He was sworn to secrecy. But he wouldn't let me out of Tartarus without telling him. He said he needed to know so he could be better prepared."

"Gods, what does that mean?" Hecate couldn't help but roll her eyes. "This has disaster written all over it."

Hermes shook his head. "No, honestly, it's a good thing. I haven't seen him this nervous and excited about anything in the longest time. He even had me trim his hair."

Hecate almost spit the wine she had just sipped at the visual. When she laughed, Hermes tossed a fig at her.

"That's enough."

"So that was what you meant earlier by odd jobs?" Hecate grinned.

He popped a piece of bread in his mouth. "Very funny."

"I think it's sweet, actually. That he's putting his best foot forward."

"He knows he needs to behave. I will bring him at one o'clock for lunch tomorrow, and we will see how it goes."

Hecate held up her wine glass. "Here's to a couple falling in love."

Hermes lifted his glass and clinked it against hers. "I'll drink to that. Twice."

5

Hecate had just put the final touches on the flower arrangement for the table when there was a timid knock at the door. When she opened it, she found a nervous Persephone holding a dish filled with dried figs and apricots dotted with fresh basil. Hecate ushered her in, taking the dish from her and placing it near her fruit bowl.

"You look beautiful, Persephone. I haven't seen you with your hair down for quite some time. The flowers are a nice touch."

"I generally braid it. Are you sure I look okay?" She paced the room, wringing her hands. "I'm not sure I should be doing this. What if he doesn't like me?"

Hecate placed her hands on Persephone's shoulders which stopped her nervous movements. "He will be captivated; you just wait and see. I have a really good feeling about this." She gave her a quick hug then sat her down at the table. "I'm going to give you a bit of wine to take the edge off. I think we could both use some."

"Can I help with anything?"

"No, I have everything ready. You stay put." She handed Persephone the half-filled glass and watched as she took the first few sips. "You should feel better in a few minutes."

"Thank you, Hecate. I'm so glad you had me come over earlier."

"Me too. I did want to explain that today is merely so the two of you can meet and see if you suit one another." Persephone nodded. She had a dreamy smile on her face that gave the impression she wasn't listening to half of what Hecate was saying. "You are under no obligation to see him again."

"Do you think that perhaps we won't like each other? If you tell me his name, I might be able to put your mind at ease. I am familiar with some men, even though my mother is so protective."

Hecate smiled at the goddess's innocence. "I'm not sure you are very familiar with this one. He has been told you are off limits."

"By whom?" Persephone was shocked. More so, she seemed angry. Hecate watched the emotions flicker across her face, and she realized that perhaps she had underestimated the young lady.

"Your mother as well as Zeus."

"Unbelievable!" She paced the room with her wineglass, drinking from it as she vented. "I'm a grown woman who is perfectly capable of making her own decisions. I realize they thought they knew best when I was younger, but at some point, they need to let me go. I should be left alone to live my life!"

"They are just doing what they feel is right. But I agree, you should be able to make your own choices. You are the only one that walks your path, only you can make choices at its crossroads."

Persephone's smile lit the room. "You always have the best way of putting things, Hecate. I'm so glad to at least have one person on my side." She sat across from her at the table and drained the rest of her glass. Her eyes were mischievous, and her tone hushed. "So, who is this person that neither of my parents want me to get involved with?"

"It isn't so much…" A knock sounded at the door, and Hecate rose to answer. Persephone calmly stood near her chair, looking much more relaxed than she had been earlier. It seemed the effects of the wine were kicking in.

Hecate opened the door, and the smoky musk of the man that filled the doorway wafted in. She had forgotten how tall he was, and she took two full steps back to allow him to enter. He ducked his head momentarily shielding his face from view as his black shoulder-length hair fell forward. Hermes had done a good job trimming it, and Hecate tried to remember how long it had been since she had seen Hades clean-shaven.

She tipped her face to receive her obligatory peck on the cheek then greeted Hermes with a smile. He closed the door behind him then handed Hecate a bundle of rosemary wrapped with some twine. She wasn't sure where he had gotten it since the crops had been so poor. When she looked up at him, he gave her a wink. The bundle would be more than enough for her Samhain celebration.

Hades walked straight to Persephone who drank him in with eager eyes. His powerful presence filled the room as did his voice when he addressed her.

"I'm glad we have this opportunity to get to know one another better." He took her hand in his and raised it to his lips, never once dropping his eyes from hers. Persephone's smile widened as she accepted the small bouquet of field flowers he handed her.

"Me too," she said quietly. "Thank you, Hades. These are beautiful." She didn't seem nervous, in fact, it was quite the opposite. Persephone was looking up at Hades with a coy smile that had him fidgeting. Hecate had never seen him so hesitant.

"So, you do know me?" The comment was almost a purr, that Persephone lapped right up.

"How could I not?" She definitely had her flirt on, and Hecate thought perhaps the wine hadn't been a good idea. She was seeing a side of Persephone that she didn't realize existed.

Hecate caught Hades's eye, and she noticed the slightest question in them. Persephone lifted the flowers to her nose to breathe in their scent then finished her thought. "I daresay there is a man, woman, or child that doesn't know who you are, God of the Underworld and all. Besides, Hecate has told me a lot about you. I was pleased to learn you like to draw."

Hades shot another glance to Hecate, his eyebrow raised. "Are you now."

Hecate avoided his amused expression and made herself busy bundling the rosemary to hang near the fireplace. She was sure she would get an earful later about the fact that she was talking about him. Hades liked his privacy.

"Well, you will have to let me know what else you two have talked about. And what else you are pleased by." His deep tone and soft chuckle had the right effect. Persephone hung on his every word, and if Hecate wasn't mistaken, she heard a longing sigh.

They drank each other in with their eyes, and Hecate attempted to cut through the sexual tension. "Please, everyone, have a seat." There was chemistry between the couple, so much so it permeated the room. It was starting to affect her in ways she didn't have time for.

"Lunch is ready, I just need to get a few things out."

Hermes walked up to her, and when he placed his hand on her shoulder, she about jumped out of her skin.

"Sorry," she whispered. She was nervous about the repercussions from the day, Hades being the least of them. She knew Hermes understood, they had spoken about the fact the day before.

His open smile soothed her. As did the gentle rub across the top of her back. He gave her a squeeze and a kiss on the cheek. His arm dropped from her shoulders before she could acknowledge the embrace. "What do you need me to help with?"

"Perhaps you can fill the wine glasses?" She glanced back at Persephone who was seated next to Hades. They were chatting about their hobbies, and she noted that they were both leaning in with interest. It seemed that Hecate's earlier transgression of sharing too much about what Hades did in his down time had been forgiven. If anything, he seemed to be sharing much more than she thought he would have been comfortable with.

Persephone was just as bad. Her contagious joy filled the room, and Hecate noticed she had a habit of touching Hades's upper arm when he said something that made her laugh. It seemed that the innocent girl she had worried about, wasn't so innocent. She reconsidered giving her more wine, but Hermes had already delivered the glasses.

The couple continued their conversation, ignoring the wine. He walked back over to Hecate and took a plate of meat and cheeses from her hand. "I don't think they will be interested in any of this right now," he murmured.

"I think you're right," she whispered. She glanced back over to the couple who were clearly into one another. Their animated conversation made her smile, she was starting to feel better about it. They were talking about their favorite things to read, and Hades promised to bring a book of sonnets the next time they met.

"Why don't we take some of this outside?" Hecate suggested. "We can have a picnic and give them some privacy."

Hermes was taken aback at first, then a smile crept across his face. "You're sure?"

She nodded. "I am. I don't think they can get into too much trouble with us close by."

"Not sure about that," he chuckled. But I agree some fresh air would be welcome. Lead the way."

They split some of the food off and left plates on the table before heading out the door. Neither Hades nor Persephone noticed they were leaving, their conversation continued as Hecate closed the door quietly.

"They don't even know we've left." Hermes shook his head. "I have never seen him so smitten."

"I'm glad for them both, but this means we will have some explaining to do when the time comes."

He followed her back to a small table and set the plate on it, before pulling up a bench. She sat across from him and sipped her wine. A deep belly laugh sounded, and she shot an unbelieving look at Hermes. The tinkle of female laughter soon followed.

"I'm not sure what I will say when the time comes." He was baffled. "How can we possibly explain Hades acting like this? He doesn't laugh."

"Well, he does now."

"Apparently," he laughed. "I've never seen anything like it."

"It's nice to see," Hecate said. "I hope it works out for them, but Demeter won't be happy about it. Especially when she hears about our role in the whole thing."

"What she doesn't know won't hurt her," Hermes shrugged. "It's honestly how most gods and goddesses handle things. It's amazing the secrets I'm privy to by being the messenger."

"I'll bet. For the most part, that is why I stay here. The intrigue in Olympus is tiresome."

"Tell me about it." Hermes popped a cube of cheese in his mouth. "I can talk to Hades if you'd like. Let him know that his interest needs to be kept on the quiet side for now."

"That would be great, Hermes. Thank you."

She nibbled on some cheese and attempted to ignore the weight of his stare. She knew what was coming next, and she wasn't sure she was ready for it.

"Hecate, about our deal…"

She looked up, waiting for him to finish his thought. He looked as if he was struggling with putting it to words, and she wondered if he had changed his mind. What surprised her was the realization that if he had, she would be disappointed.

Her response was breathy. "What about our deal?"

He reached his hand across the table, and she linked her fingers with his. The movement was as natural to her as breathing, and she marveled at the thought. The smile on his face warmed her as did the gentle squeeze of his hand. "I want to know what you'd like to do on our date."

"It's a date now then?" The question came out as a whisper.

Hermes looked nervous, as if he were gauging her reaction. "It always was for me," he said simply.

Relief pulsed through her at the thought that he still wanted to see it through. "I guess I'm okay with that."

He lifted their linked hands and pressed his lips to her knuckles. "I'm so glad to hear you say that. Anything you desire, Hecate, it's yours." He lowered their hands back to the table but kept hold of her fingers. If not for the butterflies in her stomach she would almost believe the moment had never happened. "Anywhere you want to go, I'll take you."

"What if I'm happy staying at home?"

He smiled at the comment. "Then that is what we'll do. I just want to spend time with you. It doesn't matter to me where we do that."

"You can be very sweet at times, Hermes."

"That will be one more thing we will keep on the quiet side."

She looked into his smiling face and wondered why now, after all these years? Why was it that she was seeing him for the first time? Life had a funny way of doing that, she supposed. As far as she was concerned, her attraction warranted investigation. "Your secret is safe with me. And I am happy with whatever plans you decide on."

Thinking it was abnormally quiet, she stood to make her way back into the house when she heard another round of laughter. Her steps slowed and she felt Hermes come up behind her. His hands were calloused as he ran them up her arms and circled her shoulders. As his rich voice tickled her ear, the reaction in her body was uncontrollable. She was glad she had worn her hair up; he was able to get closer that way.

"He promised to behave today. If nothing else, he is a man of his word."

There were murmurs of conversation coming from the house, but they were drowned out by the beating of her heart. Her question came out in a breathy whisper. "And are you a man of your word, Hermes?"

He spun her around and slipped his arms around her waist. Her arms came up around his neck, her fingers gravitating to the curls on the back of his head. He pulled her closer and surprised her with the embrace. She could feel his lips grazing her shoulder as he responded to her question.

"I am also a man of my word, my sweet. And I promise you I will spend the rest of my days happily seeing to your needs, if you'll let me." He held her tight, resting his cheek on the top of her head.

She closed her eyes and allowed the moment to fill her. It had been so long since she had felt this way, like she was precious. Hermes knew she was capable, there had never been a question of that, but he also had a way of embracing her independent nature. Men had a tendency of taking charge, but Hermes found ways to support the decisions she made for herself and be a true helpmate. Their balanced natures worked well together; perhaps it was time to take a chance on him. Her heart finally aligned with the message her body had been giving her all along.

Hecate moved in Hermes's arms, tipping her head back and causing him to look down into her face. Her timid smile gave him the courage to move his hands up to caress her cheeks. His thumb brushed her lower lip, and they stood in silence, each waiting for the other to decide for them both. Their lips met tentatively; she wasn't sure who had made the first move, but it didn't matter now.

"Hermes."

Her sigh gave license for what came next. Hecate wrapped her arms around him as he crushed her in his embrace. His mouth ravaged hers as she pressed her body to his. The floodgates had been opened, and pent up frustration flowed over them both. They were pulled into the waves, both equal in their passion as they tried to find purchase in the storm. She was having a hard time keeping her feet on the ground, then the ground was gone, and they were moving, gliding backward toward the shed. Within seconds, they were around the corner, and he sat her on the newly made bench.

His body was wedged between her legs, and his rough hands rasped against her skin, exciting her. She couldn't get close enough and gripped his face as his tongue met hers. Her dress was hiked up high on her legs, and she scooted closer, tucking herself closer to his warmth. Their abandon was equal, and when his mouth lowered to her neck, she tilted her head to give him access. His hands slipped around the crease of her upper thigh, causing her to moan, as did his thumbs circling the place she truly wanted him to be.

"I've waited so long," he mumbled against her skin.

"You make me reckless."

"I like hearing you say that," he said. His thumb grazed her, and a wicked smile widened as a small whimper of need fell from her lips. He slid one hand behind her and pulled her in tight against his waist. She wrapped her legs around him, her core against his hardened belly and his magical hand. Pulses of anticipation shot through her as his fingers filled her, and he swallowed her cry with his mouth. Frantic, she pulled the fabric of her dress aside then heard a voice.

She tensed, and the kissing stopped. "Did you hear something?"

"Only the pulse of my heart."

The kissing started anew, but she was distracted. He pulled back. "What's the matter?" His hand slipped from her legs.

"I thought I heard something," she whispered.

"Hecate? Where did you go?"

"Mother goddess, it's Persephone." Hecate slipped off the bench and was adjusting her dress as Hades came around the corner. A grin split his face, and he shot a knowing glance to them both before winking to Hecate. Then he turned and stepped back around the corner.

"Let's give them a few minutes," she heard Hades say. "I think we interrupted an important conversation."

Persephone's sweet voice faded as Hades led her away. "Okay, we can wait on the other side of the house. There's a place I like to paint that I can show you."

Hecate looked over at Hermes who was stifling a laugh.

"It isn't funny, we are supposed to be chaperones!"

"That's the funniest part," he laughed. He turned her into his arms and pulled her into his warmth. What she wouldn't give to stay there in his arms, but she could feel the effects their tryst had on him. She pulled back to give him some space. They had guests to attend to.

"We should go find them," Hecate said nervously.

"Hecate." She realized she was avoiding looking at him when he called her name a second time. "Hecate, look at me."

She looked up; tears of embarrassment fueled by frustration brimming in her eyes. "I'm not sure what came over me. I'm sorry, Hermes, but I really should go check on her."

The pain in his eyes made her flinch, as did the resignation in his tone. "Go then. I'll be right behind you."

Hecate made the last of her adjustments then walked from the place where the world had ceased to exist for them both. She looked back over her shoulder and almost wished she hadn't. Hermes stood with his head lowered and his shoulders drooped in defeat. It made her feel terrible, leaving things undone between the two of them. But she had no choice.

Persephone was her priority for now. Her life could wait, it had waited this long, but she couldn't help the niggling voice inside her mind. The one that voiced the question she had been asking herself more and more in recent days. How long would Hermes wait for her to decide?

7

Hecate walked around the house to the place Persephone had mentioned to Hades. They were seated next to each other on the bench that overlooked the fields, and true to his word, Hades was keeping his hands to himself.

Hecate called out as she strolled up to them. "That is my favorite place to sit. It is one of the nicest views nearby."

Hades spoke over his shoulder, his voice hinted of mischief. "Oh, I don't know. There seem to be other places to sit that have lovely views. Wouldn't you agree, Hermes?"

She glanced behind her, surprised to see Hermes a few steps behind. He smiled sadly then answered Hades.

"I believe that to be true, although beauty is always in the eye of the beholder."

"If there is another site to paint, I should love to see it."

"Perhaps I will show it to you one day," Hades said. He lifted a lock of Persephone's hair and rubbed it between his fingers.

"I should like that very much," she said sweetly.

Hades took her hand and kissed it gently. "I believe we both would." He stood and gave Hecate a wink before nodding to Hermes. "But for now, I must go. I have some things to attend to."

Persephone stood, the pout on her face caused Hades to bend down and whisper something in her ear. When he stood, she was all smiles.

"Come, Hermes, it's time to go. Good afternoon, Hecate. It's been an eye-opening experience."

Hecate no sooner felt her cheeks flush, then they were gone in a black puff of smoke. She was disappointed that she wasn't able to say goodbye to Hermes but thought it might be good for her to spend some time away from him. He had a way of clouding her better judgement.

"Oh, Hecate, I really like him," Persephone gushed. "We have so much in common! Do you know he likes to play Mah Jong as well?"

Hecate smiled. "No, honestly, I didn't know that." It was hard not to get caught up in her enthusiasm. "Did you make plans to see each other again?"

"Yes, he mentioned coming back tomorrow. He's bringing his supplies, and we're going to paint. Is that okay?"

"Absolutely, you're always welcome here. I should be around."

Persephone gave her a hug. "You're the best, Hecate! Have to run, the nymphs will be wondering where I've been off to." She hurried out of the yard and down the path, her steps light and youthful as she made her way back to the fields where she lived.

Hecate watched as her image faded and closed her eyes, taking a deep breath and allowing her worries to disappear. The couple's fate was no longer in her hands, what they chose to do moving forward would be left to the Universe. As was in her nature, once their choice was made, Hecate would support it to the fullest. She wished she could be so decisive in her own life.

Deciding Hermes wouldn't be returning, she walked back to the house. She didn't know what she expected, since she had effectively doused his heated pursuit with the cold water of indecisiveness. She really needed to decide what to do with him; it wasn't fair to either of them to keep up this way. Perhaps it was time for a clarification spell. She would have to check if she had all the ingredients.

Inside, most of the food had been left untouched, but it looked as though some of the fruit had been eaten. Strange, she didn't remember serving strawberries. On closer examination, the red fruit dotting the plates made her heart sink. She looked in her fruit bowl, and sure enough, one of the pomegranates Hermes had brought her was missing.

"Oh, this is a disaster," she cried. She paced the floor and considered where it was that Hermes could have picked up the fruit. "Perhaps a market," she said aloud. "Or a farm nearby." As much as she hoped for these things, she already knew the truth. She connected to Hermes in her mind and asked him to come to her. He was there within seconds, opening the door and walking to her side.

"What's wrong?" He looked to her face to find the answers, and she struggled for what to say. "Please, tell me."

"Hermes, where did you get those pomegranates?"

A look of confusion crossed his brow then a smile. "Is that all this was? Zeus's beard, you scared me. I thought you were going to tell me…"

"They ate a pomegranate." She paused, but his look was still of confusion. "Hades and Persephone ate…a…pomegranate."

The expression on his face the moment he realized what she was saying covered her in a sense of dread. "You're sure?"

"You brought me two, and there is only one left." She pointed to the plates on the table. "I believe that is what remains of the other."

Hermes looked at the plates then to her with realization. "You know what this means."

"Of course I know what this means!" Hecate couldn't help the shrill tone of her voice. "It means that Hades has himself a new roommate." She paced the floor, gesturing with her hands as she vented. "He said he would be on his best behavior."

"And by all rights, he was. He kept an appropriate distance from Persephone, and you would have known from her if it had been otherwise."

"She is completely enamored of him! I hardly think she would say a word. But now the choice has been taken from her entirely. She wouldn't have known that eating something from the Underworld would send her there. That was unbelievably selfish of him. Where is he now?"

"He was feeding Cerberus when you called for me."

"You need to go back and tell him we need to talk. Assuming he has designs to bring Persephone to the Underworld, we need to come to some sort of agreement. If Persephone is taken away from Demeter for eternity, she will destroy the planet."

"I'll be right back." Hermes opened the door, and with a flash, he was gone. Seconds later, he was back in a cloud of black smoke with Hades.

"You have a question for me?"

Hecate wasn't in the mood for his smug expression. "You had no right to trick her into eating that fruit."

"I didn't trick her," he said. "As a matter of fact, I tried to stop her, but she wouldn't listen. I like that about her you know, her strong will."

"What did you tell her precisely?"

"That if she ate anything that came from the Underworld, that I would be back for her."

"Sounds like you left out the part about her having to live there for all eternity," Hermes said. "Hades, you gave your word."

"I did," he said quietly. "But she touched something inside me. I'm not proud of what I did, but I can tell you that I will do everything in my power to make her happy."

Hecate saw truth in his eyes, and his words were sincere. "Against my better judgement, I'll help you, Hades." The God of the Underworld's face beamed. "But you must agree to my terms exactly."

"Anything," he said. "You must know I'd do anything for her."

"Good. That's a start." Her next comment was addressed to Hermes. "Bring back Zeus and be discreet about it."

Hermes left in a flash, and Hades groaned. He looked into Hecate's eyes and nodded. "I had intended to talk to him eventually."

"Well, there is no time like the present. When he gets here, you are going to do the right thing and ask for her hand."

Hades nodded. "Of course, I will."

Hermes was back, and then a flash of lightning cracked outside Hecate's door. The next moment, Zeus entered, his booming voice shaking the walls of her tiny home.

"You will what, Hades?!"

8

Thankfully, the negotiations between Zeus and Hades didn't take long. Hades prefaced the conversation with the admittance that he had fallen in love with Persephone and that he had chosen her from Zeus's daughters to marry. Hecate hadn't realized until then that Zeus had made that offer to Hades. She should have known.

Their conversation was brief, and Zeus had no desire to know the details. However, he did promise that when the time came, he would be the one to speak to Demeter, which calmed Hecate's nerves. Zeus was gone quickly, leaving Hecate, Hades, and Hermes to make their plans.

"There is no doubt in my mind what will happen if you take Persephone to the Underworld and her mother can't see her." Hecate paced as Hades popped the remaining pieces of pomegranate in his mouth. "She will be in such torment that her emotions will wreak havoc on the weather patterns and crops. Things are bad enough now. We can't let that happen."

Hermes dreaded the message he would have to deliver to Persephone's mother, it showed in his face. He paced as well, crossing Hecate's path in the small kitchen every few steps. "Not to mention once Demeter finds out we had anything to do with it, she'll have our heads."

"There is no reason for Demeter to know either of you were involved," Hades said quietly. "I have a solution that might suit us all. However, I need to speak to Persephone to make sure she is willing to have me. Hermes, will you request an audience with her please?"

Hermes gave a quick nod. "I'll be right back."

Hecate looked at Hades with fresh eyes. Perhaps this match would be good for him. He seemed more grounded, and the peace on his face was refreshing. "What do you have in mind?"

He shrugged. "I'm going to ask her to marry me. Then, once I know she'll have me, I'll ensure Demeter has no idea that you and Hermes had anything to do with us meeting."

"How on earth will you pull that off?" Hecate's tummy twisted as a grin split his face. Whatever he had planned wouldn't go over well with Demeter. He stood facing the door, as the sound of Persephone's musical voice came to them. He glanced over his shoulder at her and gave a wink. "I'm going to whisk her away."

Before Hecate had a chance to question what he could possibly mean, Hermes and Persephone walked in the room.

Hecate and Hermes stayed inside as Hades took Persephone back out to the bench overlooking the hillside. Hecate looked out the window to gauge Persephone's interest and, at one point, caught sight of Hades down on one knee in front of her. He had posed a question, and Persephone had eagerly nodded. When the couple embraced, Hecate pulled back from the window and gave them some privacy.

"I believe she said yes," she said with a sigh. "That will make things a bit easier."

"Indeed," Hermes mused. "I think you worry too much, Hecate."

"How can I not?" She paced the small room, flapping her hands like a crow. "He said he was going to abduct her. What am I supposed to think about that?"

"Well, if she said yes to his proposal, it won't really be an abduction now will it?"

He had a point. "I suppose not. I just don't like being left in the dark is all."

Hermes walked to her, and she slowed her pace. Soon she found herself wrapped in his arms and taking solace in his embrace. After a few deep breaths, she was feeling much more centered. The vibration of his voice soothed her.

"Perhaps some things should be left to chance. I find that life is much more entertaining that way."

She looked up into his face. "I suppose you're right. Although, I would argue that you are the god of mischief."

"Has nothing to do with me being right about having fun," he laughed. "To test the theory, I've decided you are no longer in charge of what we do on our day together. I'm going to make all the plans."

The thought of having someone else take care of all the details excited her in ways she never thought possible. Before she had a chance to respond to him, Hades walked in the door.

"I am pleased to announce our engagement. Persephone said yes," Hades said. "We have made our plans, and you both need to be somewhere other than here tomorrow. Can that be arranged?"

Hermes nodded. "I think we can find something to do." He spoke then to Hecate. "I'll plan on being here tomorrow morning at 8."

Hecate glanced between the two men, knowing she didn't have a choice in the matter. She would be having her date with Hermes tomorrow, and she had no control over what they would do.

"I'll be ready."

"Good," Hades said. He kissed Hecate on the cheek then nodded to Hermes. "Let's go, I have a lot to prepare."

Hermes gave her a quick wink before leaving with the God of the Underworld in a puff of sulfur. The final words she heard Hermes mutter gave her unexpected butterflies.

"Me too."

As promised, Hermes was there first thing in the morning. Since she wasn't sure what to expect for the day's events, she decided to wear the trousers and shirt he had given her. She was happy to see that he was dressed similarly.

"Ah good," he said. "I was going to have you change into those since we will be doing some hiking. You'll want to wear comfortable shoes as well."

"I have my sandals right here," she said as she tied them on. "So does Hades have everything ready for his…"

Hermes shook his head. "We won't be speaking of Hades today," he said softly. "You are all mine for twenty-four hours, and I don't want to waste another minute speaking of his plans. Just know that he has everything in place, and Persephone will be well cared for."

Hecate nodded. He was probably right; the less she knew, the better off she would be. "Okay, I'm ready. Where to first?"

His smile lit his face, his enthusiasm contagious. "You'll find out when we get there." He pulled her into his arms, and they shot to the sky. His winged shoes flew them to their destination faster than any bird could soar. His arms were strong around her, and she settled her face into his chest as they raced past the landscape. When he landed, it took her a moment to piece together their location.

They were on a sloped hillside, with grapevines as far as the eye could see. He led her down past the sweet-smelling grapes to a small building with an adjacent courtyard. It was evident that it was a working farm, but it seemed they were the only ones there. He brought her to a small table that held an array of pastries and fruits and motioned for her to sit.

"I thought we should start with breakfast." He pushed her chair in then settled in a seat across from her. "We won't be bothered."

"Is this vineyard yours then?" She slathered butter and honey on a piece of bread that still felt warm from the oven.

"It actually belongs to Dionysus. It is one of many that he operates."

"I had no idea he owned vineyards, but I suppose it makes sense."

"Once we finish up here, I have a place just over that hill I want to show you. I think you'll like it."

Hermes picked at the pastry he had selected. It seemed strange to her that after all this time he would be flustered and wondered at the reason. Perhaps it was that he had finally gotten what he had asked for and wasn't sure what to do about it.

"I'm sure I will," she said honestly. "It's lovely here." She was enjoying herself already. It was amazing to her that the mere decision to allow more spontaneity into her life could alter her mood in such a way, but there they were. Allowing someone else to make all the decisions for her was refreshing.

Once they finished eating, Hermes took her hand and led her toward the hillside. "I've learned a lot from the farmers here. A few years back, I decided to start a farm of my own and have a few locals run it for me. It's just over this hill."

"You grow grapes as well?"

Hermes shook his head. "No. The soil is different there, more conducive to something else. It's been a challenge with the weather, but the climate seems more temperate here. Perhaps because we are farther away from Demeter's influence."

"That could be," Hecate agreed. They crested the hill, and she gasped at the lush green valley below. The winds carried the scents to her where she stood. First came the smoky scent of sage and then the delicate smell of lavender. Last she caught the pungent tang of the herb that was dearest to her heart. "Rosemary."

The whispered word brought a smile to his face as did her look of delight. "Yes, rosemary. I thought you might like it. Let me show you what I've been up to."

After strolling through his gardens, which she didn't want to leave, they made a quick stop in Rome for lunch. After, they took in some sites in Thebes and had drinks near the Nile river. Their time together had been enlightening. Hermes had always shown his sweet side by bringing her gifts, but the day together had shown her glimpses of his true feelings about her. Her assumption had always been that it was all about sex for him, but his insight into her likes and dislikes had been telling. The day's experiences catered to her needs and included activities that he would have only known about through his quiet observations.

The moon was high, and the stars dotted the skies on the flight back to her house. They had been active for well over sixteen hours, and she was ready to unwind. She had hardly given the situation with Hades and Persephone a second thought all day, but as she settled into her routines, her mind touched on them. She didn't give voice to her worries; there were a few more hours on their date, and she owed Hermes her undivided attention.

She threw a log on the embers and stoked it until it flamed. Once she hung the bundles of herbs they brought back from his farm on the hearth, she turned to catch him watching her. His desirous expression was no longer exasperating, it excited her in ways she was ready to act on. "I'm going to make some tea. Would you like some?"

Hermes nodded slowly, almost as if answering an entirely different question. The thought occurred to her that she would like it if he were there as a matter of habit. Perhaps the demand on Hermes's time would loosen once Hades had a new bride. The day together had shined a new light on their relationship, and she had to consider that they were actually perfect for one another. Once the couple was married and things settled down, she owed it to herself to investigate the feasibility of a future with Hermes. Why had she wasted so much time?

"You're quiet. Is everything okay?" The worry that flickered across his face squeezed her heart. She didn't want to hold him at arm's length any longer. He deserved better as did she.

"Everything is perfect," she said softly. Putting the kettle aside, she crossed the room and sat beside him. As her head pressed on his shoulder, his arm wrapped around her. The motion was as natural as breathing, and his presence was strong and warm. She knew she wanted more of what he was willing to offer. No more holding back, she was ready to leave some things to chance.

They sat watching the fire, both content in their thoughts. She looked above at the bundles of rosemary they had brought back and smiled. "I still can't believe the things you're growing at your farm. Thank you for sharing it with me."

"You are the only other person I've taken there. Not even Hades knows about it."

That made her smile, and she snuggled closer to his side. "That makes me feel special."

He kissed the top of her head. "You are special. And you are welcome there anytime."

"Hermes?"

"Yes?"

"I was thinking about our earlier agreement." She was close enough to feel the pause in his breath.

His voice cracked slightly as he responded. "The clothes stay on agreement?"

She nodded as she responded. "Yes, that one," she whispered. He had been a complete gentleman the entire day. While she liked their normal playful banter, their day together showed her another side to him that had her making her move. Since she had stopped him cold before, the next step would have to be hers.

He shifted in his seat, and she took the opportunity to slip off her chair and turn to straddle his lap. His arms tightened around her as her arms slipped around his shoulders. His expression was one of delighted surprise. He looked at her with eyebrow raised, his tone was teasing. "Have you had a change of heart?"

She shifted closer, pushing herself down on his hardening length. "I have." A moan crossed his lips, and she whispered in his ear. "I want this. Hermes, I want you."

"I'm yours." He adjusted his arms, one pulling her closer to him and the other cupping her head as he ravaged her mouth. She had turned at her crossroad, and there was no denying where they were headed next. "I've always been yours."

Those two words solidified her decision. "To the bedroom then," she whispered and squealed with delight when he lifted them both off the seat and flew up the stairs into her bedroom. They were on her bed in seconds. The shirts were the first to go, and Hecate hadn't regretted wearing pants until that moment; a toga would have been much easier for him to get under. The kisses were frantic, as were their hands that grasped and stroked.

Once they were blissfully nude, he slowed the kisses and pulled back to look at her. Her dark hair was fanned out behind her, and a lazy smile curled on her face. The moment felt right. His eyes drank her in, and his hands smoothed over her breasts and down to her hips. His voice was awestruck. "So perfect." He lowered his face to run kisses along her neck, murmuring devotions as he paid homage to each breast. "Tell me what you want."

"Anything. Everything. Take me to the stars."

Hecate woke the next morning tangled in sheets and smelling of man. Hermes was spooned behind her, his arm draped over her and tight as he pulled her against him. He kissed the back of her neck and nuzzled his face against it. She could feel his contented smile on her skin.

"Good morning, beautiful."

The afterglow of their love making still warmed her. Hermes had been a thoughtful lover, and they had fallen into a contented sleep only hours before.

"Morning. You hungry?"

He nibbled on her neck and chuckled. "Ravenous. My appetite for you seems to be endless."

Hecate rolled over, and he gathered her in his arms. His hands soothed over her back, and he kissed the tip of her nose before tucking her beneath his chin. The rhythmic feel of his hand on her skin was a balm to her soul. He had always told her she was beautiful, but she'd never trusted the words. Last night, the words were laced with passion, and there was no longer a doubt in her mind just how precious she was to him.

She allowed herself a few more minutes of warmth before moving. "As nice as that is to hear, we really should get up and face the world."

Hermes groaned. "Do we have to?"

"I'm afraid so," she laughed.

"I would rather spend the day in bed with you."

"I would like that. Perhaps one day soon."

"I'm holding you to that." He kissed her softly. Passions rose, and hands started their journey before a pounding at the door stopped them.

A woman's voice yelled. "Hecate? Are you there?"

Hecate looked at Hermes with wide eyes. "It's Demeter!"

"Hecate, open up! I have to talk to you. It's urgent."

Hermes bolted into action and pulled his clothes on. "Do you want me to leave? I don't have to take the door."

Hecate shook her head. "No. As far as I'm concerned, we are together. The sooner everyone knows, the better off we will be."

His smile lit the room. "It's amazing to hear you say that. I'll go down and let her in then. You finish getting dressed." After a quick kiss, he was gone. The next second, she heard the creak of her door and Demeter's frantic voice.

"What are you doing here, Hermes? And where is Hecate?"

10

Hecate belted her toga as she bolted down the stairs. Hermes was putting the kettle on to boil, and Demeter was pacing the room. As distraught as she was, she still managed to look utterly perfect. There wasn't a golden lock of her hair out of place, and was that a new necklace?

"Demeter, what is it?" The surprise she attempted to put in her voice sounded tinny. She was a terrible friend.

Demeter stepped into Hecate's open arms, and her words came out in patches between sobs. "Hades…he abducted my baby… Oh, Hecate…she's gone."

Hecate looked into her friend's porcelain face and couldn't help her sense of amazement. Demeter was one of the only women she knew whose face didn't look like a bloated red mess when she cried. "Demeter, you need to calm down." She pulled her to the table and sat her down. Hermes placed a cup of tea in front of her, and Hecate placed Demeter's hands around it. "Drink the tea, it will help."

"I don't want to drink tea!" She wailed. "I need to find my daughter! She's been gone since yesterday." Turning in her seat, she pointed to Hermes accusingly. "You're with him all the time! You helped him!"

Hecate sat next to her and pushed forward some magick to soothe her friend. She really needed to calm herself. "Hermes didn't help anyone do anything; he was with me all day yesterday." She glanced over to him and caught his grateful smile. He blew a kiss when Demeter turned her head. "Now tell me what happened?"

Demeter told her version of the story. "The nymphs were with

Persephone in the nearby field picking flowers. They told me that they felt the earth move then watched in horror as it split open and fire came spewing from the crack."

Hecate listened calmly attempting to pull the facts from the exaggerated account that Demeter was sure to give.

"An ebony chariot pulled by fire-breathing horses flew out of the crack and raced toward Persephone. The nymphs confirmed it was Hades who reached from the chariot and swept my daughter into his arms. He drove back into the earth, and the crack closed on the sound of my daughter's screams."

Demeter lowered her head and sobbed once more. Hecate looked over to Hermes and mouthed the words "what was he thinking?" Hermes shrugged as he tried to squelch his signature grin. It made her wonder if perhaps he had been in on the planning with Hades. It was convenient that the abduction had happened when they were both out of town. It seemed Hades had held up his end of the bargain, and now it was time for Zeus to hold up his.

"Hermes, please ask Hades to bring Persephone here then go get Zeus." She tried to keep the exasperation from her voice. She just wanted to get this sorted so that she and Hermes could get back to what they had been doing. Selfish? Yes, it was. But realistic? Absolutely.

She knew the couple was ecstatic to be together and that even Zeus, himself, had agreed to the nuptials. The only one that needed to be convinced it was a good thing was Demeter, and from the way she was behaving, she wasn't sure Zeus would be able to pull it off. Hermes gave a nod then was out like a flash. He had left the door open, but knowing everyone would be arriving soon, she left it ajar.

At the realization that she'd be seeing Zeus, Demeter stood and excused herself to the bathroom. Hecate would bet her best set of runes that she was checking her face. When the others were brought back and the voices filled the room, Demeter came out to join them. Hades and Persephone were arm-in-arm with faces beaming. Demeter wouldn't look Hecate in the eye and kept a clear distance from the daughter she had been worried sick over. When Zeus entered the room, she ran right into his embrace.

"Come now, Demeter. Look how happy they are," Zeus soothed.

"Well, what about me? What about my happiness? Now I have neither you nor my daughter. I'll be alone, for all eternity."

The tears started anew, and the skies darkened. Within seconds, the winds howled, and the rains came. Zeus glanced over to Hecate, who looked at him expectantly. He needed to do something about her, or any crops she had left would be ruined. He gave Hecate a nod then led Demeter toward the door.

"Let's go for a walk to sort this out. I need you to calm down and bring the sun back, my love."

Demeter's head perked up at the endearment. She wiped her face and gave a quick nod. The sun was back as if the storm had never happened. Zeus opened the door and led Demeter outside. Then he called back over his shoulder, the thunder in his voice leaving no mistaking that it was a command.

"This means the both of you also. Come along Hades…Persephone."

Persephone ran to Hecate and gave her a hug. Her excited whisper confirmed her happiness. "Thank you so much for all you've done."

"You're happy then?" Hecate asked the question, already knowing the answer. It was written all over Persephone's face.

She nodded with a smile. "I am extatically happy. I couldn't have picked a better person to spend the rest of eternity with." She looked over to Hades who blew her a kiss then put his hand out for hers. She called back over her shoulder with a grin. "And I'm now a queen!"

"Come, my sweet. It's time to calm things down with your mother."

Persephone left Hecate's side and took her husband's hand. As he led her out of the doorway to join her parents, their united front made Hecate's heart warm. They spoke quietly, but Hecate heard bits of their conversation.

"She'll want me to stay," Persephone said quietly.

"She doesn't have a choice, my love. Would you want to stay here?"

"I want to be with you, but if I didn't at least visit, I would miss her terribly."

"Don't you worry, you will still get to visit a few months out of the year. And then the rest of the time, we will…."

Hecate didn't hear the rest of what he said, but Persephone's tinkling laugh told her what she needed to know. They would make each other blissfully happy; she was sure of it. The added bonus was that Persephone was now in control of her own life and had found purpose in that. She would make a wonderful queen. She looked at Hermes who had stood quietly and taken it all in. They met each other in the center of the room.

He kissed the tip of her nose then pulled her into an embrace. "A sad Demeter a few months out of the year could work to your benefit."

She smiled and looked up into his beautiful face. "That it could. A few months of winter will give the earth a chance to recharge. My gardens will be splendid moving forward. I wonder who came up with the idea?"

"Hades, of course."

She laughed. "Is that so? Are you sure about that?"

The mischief in his eyes gave her the answer, even if he gave credit to the God of the Underworld. "The only thing I am sure about is that I would do anything for you, Hecate," he said softly. "Even change the seasons."

"Well, it seems that you have given me all that I desire."

"Have I now? Are you sure about that?"

"Perhaps not," she grinned. "I think I can come up with a few more things I could have you do."

"I like the sound of that," he said. He took her hand and led her toward the door. "Come on, let's get everyone settled so we can get back to your list. In addition to all of the things I want to do to you later, we have a Samhain celebration to get ready for."

"We do indeed. Let's go put our order in for a brisk fall day."

"Anything for you, my heart."

To Jen

I can't thank you enough for all
you have done for me.
I love what we have created together.
Can't wait to see what the future holds! XO

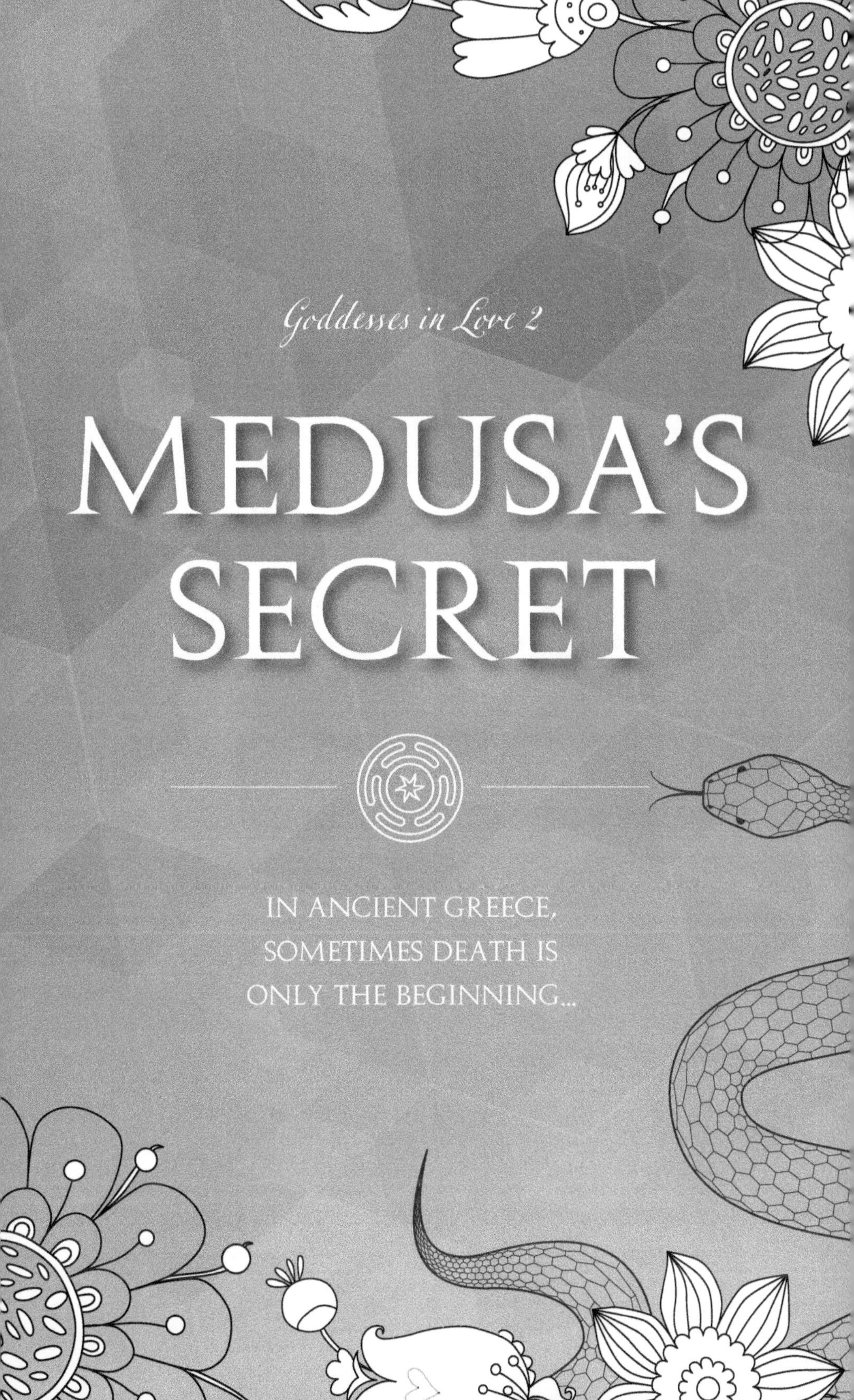

Goddesses in Love 2

MEDUSA'S SECRET

IN ANCIENT GREECE, SOMETIMES DEATH IS ONLY THE BEGINNING...

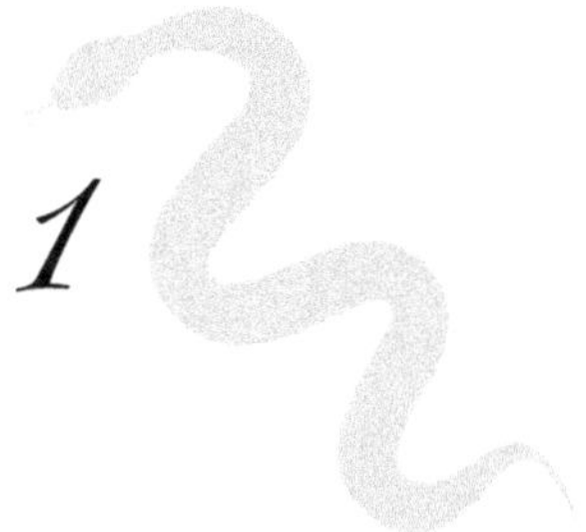

1

The thought crossed Medusa's mind that Persephone must be in a fantastic mood. She supposed she would be as well with the attentions of a god as hot as Hades, although she would never voice it. Persephone was a bit on the jealous side as were most of the gods and goddesses she knew. But today, the Goddess of the Underworld was smiling, and Medusa couldn't avoid being swept away by the beauty of her glorious morning.

Hands warm in the soil, she tended the herbs bursting with their heady fragrance. Eyes closed, she tipped her head back and allowed the brilliant sun to warm her pinkened cheeks. She had been spending a lot of time in the gardens of late, and the memories quickened her pulse. The bird's song added to her mood, and she could hardly contain the joy in her heart. She stood, lifted her basket of freshly cut rosemary, and traveled with a light step along the winding stone path to the entrance of Athena's temple.

Medusa had been with Athena from the start. She had overseen the construction of the Parthenon in Athens, along with the adjacent living quarters where she now lived. While a human form was something that typically evaded a Gorgon, one had been granted to Medusa long ago in exchange for her loyalty to Athena. Her humanity had been worth the cost—until now. The past few months had been the most wonderful of her life, but she wanted more.

Her steps echoed on the marble floors as she delivered the herbs to the kitchen. She had a few more chores to complete before Athena arrived. Being high priestess to the goddess was no easy task since she liked things just so. The floors had to be polished to a mirrored shine, and she ordered her altar clear of the countless items people gave her in tribute. It was Medusa's job to make sure everything was exactly right for the goddesses' return each day. She didn't mind; Athena wasn't only her patron goddess, she was also her friend.

With the return of Persephone's spring, there were larger groups who came to the temple in search of Athena's wisdom. Even though she was primarily known as the Goddess of War, she also had ancient skills in handicraft which she shared with the community who loved her. Many of the women who worshipped her had spent their winters practicing the new skills she had taught them, and they were anxious to show off their tapestries. Medusa had just finished folding the piece of fabric from the altar when Athena arrived. The goddess removed her helmet and flopped dramatically onto her throne.

"I swear by Zeus, things are getting tense in Athens. It took me most of the night to calm Ares down. The morning couldn't come soon enough."

Medusa loosened the straps on her mistress' sandals and put her bare feet in the warm water she had waiting. She kept her tone soothing and conversational. "He's always been on the volatile side. I've often wondered why Zeus didn't put him in charge of the Underworld instead of Hades."

"Ares would have that place filled in no time." Athena sighed as Medusa wiped the dust from her lower legs and rubbed her calves. "Hades is much more level-headed as far as all that goes."

"I suppose that's true," Medusa agreed. "Even more so now that he and Persephone are married."

"That was a good match, they are wild for one another." Athena nodded. "Hecate and Hermes knew what they were doing. Perhaps they could find such a match for you."

Medusa caught her breath then looked up to see if Athena had noticed her reaction. Thankfully, the goddess had her head tipped back with her eyes closed. She tried to keep her voice level as she responded.

"I am happy serving you, my goddess. This is my home." Medusa dried Athena's feet with one of the silk towels brought as an offering. It bore the scene of Athena's birth as she emerged from the forehead of her father, Zeus.

Athena opened her eyes and tipped her head down, her gaze examining Medusa's features. "I realize that, Medusa, but you have been a faithful priestess for some time and deserve some happiness too. Don't you want a family of your own? Should that be your choice, it would bring my heart joy to see you in love."

Medusa paused before her response; her loyalty had been tested before. Could it be that Medusa's secret had been realized? She cleared her throat of the lump that lodged there. "Thea, I love serving you and the temple. It has given me purpose, a home, and the humanity I sought for so long. I strive to make you proud."

"And you do." Athena's steely gaze searched Medusa's features for the truth of her words. After a moment, she nodded as if a decision had been made. "But if that ever changes, please know you can come to me."

Medusa wasn't prepared to discuss her future just yet, and Athena's intuition was impossible to avoid. She lowered her eyes against the piercing gray of Athena's stare and concentrated on lacing up her mistress' sandals. The leather laces crossed and knotted like snakes in a pit, not unlike the truth of her situation. Her future laid out like a tangled path, one she no longer wished to walk alone. But the choice wasn't entirely hers. For now, a change of topic was what she needed. Medusa searched her mind for an adequate distraction, finding it soft against her fingers as she tidied her workspace.

"This silk towel is lovely. The maiden who brought it thanked you for taking extra time with her this past winter."

Athena admired the towel, her face beaming with pride. "That is excellent craftsmanship. What was her name?"

"Arachne, I do believe."

She plucked the damp towel from Medusa's hands and ran it between her fingers. "Soft and delicate but also strong. The threads she used are amazing, almost as though they are fused with magic. Look at the shimmer." Athena shook the towel out and held it in front of her. Medusa could see the scene on the backside of the cloth. "She is highly gifted, but she doesn't come to mind. I should pay her another visit. Find out where she lives for me."

"Yes, my goddess."

"In the meantime, I don't want to leave Ares long—there is no telling what trouble he will get into. The last time I left him alone, he stirred up trouble with Sparta. His warmongering is exhausting." Athena sat up straight and huffed, blowing a stray ebony lock from her forehead. The visits would need to be quick. "Show those who are here inside, and I will listen to their prayers for the next hour."

Medusa took the towel Athena passed to her and gave a low bow. She hurried from the main hall to the foyer where the worshippers were gathered, eager to do her goddess' bidding. It would keep her out of Athena's scrutiny, which suited her. A little while longer and she would figure out how to broach her own topic.

The masses waited patiently on the steps, ready to take their gifts and concerns to the one who would help them navigate their decisions. Medusa let in small groups at a time to humble themselves before their goddess. Medusa hid in the shadows of the throne room and watched the countless genuflections. The gifts were endless, made with the same love and devotion the people felt for their patron goddess. She wished sharing her desires with Athena was as easy as it seemed to be for her worshippers.

Relief flooded her as she took a cleansing breath. She had successfully diverted the earlier discussion and thus avoided Athena's questions. But, knowing Athena, she didn't have much longer until the discussion would be brought up again, and she would have to face her judgement. She could no longer wait. The time had come for Medusa to speak to the man who had captured her eye. If he desired a future with her, he would have to speak up. They both would. Her heart had already made its choice, but she needed to be sure of his true intentions. In her earlier conversation with Athena, time didn't seem to be on their side.

According to the shadows on the sundial, Athena stayed closer to two hours before she left to check on Ares. She hardly rested, only taking a piece of fruit from the table to break her fast. Medusa finished packing up the offerings and separated them between things that Athena would want to keep and things that would be used elsewhere in the temple. Athena had pointed to very few items this time, and Medusa was surprised that she didn't want the lovely plum colored silk brought by the woman who needed help choosing between two suitors. As she held the cloth up against her chest and rubbed her hand down the smooth fabric, a deep baritone startled her.

"That color is stunning on you. I should like to see you wear it."

Medusa turned her head and caught the golden glow surrounding the man, before averting her gaze and lowering in a curtsy. "You honor me," she said softly.

Mesmerized by the man who moved toward her, she kept her head lowered against the power he radiated. She recognized the god by the trident he carried. Poseidon's steps halted directly in front of her, and she kept her gaze lowered. It wasn't wise to look up from a position of reverence, she had learned that the hard way with so many powerful men before. The gods were no different than a human man. If anything, they were worse. She knew what she would find by the gravely tone in his voice. The rumors about him preceded him.

"And I desire that you honor me." He squatted down, startling her enough to catch her glance. He tipped his head in bemusement. "You certainly can't do it from that position. Please rise." Then, unconventional for a god, he stood and reached his hand out to help her.

Against her better judgement, she accepted his aid. Clutching the fabric against her, Medusa took Poseidon's hand. Electricity pulsed between them, hot and fiery as if they were lightning bolts created by Zeus himself. Medusa's pulse fluttered, and she felt as if every nerve ending was aglow. She cleared her throat around her husky reply.

"Thank you, Theos." His grip was firm, and he didn't let her hand go even after she stood. She glanced into his fathomless eyes and decided she didn't really want him to. He was intriguing, and she was compelled by the possibility of his godly interest. Transfixed. She broke their gaze and, in looking down, confirmed her intuition had been correct. He was aroused. The point of his erection was barely hidden by his loose-fitting robes.

His eyes squinted, and a smile tickled his lips as if she were some great riddle he needed to solve. Perhaps that was just what she was. It was possible that he sensed the internal battle she fought every day, between staying true to her chosen path or allowing herself to embrace her desires. Seeing the glow of passion in Poseidon's eyes was thrilling but, at the same time, terrified her. It wasn't his passion that she desired. Or was it? His presence confused her senses.

"What is your name?" It wasn't so much a question but a demand, one she was compelled to respond to much as she fought to avoid it.

"Medusa," she answered quietly. She lowered her gaze to his feet, hoping that the excitement she was feeling was the result of the magick in his eyes. Each of the gods and goddesses had their own set of abilities through the power of their gaze. It was why Athena warned her priestesses never to make eye contact with them. His pull was bordering on irresistible, his power clearly tied to his prowess. Her heart fought the urge to give in to him. It wasn't possible to hold the fabric to her chest any tighter than she already did, but she tried. She knew she shouldn't encourage his attention; he wasn't a considerate lover. She knew that from the other nymphs in the surrounding temples.

"Medusa," he whispered. The tone in which he repeated her name was like the song of an Aoidos, lyrical and dripping with emotion. He raised their clasped hands and placed his lips on the inside of her wrist. Her breath caught as the tickle of his whiskers shot a pulse straight through her, and she squirmed against the feeling. It wasn't right. Tainted but, at the same time, intriguing. There was something unnatural about the way her body was reacting, but she longed for the feeling. She knew better than to be in the temple alone and should have moved to the inner sanctum when he arrived. No god or goddess ever dared to enter a goddess's private rooms uninvited, especially Athena's. It would have bought her some time.

It was too late to avoid his attention now, and even if he left, Medusa knew that he would be back. Their attraction was palpable. Athena would be enraged, but how could she possibly tell a god he wasn't welcome in his niece's temple?

"Great one, Theos, I don't think..."

"Poseidon, please."

Against her better judgement, Medusa addressed him by his given name. "Poseidon."

The smile that he graced her with sealed her fate. Unknowingly, the wheel of destiny was spun on her behalf once again, and Poseidon, God of the Sea, pulled her into an embrace.

2

The tinkling laughter of the temple nymphs startled Poseidon long enough for Medusa to break free from his hold. The further she distanced herself, the more she gained control of her senses. As the demi-goddesses entered the temple and witnessed Poseidon's godly glow, they abruptly dropped to their knees. The smile was back on his face, and he strolled toward them with a cocky strut.

"Good morning, ladies." He turned to wink at Medusa and stood before the group. "Or should I say afternoon?" Their heads remained lowered as he approached. "Let me have a look at you. You may all rise."

The nymphs all stood, their gauzy togas catching the light from the torches nearby. Two of them were wary of their guest and looked to Medusa for her reaction. She tried to keep her features neutral, but relief flooded through her. Medusa was never so glad to see her friends, and Cleodora and Melia picked up on exactly what was happening with a side glance and a pained smile. The third nymph, Thyia, was utterly enthralled, and it was she that Poseidon honed in on.

"It seems my visit has been cut short, and I'll be taking my leave." He put his finger under the smiling nymph's chin and locked gazes with her. "I should like some company on my way back home."

As his hand lowered, he brushed against her pebbled breast, dark against the sheer lavender fabric she wore. Her whispered response came out on a moan. "I shall be honored to attend to your needs, Theos."

His predatory smile sickened Medusa, and as much as she wanted to save her friend, she didn't dare.

"Excellent," he said softly. Thyia gazed adoringly into his face as he cupped her cheek. The other two nymphs kept their heads lowered, their weight transferring from one foot to the other. Their distress reached her from across the room. They all realized their friend's fate, yet they were all powerless to say or do anything. He was a god after all.

Poseidon glanced over his shoulder and addressed her one last time in a voice laced with the promise of passion. "We aren't done, protectress. I'll be back for you."

Medusa lowered her eyes against the magick he wove, and like Cleodora and Melia, she awaited his choice. She knew from the rumors, it could change in an instant. She thanked her goddess that the feelings she had earlier didn't seem to be real. Either way, illusion or not, she also knew there was nothing on Earth or in Olympus that would grant her the strength to fight his appeal if he chose her.

As Poseidon took Thyia's hand, Medusa was heartsick with the knowledge that her friend would no longer be welcome to serve the goddess. Once Poseidon had his way with her, Athena would execute a harsh and swift judgement. It wasn't fair, but it was the way things were, especially when it came to him in particular. His bickering with his brother, Zeus, was legendary, and it was no secret that Athena was favored by the ruler of Olympus. The animosity she and Poseidon had for one another had been there from the start and hadn't faded with time, so the easiest solution was to steer clear of him. She hoped the fact that Thyia had nothing to do with his impromptu visit would lessen her punishment.

A quick glance to Melia and Cleodora confirmed they kept their heads bowed against his appeal. Thyia, however, didn't. He gestured for her to start walking, and her hips swayed provocatively, urging her lover forward. The last thing she heard was the nymph's giggle as Poseidon placed his hand possessively on her lower back and splayed his hand over the top edge of her buttocks. He glanced over his shoulder once more, looking right into Medusa's eyes, and blew a kiss before leaving the building. She waited to move until he was no longer visible.

"Oh, Melia, Cleodora, are you both okay?" The nymphs' hurried steps brought them into her embrace. They both held fast to each other and her.

Cleodora was the first to speak. "We had no idea he was here, otherwise we would have never brought her in here."

"She has always been susceptible to the charms of a man," Melia added. "Poseidon is notoriously irresistible."

"We must pray to Athena that her experience will be satisfying and loving." Medusa led the two nymphs to the altar where they lowered themselves before the statue of their patron goddess. "It is the only way we can help her now. Goddess be merciful."

"She will never be allowed back," Melia whispered.

"That may be the least of her worries," Medusa answered.

"If the stories of Poseidon are true, it will be," Cleodora said.

They joined hands and lowered their heads as Medusa led the prayer. "Oh Great Athena, Goddess of Wisdom, hear our plea. Your humble servant, Thyia, has fallen under Poseidon's spell. Please buffer his nature with your calming presence and provide Thyia the opportunity for a truly loving experience."

"May Athena show mercy." They all whispered then offered their own prayers to the goddess.

Medusa's prayers included Thyia's name as well as her own. Soon, her secret would be known, and a choice would have to be made. She just hoped that when that day came their friendship would temper Athena's judgement.

After their prayers, Medusa sent Cleodora to Athena's inner sanctum to pull down the tapestries. They swapped them out seasonally, and they had received some lovely spring scenes that Athena would enjoy during her visits. Melia stayed behind with Medusa and was helping her clear out the ashes from the fire pits. She put a voice to what they were both thinking about.

"Thyia will be okay. She never liked serving Athena and was always looking for a way out."

"It doesn't excuse it," Medusa said. "Nor does it lessen my guilt at being relieved that you came when you did, and I avoided her fate."

"It's only natural," Melia soothed. "I feel the same. But we are here for the will of the gods and goddesses we serve. Athena can only provide so much protection."

"I know. I wish she were here more. If she were, this could have been avoided. It just doesn't seem right somehow."

"It's not, but we are powerless to change things. Although, I believe that you, out of any of us, do hold the power to change your fate."

"How so?"

Melia stopped her task and looked across the altar at Medusa. Her head was tipped, and a question crinkled her brow. "You are friends with the goddess you serve, that in and of itself is something we don't all have. And if I'm not mistaken, you do have the interest of her half-brother."

Medusa's breath caught. Her friend's observance had gone entirely unnoticed. "I don't know what you mean."

Melia's eyes lit with playful mischief. "You know exactly what I mean, or I should say who. And if you ask me, he feels the…"

"Athena, are you here?" A masculine voice called out, sending shivers down Medusa's spine. Her pulse quickened, and she shook her head and put her finger to her mouth gesturing for silence.

Melia nodded slowly, a knowing grin on her beautiful face. She shrugged and went back to her task and let Medusa greet their guest. Melia knew more than she let on, and Medusa wasn't sure how she felt about it. She should have been more cautious; the priestesses were excellent at keeping a low profile. There enough to perform their duties but invisible the rest of the time. It made her wonder how much of her secret was known and by whom.

She moved forward and made it to the front of the temple just as Perseus walked up the last marble step. He looked from side to side then glanced behind her. Medusa followed his line of sight and watched Melia stand and lift the soot bucket.

She called out as she walked toward the bedrooms. "I'm done here,

Medusa. I will go help Cleodora finish up. I can't imagine it will take more than an hour."

"Thank you, Melia," Medusa squeaked. She watched as the nymph disappeared through the curtains leading to Athena's bedroom then turned back to her guest. The demi-god was dressed casually, no hint of the weapons he generally wore, although Medusa knew better. He never went anywhere without his knife.

"Athena's not here, my lord."

He took a few steps forward until he was within inches of touching her. The heat of his breath warmed her cheeks, and the scent of peppermint surrounded her. He made a habit of stopping in the herb gardens before entering the temple. She looked up, taking in his strong jaw and higher yet to his playful eyes. The raised eyebrow and barely suppressed grin tickling his face had her wondering how she could have ever been attracted to Poseidon. The God of the Sea was nowhere near as compelling as Athena's half-sibling.

"That's a shame," he said. His next comment was but a whisper. "I suppose you'll have to keep me company until she arrives."

"She's only here in the mornings," Medusa answered. She could hardly hear her response over the sound of her heartbeat. His hand lifted, and she closed her eyes against the caress she knew would be next. His fingertips rasped against her cheek, sliding slowly down her neck and resting on her shoulder. His thumbs drew slow circles around the hollow of her neck, and like all the other times before, it drove her mad with desire.

"So I've been told," he said on a sigh. "Which is precisely why I'm here in the afternoon." His smile warmed her. "I shall wait for her in your company. Is that alright with you, Medusa?"

His hand dropped, and she missed the warmth of his touch immediately. The feelings she had for him were as real as the marble pillars that lined the front of the temple, although not nearly as cool. No, what she felt for him could never be mistaken for anything but a burning flame. At first, she hadn't believed it was true, and then she allowed the hope to bloom. Now, taking in the passion in his eyes, she knew Melia had been right to presume there was something going on between them. His sporadic visits since the day they met were much more regular now, and he hardly came in the mornings anymore, electing instead to come when he knew his half-sister wouldn't be present. The reasons had all but been confirmed with his smoldering gaze.

He waited for her response as she took his hand and pulled him through the throne room to the doorway that led to the gardens. She led him in silence as she had done so many times before and, once through the doorway, walked quickly down the marble steps into the formal garden. Their steps were hurried, and the excitement contagious. Once they were through the opening of the hedges that formed the labyrinth, he stopped and pulled her back into his arms.

"Not one more step," he said with a playful growl. "I need a kiss from you before I waste away. It's been far too long."

She went into his embrace willingly and placed her hands on his cheeks. They were clean shaven and smooth beneath her fingertips. The essence of musk and frankincense came to her, and she pulled in a deep breath of the comforting scent that she would forever connect to him. "Just a kiss?" His eyebrow raised at the bit of sass in her tone. "And wasn't it just last week we walked the labyrinth?"

He turned his head and kissed Medusa's palm then pulled her closer and leaned his forehead against hers. "Far too long ago for my taste, my love. And I don't recall that we did much walking that day."

Medusa's eyes grew wide, then she put her finger on his lips and shushed him with a whisper. "Someone will hear you."

He pulled her hand from her lips and kissed the inside of her wrist, making his way up her arm to the crook of her neck. "I doubt anyone will be out this time of day, and it's true we didn't walk." He pulled her closer, and she could feel his breath on her ear. His next words were whispered. "I recall you sat, and I was kneeling before you. Feasting on you as if you were my personal buffet."

Her eyes were closed and her head tipped back, visualizing what they had done on the marble bench not ten feet from where they now stood. His arms pulled her tighter against him. "The day is young, and we have an entire labyrinth to explore. Lots of hidden treasures we have yet to uncover." As his lips met hers, all doubt and hesitation left her mind like smoke from a flame. His hands scooped behind her, and she was soon straddling his waist as he walked her to their favorite bench. He sat down and tucked her legs on either side, snug up against his groin. She was glad for his casual dress. His armor was much harder to work around.

"We have but an hour," Medusa whispered.

His hands swept under her gown, and she felt the cool breeze on her thighs. "I will take any amount of time I can get with you. I have thought about nothing else all week."

"You fill my every waking thought. The days are torture without you."

"Good thing your hero is here to save you then." He cupped her face and gazed thoughtfully into her eyes. "You have my heart, Medusa."

Her answer was a smile then a kiss. "You have captured mine as well, Perseus." And there was her answer. She knew he cared for her, but time would tell what that meant for him in his world. A hero's life wasn't easy, especially on the families that were left behind during their travels. They hadn't spoken of a future, but if she was going to leave Athena's temple for him, she knew she wanted a family. Children.

As they shared their breaths and bodies in the garden, she tried not to worry about the future and how it would be for them. If Perseus chose a life with her, he would need to approach his father and negotiate changes to his pre-determined destiny. Zeus didn't like change, especially when it contradicted his authority. Athena was a lot like Zeus and would be Medusa's hurdle to jump.

She squelched the small voice in her mind that warned their path to happiness wouldn't be easy and found comfort in the stolen moment she shared with her lover. They would worry about their future tomorrow. For now, there was only desire.

3

Athena came back to the temple just as Medusa was serving Perseus dinner. The other nymphs had prepared the meal before they left for the night. Medusa kept her distance and watched from afar as the two most important people in her life discussed family matters over the main course. Her passions flared anew each time Perseus pulled the wineglass from his lips. She longed to taste the wine that lingered there, and his glances and secret smiles to the corner where she stood confirmed he'd allow it. Thankfully, her reaction to him was hidden by the shadows and boisterous conversation.

It wasn't right for one of Athena's virgins to be consumed by such thoughts, and if Athena knew the truth of it, she wondered if their friendship would survive the goddess' wrath. What made it worse was the fact that he was Athena's brother—well, half brother, technically, since they didn't share a mother. Although, more than Athena, it was their father that Medusa worried about. Zeus had plans for his son, and they didn't include him settling down with a family. Athena wasn't the only hothead on Mt. Olympus. Medusa needed to tread lightly, as did Perseus.

"Medusa come join us," Athena offered. She pointed to the chair near her, across from Perseus. "You are making me nervous hovering in the dark."

Against her better judgement, she moved toward the table. "It is easier to stand between the table and kitchen, especially since we are the only ones left this evening."

"All the more reason to join us," Athena smiled. "I'm sure Perseus won't mind."

"Not at all."

A quick glance was all Medusa needed to see the mischief in his eyes. He shifted in his seat then cleared his throat after the warning glance she shot him. Now was not the time or place.

"Very well," Medusa demurred. "I will be honored to join you. Thank you, Thea."

"You don't have to refer to me as goddess, Medusa. I do have a name. You may call me by it."

"I don't feel it is proper when we aren't alone."

"Well, the others have left, and Perseus is family, so I insist you use my given name."

"Very well. Thank you for the honor, Athena."

Athena smiled in response then glanced between her two guests and raised a glass. "Long life and health to my two favorite people."

"I'll drink to that," Perseus said. "And thank you, sister. Your love and friendship mean the world to me."

"I would do anything for you, my brother." Athena took a bite of cheese before addressing Medusa. "So, I understand Poseidon has taken another one of my nymphs to be his plaything?" Her tone was conversational, but Medusa could feel the anger coming from her in waves. Athena didn't like it when her nymphs were bothered and was especially irritated when they were taken from her temple. Poseidon was the worst of the offenders. Medusa often wondered if it had more to do with their dislike for one another than it did Poseidon's libido.

Medusa nodded. "It was Thyia, mistress."

"I understand that when she and the others arrived, you had been here alone for some time with Poseidon."

"That is true." She glanced at Perseus, who was attempting to seem indifferent to the conversation but his grip on his wineglass told another tale. His knuckles were white against the goblet, and his jaw tight. His anger grew as she tried to diffuse the situation Athena had caused.

"He came to pay his respects to..."

Athena slammed her goblet down on the table. "Don't be ridiculous.

He came here to see you."

Perseus stood up from his chair and paced between the table and fireplace. His nervous energy shook Medusa to the core. She had never seen this side of his demeanor, and it unnerved her.

She lowered her head to hide the tears that were forming. It seemed that no matter what she did she was fated to disappoint her goddess. "Mistress, I didn't…"

She felt Athena's hand on her arm. "I'm not angry with you, Medusa. Poseidon is another story."

"Poseidon is a pig," Perseus murmured.

"Most would agree," Athena said. "Although there are some that see nothing wrong with his behavior."

"No man should ever have the right to treat women the way he does. As a god, he should serve as a better example."

"He's a bit overbearing, it's true. But nothing happened."

Perseus posed a question before Athena could respond. "Did he touch you?"

Medusa glanced at Athena, who patiently awaited her answer. Perseus waited as well, a vein in his neck pulsing with the beats of her heart. The small gleam in Athena's eye was disconcerting, and Medusa struggled to understand its meaning. Her lack of response brought Perseus back to the table. He leaned forward, hands in front of him, and posed his question again. He was taut, like a tiger ready to pounce.

His voice deepened, his tone serious. "Medusa, did he touch you?"

The tears fell, and it upset her to no end that she couldn't remain strong, but the stress of her secret and the decision she would now have to face was too much for her to bear. The pain of it dripped down her cheek as she shook her head and answered her lover's question. "Only my hand and a kiss to my wrist."

Perseus pounded the table then stood and addressed Athena. "There are things I need to attend to. Thank you for dinner, but I must take my leave."

"I understand. Safe travels, brother."

They watched as Perseus stomped out of the temple. The muscles in his arms bulging, and his chest puffed. He was a man on a mission.

While Medusa was flattered that he would be upset about Poseidon's visit, she was simultaneously terrified. A demi-god had no strength against one of the ancients. Athena, on the other hand, seemed pleased with herself.

"He's quite taken with you," she said with a smirk.

Medusa glanced back to her face. Athena looked very much like a cat who had been in the cream. She turned back and looked for one last glimpse of Perseus, but he had disappeared. Medusa rose and walked toward Athena who had moved to the fireplace. Her head was bowed as she watched the flames dance.

Medusa investigated the back of Athena's form for any indication that she might be upset about the fact that she had fallen in love with her brother. So far, the indications seemed good, but she wasn't taking any chances.

"Poseidon isn't any worse than any other man I've had to deal with. Perseus is too much of a hero to let something like that go, but I wish he wouldn't waste his efforts on me."

Athena turned around, her smile softening and her head tilted in thought. "Perseus has no other choice but to defend the woman he cares for. It is in his nature. But no matter the outcome of the future you pursue, decisions must be made by you both. Until you commit to your path, Poseidon is going to be a regular visitor to my temple, and I have no desire to keep losing my nymphs to him. It needs to stop."

"They find him irresistible, Thea, there's something about him that takes your breath away." Medusa shrugged.

"There is nothing about him that is at all interesting, trust me. He cheats."

Medusa was confused. Why would a god need to cheat? "What do you mean?"

"That damn Aphrodite keeps loaning people her belt. Poseidon was in such a habit of borrowing it that she finally made him a pin for his toga out of one of the links. She had Hephaestus fashion it for him. The metal-working dolt will do anything for her. It has always been so."

"I had heard of her belt but never thought of her loaning it out. That makes complete sense now," Medusa mused. The confirmation made her feel better that her attraction to the powerful god was prompted by magick.

"There are all sorts of gods and goddesses using it," Athena flopped in her chair and took a piece of cheese off of her plate. "It's ridiculous, really. Love isn't something to dabble with, it should be pure. Something that grows between two people, that binds them over time. Besides, Aphrodite is the last person who should have that belt—she's already stunning."

"I would agree. It does seem rather unfair that someone so beautiful should have more of an advantage. Besides, it seems that the love she promises is fleeting. If it were me, it is the love of a lifetime that I would desire."

"My point exactly. She should be taught a lesson for giving gods and goddesses an unfair advantage over humans. However, I haven't found the best way to do that. Yet."

"You would consider going after Aphrodite?" Perhaps Athena was more vengeful than Medusa had realized. Or was she seeing the gods and goddesses now for what they really were? Jealous and petty.

"You didn't hear it from me," Athena said. "But there are a few gods and goddesses that I feel could use a lesson or two. And believe me, Poseidon and Zeus are among them."

Medusa knew that about Athena. Knew that most people thought her temper was volatile and swift, an assumption propagated by the gods and goddesses that she had tried to keep in line. It was entirely why Medusa decided to serve her all those years ago. Athena was a great many things, but she was levelheaded, and at the center of every decision she made was a sense of justice and balance.

"Your secret is safe with me," Medusa said with a smile.

Athena hugged her tight, and it made Medusa think of her sisters. Her friendship with the goddess was almost like family, but it wasn't the same. Strangely, for a goddess born without a mother, Athena was the most loving and thoughtful goddess out of the entire Parthenon.

"I know it is," Athena said. "You are truly the best person I know to keep secrets. Even your own."

Medusa flushed, and Athena smiled. "You're trustworthy and loyal, and I want you to know I'm here for you."

"I know you are, my goddess," Medusa murmured. She still couldn't look her in the eyes when it came to this topic.

"You'll be able to be honest with me when the time comes?"

Medusa pulled back from the hug and nodded. "I will. It will be soon. I would have told you already, but it's not only my truth to tell."

Athena nodded and walked away, calling over her shoulder. "I realize that, you know, which is why I brought it up. You need to be sure you don't run out of time. Poseidon is not one to step aside once he decides on his target. And Perseus knows that."

As the goddess walked back toward her chambers, Medusa whispered to the fire. "That is what I'm most afraid of."

Weeks had gone by, and Medusa was worried sick. There had been no word from Perseus, and Athena's visits were quicker than normal as she busied herself with the work of a goddess. The conversations between them had been brief, and Medusa had not dared to ask after Perseus. Even though the goddess had led her to believe that she was in support of Medusa reaching for her dreams of starting a family, she did also know that the gods and goddesses could be fickle. Athena, for all her good points, could be the worst of them all. Luckily, she had been in Athena's good graces up until now.

She and the nymphs were in the altar room washing down the marble statues when Thyia raced in sobbing.

"He didn't want me," she wailed.

"Well, what did you expect?" Melia rolled her eyes. "You know how the gods are and how many before you have been tossed to the side. Why would you think you'd be any different?"

She was speaking the truth, but it was cruel to point it out. Medusa looked at Melia with arms akimbo and mouth agape. She turned and took a few steps toward Thyia with arms wide. "Don't listen to Melia, it's a mistake any of us could have made."

As Thyia sobbed in her embrace, her response was muffled against Medusa's chest. "It's not a mistake you would have made, Medusa, you're too wise for that. Oh, what am I to do? I won't have a home, Athena's going to kill me."

Medusa pulled back from the embrace and shook her head. "Don't be ridiculous, Athena doesn't kill anybody for stuff like that."

Cleodora's comment echoed through the room. "No, she just turns people into monsters and lets them live."

Medusa whipped her head around and glared at her.

Cleodora shrugged with a sheepish look. "What? You know it's true."

Medusa shook her head in frustration and turned Thyia toward the entrance. She led her out with her arm around her shoulders.

"Don't listen to Cleodora, you know Athena is fair in her judgments, and the only thing you did wrong was follow your heart. You didn't know Poseidon was going to be that way. I know I certainly had hope for you when we hadn't seen you in a few weeks. I'll talk to Athena on your behalf later and see what I can do. Perhaps there's a demigod in need of a seamstress. Your dresses are stunning, so maybe we can find a good use of your talent."

Thyia's shoulders straightened, and she stood a bit taller. "You're a true friend, Medusa," she said. "I can't thank you enough. I'll come back later tomorrow to see what she said."

Medusa agreed. "The more I think on it, the more I know that is the right path. At the very least, I know Athena will still want you to work on her gowns."

"Thank you, Medusa." Thyia turned and walked away, her head a little higher than it was when she entered. It broke Medusa's heart to see her friend become one of the countless women tainted by the whim of a god. It happened all too often. The broken hearts upset her, they always had, which was part of the reason she had made up her mind to serve the virgin goddess in the first place. But, like Thyia, she no longer could do so.

Athena's hints that she was aware of Medusa's secret were enough to make a drastic change. And she was lucky that she did hold the goddess' friendship, otherwise she, too, could have been turned into any number of beasts that suited the goddess' whim. Perseus hadn't made his intentions known, yet she couldn't help but be caught up in the passion every moment she was with him. She was in love with him, and she believed he was in love with her in return. But until he fully committed to her, and she was sure his vision for a life outside the temple aligned with hers, she wouldn't be able to move forward with him. No matter what the goddess guessed was going on, Medusa couldn't be truthful until she knew Perseus's mind.

No longer able to serve Athena and unsure of her future with the man she had given her body to, Medusa's options were sparse. But there would be a time, soon, when she no longer had the luxury of avoiding her fate. She knew that time had come, and Athena's imagined wrath was now the least of her worries.

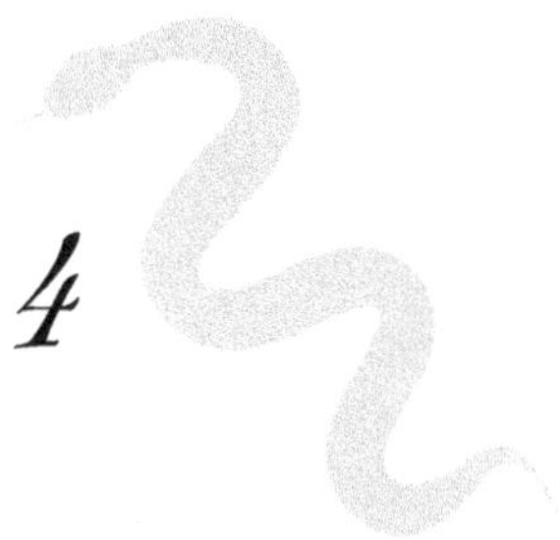

4

Athena came back late the next day and immediately called for a bath. Medusa took care of the task herself, scattering rose petals in the water and lighting candles. She had gotten good at gauging Athena's moods, and from her mistress' demeanor, it could go either way. The goddess sat in the tub, allowing the weight of the day to float away with the ripples in the water. Medusa sat behind her on the edge of the large sunken tub, running a brush through Athena's raven-colored hair. She was happy to see there weren't many tangles, it would make for a less painful conversation for both of them.

"Thyia came by yesterday, my goddess," Medusa said softly. She made sure when opening potentially volatile topics that she used soothing tones.

"She's alright then?" Athena's tone was relaxed. Medusa wondered if she was truly registering their conversation.

Medusa put down the brush and massaged Athena's scalp, circling her temples in a soothing motion. It would be wise to relax her, with Thyia's fate still in her hands. As was her own, if she honestly thought about it.

"She knows she can't come back, mistress. However, she had hoped you would be merciful when you passed judgement."

"I'll bet," Athena murmured. The conversation could still go either way. Medusa's fingers were cramping, but she kept rubbing. Soothing circles, positive intent.

Athena pulled in a deep breath and let it out on a sigh. "Thyia was always a wonderful help. I'm not nearly as close to her as I am to you though. I'm not sure I should be as lenient as I would be with you, Medusa." Athena tipped her head back and looked into Medusa's face. "You do understand what I'm saying to you, right?"

Medusa lowered her eyes and nodded. She had told her, without coming out and saying it, that she valued their friendship. She just hoped that when the time came it would be strong enough to overcome the web of secrets that bound them. There was so much more at stake than her friendship with a goddess or where she would live. She would be changing a hero's destiny, from that which had been written in the stars by the king of the gods himself. Having sex with Perseus was one thing, asking him to commit to a wife and family was completely another. Medusa had never wanted anything less. Falling in love with a hero wasn't something she had ever counted on. But now that she had, there was no turning back.

Athena turned back and sank lower into the tub. "In your opinion, Medusa, what should Thyia's fate be? She has consorted with my uncle and could possibly be carrying his child, so I do feel some obligation to help her. However, all my girls have been told to avoid being alone with him, especially since we know he is someone that will never change— at least not until I can figure some things out." She chuckled at her own comment.

Medusa smiled. Thankfully, her mood had changed for the better. "Many of us are not as empowered as you are, mistress. We can't control our own destinies."

She responded with a huff. "Well, that's complete rubbish, and you know it, Medusa. Demigods and humans are probably more capable of controlling their fate and destiny than the gods and goddesses are. We were created for a single purpose and are deigned to enact that purpose whatever it is, even if it goes against what we know is right. We are creatures of compulsion. It is our nature."

"I didn't mean to upset you, Athena."

"You aren't upsetting me, my friend. But it is important you understand that we didn't ever have a choice. We were born to our duties. It's not the fact that women are following their desires and having sexual relations with whoever they want that upsets me. It's the fact that I can't. That I was designed by the Universe to provide pure and untainted counsel from the forehead of my father who decided he didn't want to commit to the pure and untainted part of his duties. His transgressions are the entire reason for my existence. Transgressions, I might add, that I will never be able to experience myself."

"There are those that would say that you are better off for it."

"I would agree on most counts, but the fact that I can't choose my own fate still irritates me. My father isn't the most lenient when it comes to what his children are allowed to do or not do. However, he doesn't necessarily lead by example."

"I feel bad for Hera," Medusa mumbled.

"I've come to learn she knew what she was getting into and is doing fine simply working around it. We've had many conversations about how much of a pig my father can be. Her temper tantrums are more than warranted, in my opinion—not that I would ever voice that to my father."

Medusa lowered her hands to Athena's shoulders and kneaded. It made her sick to think that anyone with so much power was unable to change their own destiny. It didn't bode well for those without it. This was the most Athena had spoken about her inner thoughts in a long time, so she did what any good friend would do and listened. As Athena vented, Medusa kept up her ministrations. Her fingers were sore, but the goddess' shoulders were tight. She kept rubbing until Athena relaxed.

"I don't blame you for any of it. I wouldn't want to suffer the wrath of Zeus either." She thought about her own situation and how protective he was of Athena. She realized now that it wasn't a father being protective of a daughter, necessarily, but more that he was protecting the piece of his soul he had pulled from himself to create her. Not only was he a pig, but he was also self-serving. He had just lost the last of the respect Medusa had ever had for him.

"It is why he must never know Hera and I are close now. Women must always stick together."

"I understand and will always keep your secrets safe, Athena."

"I know you will," she answered. "So, now what of Thyia? I'm feeling relaxed and generous."

"While I know that some have been changed into an animal or object of nature to avoid men's attentions, I believe Thyia would be happy doing something else."

"I hate that people think I do that out of spite," Athena groused. "They all wanted to be left alone, and they can shift back to human form at will. They don't always want to, by the way, and they know I am just helping them out."

"I know that. Your heart is always in the right place."

"Thank you, Medusa."

"I wish all truly knew you as I do," Medusa said honestly. The knots she massaged had all but disappeared, and the goddess sunk deeper in the tub.

"You are a kind person. I have never known anyone so generous and loving. My brother is a lucky man."

Medusa blushed, still unsure that she should acknowledge her relationship with Perseus. Athena was already changing the subject. "What do you feel Thyia's fate should be? She is lucky to have you looking out for her."

"I don't think that Thyia necessarily wants to run from men. She seems to really like them, actually."

"You are right about that," Athena laughed. "She was never cut out to be one of my priestesses. You know, it isn't the sex that bothers me, it is the poor choice in partners."

"I get that. Not all partners are loving."

"That is a fact."

"She loved being here also, serving the temple and its people, so what about a shop? Somewhere where she can make clothing and continue to do the things that she is really good at?"

Athena nodded, her eyes remained closed. "She is an excellent seamstress. That is a wonderful idea. I do love the gowns she fashions for me."

Medusa continued to soothe Athena's shoulders and neck as she stated her case.

"Yes. And she could continue to serve you in that capacity as well as other goddesses whom you grant favor."

"Perhaps she can work with Arachne. I did go see her, you know," Athena said. "The fabrics she weaves are finer than any silk I have ever seen, on Earth or in Olympus. It would be amazing to have Thyia fashion things from the fabric."

"What a wonderful idea, Athena! Perhaps I could go to town and find a small building that would make the perfect shop." Medusa was excited, this idea felt all kinds of right.

"In a bordering town, perhaps Thebes? Give the landowner anything they want, and we'll set her up in a shop. In return, the ladies can make my dresses among other things. I will approach Arachne. I have another matter I must speak to her about."

"Thank you, Athena. I can't wait to tell Thyia. She will be thrilled. When I find a place, we can all meet to discuss the terms."

"I will leave you to handle it, Medusa," Athena said on a sigh. "I trust your judgement, and if you need me, you know how to call me."

Medusa nodded and placed her hand on the single stone that hung from the necklace Athena had given her. As high priestess, she had never used it but knew that she only needed to hold it and recite the words she had been given to bring the goddess to her side.

"I appreciate all you've done for me and my family, Athena. It will not be forgotten."

"You and your sisters have been loyal to me, and I am eternally grateful. Anything you need, it will be granted." She stood with her arms outstretched and waited until Medusa wrapped a linen around her. As she stepped out of the tub, she shot Medusa a playful grin.

"By the way, you should find some more nymphs for my temple. Of late, my priestesses seem to have other ideas of what they want to do with their lives."

Medusa inwardly cringed while she helped her to her dressing table. "Right away, Thea." The amused smile on Athena's lips didn't soothe the knot in Medusa's stomach. She hated lying to her mistress. Planning a life outside the temple with a man was one of the worst things a virgin priestess could possibly do.

The next day, Medusa met Thyia in an artisan village between Athens and Thebes that she loved to shop in. The town was filled with talented artists who created everything from marble sculptures to jewelry, and the commerce was booming. The town was getting new shops almost daily, and she had been there often enough to know that there weren't many textile shops there. Thyia's talent would be highly sought after.

"I still can't believe that Athena suggested this," Thyia gushed. "It's like a dream come true."

"She recognizes talent when she sees it," Medusa answered. "Arachne makes some beautiful fabric. Between the two of you, I believe you will be extremely successful." Medusa pointed to a quaint cottage at the end of the street. There were herbs in flower boxes that lined either side of the house. "That is the house I was telling you about. I thought the herbs could be used to create sachets."

"How much is the rent?"

"We will need to find out, but Athena isn't worried about that, since you will be the head seamstress to the temple. You can pay your debt off that way. She already has a few jobs lined up for you."

Thyia giggled. "I bet she does." She threw her arms around Medusa and gave her a quick hug. "Thank you so much, my friend, you are a miracle worker. You just saved my life."

Medusa hugged her back then tensed as she saw who was approaching over Thyia's shoulder.

"Where's my hug?"

Poseidon's voice startled Thyia, who turned around to face him. "You had more than your fare share and decided you didn't want them anymore." Her hands were on her hips, her weight on one foot. The other tapped angrily.

"I didn't say I wanted one from you," Poseidon said dismissively as he walked around her and right up to Medusa. Much as Medusa didn't want to engage, she didn't want Thyia suffering the wrath of a god either. Her hand covered her necklace just as his were placed on her upper arms. His touch wasn't as potent as it had been before—if anything, it was making her ill as was Thyia's hurt expression.

"Theos, I don't think…"

"I told you to call me Poseidon, my sweet."

Thyia turned and pulled one of his hands from Medusa's arm. "You need to leave her alone. She's Athena's high priestess. Her favorite."

"She's my favorite too," he answered. He moved closer to her, pressing his body up against hers and leaning his face down to whisper into her ear. "I will give you a life free from servitude, just say you'll be mine."

Medusa tensed and pulled her head back. "I'm honored, but I am happy serving in Athena's temple." She put as much distance as she could between them while still locked in his embrace. She turned her head, attempting to pry herself from his arms as he lunged for a kiss.

"Get your tentacles off of her." Medusa didn't need to see him to know who it was, although his tone was far from the loving one she favored. The next thing she heard was the snip of Perseus's sword as he pulled it from its scabbard. The sound caused Thyia to run in the direction of the temple. "I won't warn you twice."

Poseidon's fingertips tensed and pressed into Medusa's tender arms. He was angry, but his face still held a clenched smile. He watched her face aptly as he responded to Perseus.

"You and I both know you wouldn't survive the battle. Put your sword down, son of Zeus." The title was spat out with distaste, and Medusa now saw that it wasn't so much that Poseidon wanted her but that he didn't want the son of his brother to have her. "You can't kill a god."

"Perhaps not, but I can have fun trying." Perseus rocked side to side in a crouched stance, preparing for battle.

"And how would your lover feel if you died when she could save you?"

Perseus's concentration was jarred for the briefest of moments. Long enough for him to look into her eyes to add conviction to his next sentence. "She already has my heart. No matter what happens to me, my love for her is eternal. Nothing you do will change that."

Their secret hadn't been a secret at all. If Poseidon knew, there was no telling how many other gods and goddesses did as well. There was nothing the gods loved more than to stir the pot of humanity and see who came to a boil next. It was entirely how the night skies obtained so many constellations. Every past lover was given a place of honor there when they could no longer be together. Whatever it took, that would not be Perseus's fate.

Medusa shook her head as she caught his gaze over Poseidon's shoulder, willing him to stay with her cries. "Perseus, please don't." Poseidon's grip around her shoulders kept her wedged against his form. She could hardly breathe, let alone move her arms. As Perseus came into her line of sight, her eyes pleaded with him, but his mind was made up. He touched his lips then center of his chest, before breaking eye contact with her. It was as close to an embrace from him that she was going to receive, considering the circumstances.

Perseus completed his combat circle then stood behind Poseidon, weapon readied, and called out. "If you don't remove your hands from her, I will do it for you." Perseus moved his feet shoulder-width apart and bent his knees. He held his sword with both hands in front of him, readied for a strike. It made Medusa feel better in some small way that he wouldn't strike the first blow but rather wait for his fate to be dealt. Poseidon couldn't wield his trident and hold her at the same time, so perhaps, if she remained in his arms, it would give Perseus more time.

"You are welcome to try, demi-god."

No one dared to confront a god in this manner, and Poseidon's demeanor reflected that. His body was rigid, but he had yet to give up his prize. Did she truly matter that much to him? She didn't think so, and Poseidon had more than enough reason to deal with Perseus swiftly. The fact that Perseus was his nephew was the only thing stopping him from lashing out. That and, possibly, the thought of his brother Zeus getting involved.

Poseidon let go of one of her arms and, while still holding the other, turned to face Perseus. He waved his free hand, and his trident appeared as he called it forth. A blueish-green light crackled around the weapon, pulsing from the magick that had forged it.

She feared for Perseus and, now that her hands were free, tightened one around the stone in her necklace. With her eyes closed, she sent visions of the scene before her and recited the words that would bring Athena to her side. She had no other choice. Poseidon wouldn't let Perseus live after so many witnesses seeing them fight over her. He was too proud to admit defeat in any form. Besides, the gods always won.

Perseus kept his focus on his enemy and didn't let her distract him. It was the sign of a true hero and was why he had survived so many battles. But when the earth cracked behind him and a powerful voice rumbled, it startled him from his stance.

"Poseidon, let my priestess go!" Athena's voice roared, and she, too, had her sword ready. Medusa was never so happy to see her friend and never more unsure of the path she had chosen. Had her choice been the right one? Would her vision of the future align with Perseus's?

He glanced over, and seeing Athena's warrior stance and godly glow, Perseus once again lowered into his attack stance.

Poseidon shook his head. He sounded bored. "Athena, you know you can't stop me either, even if you do have your father's ear. I have decided to take Medusa as my bride, and you and I both know that my choice will be binding in his eyes."

Athena lowered her sword and stepped to Perseus, placing her free hand on his shoulder to prevent him from moving forward. His anger was being held by a tenuous thread, and it took all Medusa had in her not to run to him to calm him. She had already decided to go with Poseidon willingly, if he let Perseus live.

The goddess' eyes had a fire in their depths. Medusa wasn't sure at this point that any of them would be getting the future they imagined. "Very well," Athena said with her eyebrow raised. It was the same look she had every time she passed judgement on her subjects. Medusa braced herself for whatever Athena had planned. She heard the goddess' soothing voice in her mind. *Keep your eyes closed, my friend.*

She placed complete trust in her goddess and immediately closed her eyes. Quicker than a viper strike, Athena's magick surrounded Medusa, and it pricked her skin like a thousand tiny needles. The feeling was just starting to get uncomfortable when she felt her body transform. Her golden hair, once in tendrils around her face, was now weighted and moving. When she heard the hisses, she knew what Athena had done. Her arms cooled under Poseidon's touch, and when the texture of her skin changed, he dropped his hand.

"What have you done? Change her back," Perseus pleaded. His voice cracked and tore at her heart. "You can't leave her like this!"

She had been right. They wouldn't be getting the future they had imagined, and her biggest regret was that she hadn't had met Perseus sooner in her lifetime.

Medusa kept her eyes shut tight against the scene that was playing out. A scene that never in her life she would have wished on her worst enemy. Athena's voice was harsh. "I'm giving Poseidon a bride worthy of his monstrous behavior."

"Athena, you can't…"

"Don't presume to tell a goddess what she can and can't do, brother." Her tone didn't leave any room for argument. "f I were you, Poseidon, I would take her far away from here. It will be especially interesting to see how you handle gazing into her eyes as you have sex with her."

Medusa could feel her nails extending into claws, the transformation hurt as it gripped her body. Thankfully, unlike her sisters, she seemed to still have two legs, but the scales covered the sides as well as both of her arms, if her guess was right. Stheno and Euryale were snakes from the waist down but had kept their human hair. It seemed that Medusa wasn't going to be as lucky. Her head was now crowned with a nest of vipers that curved and snapped as they searched for their next target. She heard Poseidon take a few steps away but kept her eyes shut tight. Just when she thought perhaps the changes were complete, her back started to burn just under her shoulder blades. The pain was so great, it caused her to drop to her hands and knees as she prepared for what came next.

Poseidon's voice boomed over Medusa's pain-filled moans. "You are spiteful, Athena. I would have given her a good life. It seems, Perseus, that neither of us will be loving the fair-cheeked Medusa." She felt the force of Poseidon's anger as he struck the base of his trident against the ground.

"Are you happy with the outcome, oh great God of the Sea? Any more lives you want to ruin while you are at it?" Perseus's voice was pained. The three of them were arguing, but most of what they were saying was muffled by a haze of pain. Medusa's transformation wasn't something that she had ever anticipated going through, since she had negotiated to remain in human form all those years ago. Had she known how painful it would be to wait, she would have rethought her decision.

"I've made up my mind. You need to both accept it."

Medusa cried out as leathery wings erupted from her back and tore through her dress. They stretched outward, testing their ability to carry her to safety. Soon, like the harpies, she would be able to fly away from it all, if she chose to. The sound of footsteps became louder, and the snakes that surrounded her head hissed and snapped as they tried to protect her during the final stage of her transformation. Perseus's voice cut through her anguish and added to the agony she was consumed by. Her heart shattered. There was no turning back for them.

"My love, are you okay? This is all my fault." The steps stopped, and her lover's voice pleaded. "I should have told my father about you, about the life I wanted with you." Medusa cried out, her heart filling with the knowledge he had wanted the same future but breaking with the realization that they would never acquire it. "Please change her back. I'll do anything, Athena."

"Not the way her magick works," Poseidon responded. "Time to find yourself a new play-thing." His trident struck the ground once more, and with a crack of energy, he left. Medusa could no longer feel the sea god's presence filling the space which gave her a sense of relief.

Athena and Perseus spoke more freely now that he was gone. "You can change her back, right?"

"It's not that easy, Perseus. There are still some things that need to be done."

"I don't understand. What sorts of things? You had the power to change her, why can't it be reversed?"

"Poseidon was right, it doesn't work that way. Magick always comes with a cost."

"Well, why are the humans always the ones paying it?" He didn't wait for a response and moved closer to Medusa. She could feel his warmth radiating toward her. "Are you okay? Please answer me, my love."

"Remember to keep your eyes closed, my friend." Athena called to her from a distance, which Medusa appreciated. She was giving her a chance to say goodbye.

Medusa nodded then stood with wings unfurling and flapping behind her. She rubbed her hands up both arms, and they were cool and scaly to the touch. Running her tongue over her top teeth, she felt the sharp points that completed her transformation. Even if she were able to open her eyes, she wouldn't dare. She wouldn't want to see Perseus's horrified expression.

"I'm okay," she said quietly. "It's better this way."

"How can you say that?" His agony tore at her soul. If only she could soothe him.

Medusa heard his sword drop and felt his body press against hers. As he took her in her arms, she sent a message to the snakes that formed her hair to not hurt him. She wasn't sure if they could be controlled, but she thought she should try. As his arms worked around her waist and her head rested on his chest, she was glad they had obeyed. It would be the last time she would know his touch.

"This is what I should have been all along. It's my destiny," Medusa whispered. "I will be forever grateful for the time we had together."

"Whatever task I need to complete, whichever sea I need to cross, whatever beast I need to kill, it will be done. I will make this right."

He pulled back and cupped her face, kissing her with the same passion he shared in the labyrinth. With a passion she would never know again. Medusa pulled back with a cry and turned from him. Her wings settled around her like a shield—she couldn't take any more heartbreak. "Please go, Perseus. I need to embrace my new future, and it can no longer include you."

"We'll see about that." He took a few steps, then she heard his sword scrape the ground as he picked it up. Athena was still standing nearby, and Medusa dutifully kept her eyes shut tight as she had been instructed. She was sure she would find out why when she and Athena were finally alone.

"I'm not sure I can ever forgive you, sister."

"That makes you and everyone else in Greece. Although, perhaps one day you will," she murmured as he stormed away.

Athena walked around to face Medusa, taking her hands in her own. "It is safe to open your eyes, we are alone." Medusa looked into the eyes of her betrayer, her transformer, her friend, and saw what she always had before—love and sisterhood. The beauty of it filled what was left of her shattered heart.

"Well, that got rid of Poseidon. You won't ever have to deal with him again."

"Or anyone," Medusa grumbled.

"We'll see," Athena said cryptically. "I am a firm believer in the power of love, and I've come to realize that what my brother feels for you is stronger than any weapon he wields. The choices he makes moving forward will determine your combined destiny. But for now, we need to get you somewhere safe, where you won't be bothered."

"My sisters will take care of me."

"I've already sent Hermes to fetch them."

Medusa nodded in response, numb to the fact that her body was no longer her own. She allowed herself to be led toward the docks where she awaited the next stage of her fate, hardly registering the beauty of the world she was leaving behind. The love she had for her goddess battled with the hate she had for the form she had given her. Knowing that her future wouldn't include the man who had stolen her heart crippled her. Like Perseus, she, too, wasn't sure she would ever be able to forgive Athena for taking her choices away from her. But Athena made it seem as though their future was still being crafted. That gave her some hope.

Time would tell if the faith she still had in her goddess would be rewarded.

5

Medusa had been home a week, and it was already getting to her. She couldn't stop crying, and because of that, the island of Sarpedon where Athena hid her was overrun with serpents. Her sisters, Stheno and Euryale, didn't seem to mind and had already fashioned a small house inside their cave to keep some of the prettier ones in. Her hair didn't seem to mind either and kept calling the new snakes over for visits.

Home hadn't changed. If anything, it felt more like she didn't belong even though one could argue that she finally did. Her sisters had never known the world she did by virtue of her fair looks. Upper half entirely female and lower half serpent, her sisters were deemed monsters and forced to slither around the island for eternity where they were born. They never begrudged Medusa in pursuing her dreams of living in the human world, only saying that they wished she would have visited more often. The crying started anew; she had been a horrible sister.

"You really haven't," Stheno said. "Stop going on like that, or we won't have anywhere to put them all."

"You are a wonderful sister, Medusa, but you need to stop crying," Euryale said. "Or at least catch your tears before they hit the ground."

Medusa nodded and pulled in a deep breath. She dried her eyes and took the glass that Stheno handed her. It was filled with pomegranate wine, her favorite. "You're right," Medusa sighed. "The crying isn't helping anyone, but I can't help myself."

"Well, time to get over that," Stheno said snarkily. She slithered over to the rug beside Medusa and picked up her own glass, coiling her body around itself and settling in front of the fire. "Nothing good ever came of crying incessantly. Besides, we don't want a visit from Oizys, she is never much fun to be around."

"I can't imagine why, considering she's the Goddess of Misery."

Stheno rolled her eyes, and Medusa had to laugh. She had missed her sisters' bickering. It was nice to be home. "You two haven't changed a bit."

Euryale laughed. "You haven't either, Medusa, you are still the same sweet sister we had growing up."

Medusa took a sip of her wine to temper the tears that were forming. They didn't need any more pets. Considering what Athena's magick turned her into, it was the nicest thing she had ever heard. Euryale was always sweet that way.

"Always looking out for others," Stheno agreed. "Which is why I know that the fates will be kind to you now." Medusa looked in her open face and saw nothing but love.

"Why, Euryale. That is the nicest thing I think I have ever heard you say," Stheno exclaimed with a grin.

Medusa laughed as she watched Euryale's forked tongue poke out between her lips with a hiss. "That is because no one else warrants it."

Stheno slithered over to Euryale's side and put her arm around her, tucking her head on her shoulder with a smile. Her honey-colored hair was longer than the last time she had seen her and was in direct contrast to her other sister who had cut it stylishly short. The cut locks bobbed back and forth just over her shoulder blades as she returned the embrace. "I knew there was a kind heart deep down in there somewhere."

Euryale shushed her. "Don't let that get out, or this island will be over-run with humans."

Stheno smiled and shook her head. "I can't imagine that would be true with the number of snakes we have here. Perhaps we should move some over to the north side of the island."

"Good idea," Euryale agreed. "These new ones look like they will like water. I will take them over to the lily pond." She turned her head toward the rolling pile of newly formed snakes and gave a quick hiss. As she moved toward the mouth of the cave, they all followed in single file until every last snake formed from Medusa's tears was gone. After they all left, her sister started giggling.

"She thinks I don't know," she said in a whisper.

"Know what?"

"About her friend. He generally comes once or twice a week now."

Medusa wasn't as surprised to hear that Euryale had a suitor as she was that she had tried to hide that fact from their sister. "Is he someone that can be trusted?"

Stheno nodded and curled up beside her. "I believe so from what I've observed. She seems really happy, although you would never know it from her snark."

"I'm not sure anyone can change that," Medusa laughed. "I suppose that is part of her charm."

"Most certainly. I think we will be meeting him soon, especially now that you are here. She always sought your approval on things."

"Not sure that would be a good idea with what Athena did to my eyes." Stheno gripped her hand and gave a gentle squeeze. The gentle touch had her pulling back her tears. Her sisters had a lot going on in their lives as well, it would be nice to catch up with them both.

"We will figure something out. Maybe you can have your back to him or stand behind a screen."

The pain of her situation tightened her throat. She needed to find a way to channel her despair. Perhaps Athena could teach her looming. As much as she wanted to hate her, she did miss her friend, although she wasn't sure she was up to seeing her quite yet.

Stheno's hand gripping hers was a source of comfort, but the cautious tone warned Medusa that a tender topic was on her mind. "I don't want to get you worked up again, but we haven't seen you in forever. And you've been a home a week, so I thought it would be okay to ask now."

Medusa turned and looked into her sister's eager eyes. She was glad the curse hadn't extended to turning females to stone. She wouldn't have been able to bear it if she hadn't been able to set eyes on her family again. "You can ask me anything, sister."

Stheno's smile practically lit her face. "I'm interested to hear more about your suitor. Perseus?"

Medusa nodded and pulled in a deep breath. Stheno had always been a good listener, and while the topic was still fresh, she felt she should at least try to work through some of her grief. "That's right. He's a warrior from Seriphos. We met through my service to Athena."

"Her brother, right?"

A sigh escaped as she pulled together her thoughts and selected just the right words to save her from new tears. "That's right, through Zeus."

"Isn't everyone related through Zeus?" Stheno laughed and took a sip of wine.

Medusa agreed with a laugh. "Pretty much. Although, I had heard that he has slowed down a bit. He's afraid of Hera."

"Well, he should be! She's no less powerful than he is, and he needs to be reminded of it every once in a while."

"I would agree with that."

"So, back to Perseus. If he's captured your heart, he must be amazing."

Medusa smiled. Thoughts of him warmed her, and she was glad to see they made her happy instead of sad. She would remember the good times. "He is amazing and has a fantastic sense of humor. He knows how to make me laugh which is more than I can say for most men. And he seems to really care about my opinion on things. We would talk for hours about any topic you can think of. We were friends long before we got involved."

"And Athena was okay with it? The relationship I mean?"

"We kept it a secret, but somehow, she found out. She hinted as much over the past several weeks. I felt I needed to truly know what Perseus had planned, as he hadn't made his intentions really clear."

"And now?"

Medusa sighed. "Now, I realize I didn't need to wait for a proposal from him, his intentions were there all along. He was committed to me. What breaks my heart is that he still is."

"Well, what is wrong with that?"

"Look at me!" Medusa stood and paced the floor. Her arms gesturing wildly as she made her point.

"I don't see anything wrong with the way you look," Stheno said quietly. "You are as beautiful as you have always been, sister."

Tears formed in Medusa's eyes, and she paused to draw them back in. After a calming breath, she spoke. "Thank you, Stheno. It's hard to feel it when I'm in a skin I'm not used to. It's not how I've lived my life, and it will be an adjustment. What is the most upsetting is that I won't ever be able to look at him again. As much as I believe he still loves me, it isn't safe for him to be around me."

"Because of the magick behind your eyes?"

"Exactly. Athena made it so that Poseidon wouldn't want anything to do with me, but now, every man I set eyes on is in danger as well."

"Well, it's a good thing there are no men here."

"Except for Euryale's boyfriend."

"True. We will find our way around this, Medusa. Don't you worry. In the meantime, we will be sure that Euryale keeps her friend to herself."

"I feel that would be best for us all. I'm not sure any man will ever be safe around me again."

Her sister nodded and left but not before Medusa caught the pity in her sister's gaze. It caused the tears she had staunched to flow again, adding a few more snakes to the growing numbers. How would she survive an eternity in this form? She just couldn't bear to think about it, nor would she dwell on the fact that Athena hadn't given her the ability to shift back like she had with the others before her. Perhaps the goddess hadn't been happy with Medusa's secret after all.

edusa had just finished hanging the laundry on the line when Stheno came up the hill toward her. Her expression was frantic, her slithered pace hurried. "There's someone here on the island." She gestured behind her and pointed toward the pond. "He was speaking to Euryale."

"Not sure that will end well," Medusa mused. "What did he look like?"

"Light-brown hair, shoulder-length, with broad shoulders and a determined strut. He didn't have armor but was suited for it."

"Perseus," Medusa whispered. Her heart raced both in fear and anticipation. It had been weeks since she had last seen him. Even though she wouldn't be able to lay eyes on him, she was still looking forward to hearing what he had to say.

"It seems so from your descriptions of him."

"Was Euryale being nice to him?"

Stheno gave an apologetic look. "She was her normal snarky self, although it seems he wouldn't care one way or another. He looked pretty determined to get here."

"Definitely sounds like Perseus." Medusa started toward the mouth of the cave with Stheno slithering behind her. "No matter who it is though, I need to prepare a few things."

"How can I help?"

"Where was that wall mirror we used to have? I might need it."

Stheno had barely left the room when a masculine voice startled Medusa from her nervous pacing. She had barely had enough time to turn and cast her eyes down before she heard his sandaled steps shuffle against the sandy floors.

"Don't come any closer. I couldn't bear it if anything happened to you."

"I've taken precautions," Perseus soothed. Just hearing him warmed her like a cup of chamomile tea on a cool spring night.

His steps came closer, and she felt the warmth of his breath on the back of her neck. Medusa crossed her arms and soothed down the scales. She was thankful she kept her human form but worried he would recoil once he touched her. Her supple skin was now dark green and rough to the touch. His movement toward her filled her with anticipation, making her voice squeak. "What sort of precautions?" She felt the pulse of his energy now, his aura, as it lit her from the inside out and brought her a sense of normalcy.

In the next moment, his hands were over hers, and his lips caressed her shoulder. The snakes entwined in her golden locks made way for his caress as though they, too, were under his loving spell. As his kisses traveled up her neck, she moaned at the sensation of his tongue darting in and out on her skin. His love hadn't lessened, I idea of it brought tears to her eyes,. Relief and despair tangled her emotions.

"Athena told me what to avoid," he whispered as his arms came fully around her, and he pressed his length against her. "She said a direct gaze would be deadly. The mirror is a good idea." He nibbled her ear lobe, and she breathed in the feeling. She had missed his slow attentions to every inch of her body, his practical worship of every part of her.

"So nice of her," Medusa said flatly. "What of the snakes?"

"Your hair?" His voice sounded surprised. "I don't seem to be having any trouble with them. As a matter of fact, they seem to be making way for me." He laughed, and the sound of it was a balm to her soul.

"Well, perhaps I have a bit to do with that. I have been warning them that if they so much as hurt a hair on your head, I would consider shaving myself bald."

"Not sure that will be necessary, my love. They seem to like me."

After a deep breath, she succumbed to his embrace, relaxing into the shelter of his arms. "I know I do." She placed her hands over his, which circled her waist and sighed. "I've missed you, Perseus. I can bear pretty much any pain, but being away from you kills me inside."

"I feel the same, my love. I know now my life will never be the same without you."

"Yet, we still can't be together."

"Tomorrow will work itself out," he whispered. "Let's focus on the now." His hands moved slowly up to her breasts, cupping them from beneath.

Medusa sighed. "I was hoping you would say that, although I would have never dreamed it could ever be."

"My love for you hasn't changed. Neither has my desire."

"But I have."

His arms tightened around her as he whispered. "Not in my eyes."

The words he spoke were heartfelt, and her body reacted as it always had with him. Passion flooded her veins and enhanced the sensitivity of her skin. She was no longer worried about him touching it as much as how it would be if he didn't.

"But I'm not sure how much time we will have," she moaned. His touch was driving her wild. She felt his smile against her shoulder.

"Stheno told me she would give us a few hours."

Medusa laughed aloud, eyes shut tight but crinkled in mirth. "Already have my sister wrapped around your finger, I see. She must like you."

"I've been known to be persuasive when I want to be."

"That is the truth," Medusa agreed with a laugh. "My room is just beyond the fireplace to the left. I don't dare open my eyes, but will you lead me there?"

His hand slipped from around her waist, and he gripped her hand tight. She felt him tug, and he pulled her behind him.

"Did Athena send word with you on how to end the curse? Will I be able to look at you again?"

His steps slowed, and he slipped behind her, gently placing her hands on the top of her mattress. The silken blankets she brought from the temple soothed her as did her lover's hands, sliding her dress from her shoulders.

"After," he murmured against her skin. Heated from his attentions and in complete contrast to the skin-type she was now cursed with. "I need you in my arms first."

She shook her head. "I won't risk turning around, this position will have to do. Are the wings going to be an issue?"

"Not at all, and they are stunning, by the way. If I remember correctly, this was one of your favorite positions."

Medusa smiled as she pushed the remainder of her garment down to pool at her feet. "You have an amazing memory. How many other things do you remember about me?"

"Everything. You've infused me heart and soul."

Soon, his hands were everywhere, and with her eyes shut tight, she allowed him to touch every part of her body and mind. As always, he left no part of her unloved.

Hours later, they were down by the pond where Euryale typically met her boyfriend. There was a small gazebo nearby, but Medusa preferred the spot closer to the water near the large willow. She was backed up into Perseus's arms, warmed from his love making and feeling secure in his embrace. Her hair was calm as well, lulled into sleep by the orgasms he had given her earlier.

His lips had hardly left her neck, and they had been quietly sitting for some time when his voice startled her as she had almost drifted off.

"Do you trust me?"

The question was odd, but she didn't hesitate. "With my life."

He shifted behind her then brought his arm up in front of her. He was holding something small and shiny. When she saw her favorite stone adorning the ring, her heart paused.

"Will you marry me?"

She shook her head, not wanting to believe the words she had heard from his mouth. He wanted to marry her? She couldn't even look at him, but he wanted to spend the rest of his life with her? A monster? The stone sparkled in the sunlight, taunting her. It was promising a future that couldn't be hers. Not until the curse was lifted.

"How can you ask me that?" Her question was a pained whisper. She started to squirm. She needed to move.

"Because I love you," he answered simply. He stood up and followed her to the pondside but kept his distance. Her hair was just as upset as she was, and a few of them had been riled up enough to strike. Perseus was close but far enough away that they couldn't get to him.

"I love you too, but it's not about that."

"If two people love one another, what else should matter?"

"How about the fact that I'm a hideous monster? How could you possibly love that?"

"Medusa, I've always been in love with what is on the inside. You are smart and witty and always know how to get me to relax. I feel like I'm home when I'm with you, and I want to be part of your life, no matter what that looks like."

"I don't have a choice what that would look like, that is the trouble."

"If you had a choice, right here, right now, which life would you choose? The one you had or the one you feel you were destined to have?"

Medusa thought about it for a moment, weighing her thoughts as she looked out on the water. She had turned her back on her heritage to live her life as a human; had that been wrong? Had she been selfish to embrace that lifestyle and relish the fact that she was attractive and her skin supple? Other than the fact that she felt she could have connected with her sisters more often, she didn't think so. She was happy being human, and they were happy as they were. They each embraced the life they had been given and accepted each other's choices.

"I want a life with you. One where I can look into your beautiful sapphire eyes, the ones that match that stone that you are holding. I want to have children with you and be able to look at them as well without killing them."

"What would you do for that to happen?" His voice was but a whisper, but he sounded closer. She kept her eyes shut and answered.

"Anything."

"Do you trust me?" He was even closer now.

"With my life." She heard the snick of his sword, and her eyes snapped open. She saw him in the reflection of the pond just behind her, holding something that seemed to have mesmerized the snakes from striking.

"I love you," his voice cracked, and she saw the flash of his sword as it raised to his side.

She knew she could stop him, prevent him from following through with his chosen course by merely turning and changing him to stone. But she didn't. Once again, the choice was taken from her, but she didn't want to remain in this form or live without him. Dying was the least she could do for them both. She could make that choice.

"I love you too."

Before her head hit the ground from the swift blow, she heard him wail. "Forgive me, Medusa."

She was thankful his blade was sharp and his aim true. She had hardly felt the blade against her neck. She watched her body collapse near the pond where she had laid in her lover's arms, through the eyes of the snakes that were no longer a part of her but still woven in the locks on her head now feet apart from where her body lay. She watched as Perseus pulled out a sack and walked toward her, sobbing as he held the fabric in front of him.

Although she continued to hear his heartbreak as the darkness covered her sight, it brought her a strange sense of peace. She was pained for his sorrow and wished there were a way she could comfort him, but her body was no longer her own. The sense of relief soothed her agony. He would be safe and would one day find happiness.

She was finally at peace with her choice.

7

Athena had just washed the latest battle from her skin when Melia announced she had a visitor. She dried off and donned her new silk robe gifted to her by Thyia and her business partner, Arachne. Supporting their talents was the best thing Athena had ever done for her wardrobe. The ladies had been wildly successful since they opened, and the goddess had no less than a dozen new dresses to show for it.

When she entered the expanse of her dimly lit temple, she could hardly see the figure in the shadows. It was the weight of what he carried that caught her attention.

"The deed is done," Perseus said roughly. It had been days since she had sent him on the quest, and he was still unhappy with her.

"It was the only way," she responded, closing the distance between her and her brother. The canvas sack that he held had stopped moving, but she knew better. The contents were still alive. Even after days of travel, the blood still dripped from the fabric and formed snakes on the marble. They slithered toward the shadows in the corners of the room.

"So you say." He tossed the sack at her feet and turned his back to her as Medusa's head rolled out of the sack and onto her marble floor. "It killed no less than a dozen men on my journey back. Not to mention the number of poisonous vipers that now live in Libya because the bag kept leaking."

"It will be an important weapon for what needs to be done."

"You are talking about a piece of the woman I love!" His pain echoed in the empty temple, swallowed by the inky void visible between the firelight of the torches. "What you had me do to her was unforgiveable. Unfathomable. Never in my life have I ever had to do something so horrendous."

Athena flinched, not because of his anger but knowing that she had been the cause of it.

"It's time to keep your promise, and you damn well better do it. Because your role in the possibility of my future is the only thing holding me back from killing you right now."

"Keep your voice down, Perseus. You know threats to gods and goddesses are heard by others." She smiled sadly and glanced down at the head—the eyes were shut, but the snakes were watching intently. She blew a kiss to them then placed her hands in front of her as if in prayer and bowed to them. The snakes all lowered their gaze, heads bowed in tribute. She took hold of the sack and held it open in order for the rolling masses of reptiles to slip into its opening. Once the head was securely in the sack, she tied it shut.

"Now I have a weapon to threaten our enemies with. A weapon that works on both humans and gods alike. You and Medusa have done me a great service, it will not be forgotten. Now, I will keep my promise, but you must remember to keep yours as well."

"Mine won't be nearly as hard to keep. Loving Medusa was never the problem. Bringing her back from the dead could be."

"Leave that to me. On the next full moon, you may travel back to Sarpedon. Until then, you must take care of the tasks I have given you. It must remain as if she wasn't alive."

He turned to glare at her. "I will do what I have been asked but have already done more than any man could be expected to against the woman he loves. After these final few tasks, I want your promise that I will be left alone. For eternity."

"It shall be done, and as promised, I will speak to Father on your behalf. In return, you must remember your oath, Perseus. 'Til her death shall you bind your life."

"I remember, sister. It is all I ever wanted."

"Eternity is a long time."

"Not with her."

The night had finally come, and the moon was full and bright. Medusa had taken extra time with her bath earlier in the afternoon, still getting used to the changes in her body. The scales were gone as were the wings and snakes. The last thing to sprout after growing her new head was the soft golden hair that she had been blessed with as a human. She ran her hands over the spiky length and thought she may keep it short. It was certainly easier to take care of.

Her sisters had aided her during her transition, watched over her vulnerable body as it healed. Hermes, who had been sworn to secrecy, had sent them a message from Athena that no one was to know Medusa still lived, and under no circumstances was Perseus allowed back to the island until the next full moon. He left oils and herbs from Hecate to aid in the healing process, the last of which she used in her bath that very afternoon.

Medusa paced the room, worried that Perseus had given up on her, worried that the task he was required to do had taken a toll on his mind. She would know soon since tonight was when her final secret would be revealed. As she smoothed her plum-colored gown for the hundredth time, Stheno came racing into her room.

"He's here, sister!"

Medusa's hands went to her hair to check the flowers she had placed there then smoothed her dress one more time. "How do I look?"

"Beautiful, as always," she soothed. "We will be on the other side of the island for the remainder of the night. To give you some privacy."

"We will have a lot to talk about."

Stheno smiled, a knowing gleam in her eye. "More than he bargained for."

"More than we all did." The weight of it dropped into her stomach. Before she had time to dwell on it, Perseus stepped into the entrance.

Medusa's eyes went to his and instantly teared up at the emotion she saw in their depths. There was no horror, no bitterness—only love. He dropped his belongings and ran to her, taking her into his arms and squeezing tight. "Thank the goddess, you're alive."

He pulled back, his eyes full of tears and looking to hers which were dripping as well. This time, only tears formed there. It seemed the curse was fully removed. "I've missed you so much, my love. It was agony without you."

"I couldn't come." Perseus kissed her then wiped the tears from her cheeks. "I didn't want to risk it."

"I heard," Medusa nodded. "I knew what you were asked to do."

Perseus looked back at her in confusion. His face showing the attempt at solving the puzzle. "The gorgon head," she said. "It allows me to see through the eyes of the snakes. I can hear through the vibrations they feel if I really concentrate as well."

"So, the journey back to Athena and our conversation?"

"I heard bits of it, but I was still weak." She pulled him tight and murmured into his chest. "I'm so sorry for all of the pain I caused you, Perseus. I wish you could have known that I was okay."

"She had told me you would be, but I know to never trust the word of a god or goddess. Concentrating on the tasks I had been given was the only thing keeping me from going insane."

"It was exciting seeing you in action. The way you took down that sea monster was incredible."

"That was all you, my sweet." He scooped her up and walked her to the bed, laying her down on the silken covers. "I would have never been able to defeat it without the gorgon head. I only wish there had been another way."

"Nothing is ever easy when it comes to the whims of those we serve."

"Well, I'm glad that is done. I'm free now to live my life with you."

"And is that what you choose? Living here with me and my family? I can't leave, no one can know that I still live."

"It was the choice I made when the tasks were given to me. Each one I completed brought me a step closer to living an eternity with you. I love it here with your family. Stheno showed me a gorgeous site on the other side of the island where I thought we could build a home for two. If that is what you want, of course. I thought we would have more privacy that way."

"How would you feel about a home for three or four?"

His face registered surprise, then delight, as she nodded slowly.

"Pregnant?" He whispered with hope.

She nodded again, and the tears formed anew. This time, she tasted the salt of them. He kissed her then laid his hand on her slightly rounded stomach. She placed hers over his, the sapphire ring he had proposed with sparkling in the firelight.

"I will build you whatever you want, so long as you say you're mine."

"I am yours until death."

"Already did that," he grinned. "I want eternity."

"It's yours, my love," she promised. She couldn't help but smile at his grin. It was telling. Something was on his mind.

"So, you saw and heard things during our adventures? Guessing you know everything there is to know about me then after some of those conversations I had with the gorgon head."

"Well, not everything, but a lot more than I ever knew before, which I find hard to believe by the way. How could I have not known about you and your mom being locked in a wooden chest and tossed into the sea?"

"I was a baby, not really my story to tell." He shrugged and pulled her to the couch where they settled facing each other. His leg covered hers, and her thought was that she could lay like that forever. "It eventually led me to you though, so I'm thankful for that."

"I am too, although not so much the last bit we had to go through."

"It was the only way we could be together the way you wanted. I just want to be sure you have no regrets, that this form is the one you would have chosen."

"No more regrets," she agreed. "And yes, this is the form I would choose. I know my family is there for me no matter the life I decide to live."

"Your sisters are amazing. They have welcomed me with open

arms. I was worried they might have a different reaction when I returned after what I did."

Medusa shook her head. "Hermes shared what was going on, so they had time to adjust to the idea. It also gave me time to catch up with them. I shared some of the tales you told me when I was traveling back to Athena with you."

"It is so strange to think about it that way."

"Agreed. But it was a gift being part of your travels and hearing the tales at night when you rested. It made me feel as if I was there with you. Like we were connected."

"You were. You are." He took her hand and placed it on his heart. "Here, forever."

She cupped his face and pulled his head gently to hers. As their lips met, she felt the final connection to her happiness click into place. He was tender and gentle, worshipped her like a goddess, which filled her with a joy that she had only dreamed of.

"Now that the last of my secrets are out, we should figure out what is next for us."

As he untied the belt from her robe and slipped it from her body, he answered with a grin. "I am way ahead of you, my love."

EPILOGUE

Medusa stood on a cliff overlooking the waves crashing into the shore. Her shoulder-length tresses tickled her cheeks in the breeze as she searched the horizon for Perseus's return. Hands on her growing stomach, she sheltered the life that grew inside her, knowing after a visit from Hecate that the twins would be the first of many children that would bless their immortal lives.

The visions were easier to control now, coming only when she asked to see them and no longer disturbing her sleep. She could witness everything the snakes had seen and been through, keeping her in touch with what was happening in the world. Not only through the real head, but also those that used her likeness as the gorgon. It allowed her to keep in touch with Perseus on his travels.

Stories of his great deeds, completed with the help of the mystical gorgon's head, were told time and again, and her image became one of protection. The world became obsessed with placing an image of her with her snaky locks on doorways, armor, and even on shields. Athena had one fashioned for Perseus by Hephaestus, made from Olympian steel and including a lock of Medusa's human hair. It allowed the couple to communicate no matter how far apart they were, especially important with her impending due date. She could see and hear through them all and was called upon by her goddess to aid her in battle.

Medusa now had more eyes and ears than she knew what to do

with, and with the help of Hecate, she learned how to manage the great power she now harnessed as Athena's oracle. She had spent the afternoon watching Athena go around with her old head and threaten those on Mt. Olympus. Aphrodite was one of the first goddesses she threatened, not for what the head could do to her necessarily, but to all of her lovers, Ares included. With tears and wails, Aphrodite promised to take back Poseidon's pin and never to allow anyone to borrow it, or her belt, again.

She had just tuned out of watching Athena's antics when she received a call from Perseus. He called around the same time every night. "Making our way back to you, my love. How are my babies doing?"

"Babies are getting a little anxious to meet us. They have been kicking like wild stallions."

"I know we are cutting it close, but my mother really wanted to be there for the birth. We should be there in a couple of days' time."

"According to Hecate, we have until the next full moon, so there's plenty of time. The shield seems to be working great, I have a clear view of both you and your mom." Danae was standing behind her son and waved shyly. She blew a kiss then kissed the top of his head and walked off. From what Perseus had told her about his mom, they would get along great, but she appreciated the moment of privacy.

"She has more packing to do, so we should be alone for a little while. She's excited about the babies."

"I am too," Medusa said with a laugh. "I appreciate her coming, I wasn't sure how we were going to manage two at one time."

"We'll figure it out, and she will be a big help. When I get back, I plan on finishing the final room on our cottage. Eurayale's friend has already agreed to help, but he has to finish a project with Odysseus first. Have you thought of any names?"

"I was thinking Pegasus had a nice ring to it. Maybe Chrysador as well? Still making a list."

"Those are both strong names, I like them."

"Then everything is set for them. I just need you. Without anything to do, these last couple of days will be dull. I wish you were here with me, perhaps we would be able to find a way to fill the time."

"Oh, there are definitely things we could find to do," he laughed. "I have a few minutes alone if you're somewhere comfortable and are game."

"I'm always game." She settled on the blanket she had laid out beneath one of their shade trees and leaned back. She could see the clouds and sunlight breaking through the leaves as they swayed in the breeze in the background, and as she concentrated on only one set of eyes on the shield, she managed to see the smiling face of her husband. As the vision from more eyes joined, she was happy to see much more of his form until it finally showed what his masculine hands had in their grip.

She shifted her gown up on her legs and sighed. He was ready and waiting, and it wouldn't take her long to join him. Finding satisfaction together this way was one of their favorite things to do when they were apart. "What is that you've found?" She couldn't help the teasing tone, it had become another secret between them.

"One of your snakes, my love," he laughed. "Would you like me to show you?"

She answered the same way she had since he had left. "Now and when you come back to me."

"Always my pleasure."

"And you are mine as well."

Love is a choice,
which starts with self.
Only then can you let the heart
decide who to let in.
To all who are on a journey
of self-discovery…
you are loved.

ATHENA'S CHALLENGE

ONE IS HIDING THEIR IDENTITY;
THE OTHER IS TRYING TO
UNDERSTAND THEIRS.

1

The goddess Athena trudged into her temple and wound her way back to the chamber where her priestess-in-training was waiting. It had been a long day, and she was ready for the comfort of her bed. The crickets outside the entrance filled the hollow halls of her temple with their song, soothing her nerves which were frayed thin by her brother's antics. Ares' war mongering in the cities surrounding hers was exhausting.

Karisa helped her disrobe in silence then led her to the bath she had waiting for her. Athena would be happy for the warmth of it. The last few weeks, she had bathed in the rivers and streams she frequented; she was chilled through. It was times like these that she missed her former priestess, Medusa, who had always known just what she needed without reminder. But the young gorgon had left her service to marry the love of her life, Athena's half-brother, Perseus, and Medusa had been living happily on the island of Sarpedon ever since.

The couple was expecting their first set of twins, and Athena was days away from being an aunt. The goddess Hecate had shared with her that the boys wouldn't be the last set of twins that would brighten their lives. Athena was happy for her, Medusa had always wanted to be a mother, but she wondered how long it would be before she would find an adequate replacement for her. The only good thing that had come out of the entire situation was the creation of her Aegis, which allowed Athena to protect her followers more adequately. Medusa's ability to see and hear through any image of her gorgon head was an invaluable tool, but if she were honest, she would rather have her friend back in Athens.

"You forgot the lavender again, Karisa," Athena sighed. The fragrance was sorely missed, especially after the week she had. "Also, I noticed the fires were low, and the bread baskets were empty."

"I'm so sorry, Thea. It won't happen again."

So much for adequacy. "That is what you said last time," Athena muttered under her breath. Or competency for that matter. "The fires are to be perpetual; my people are welcome any time day or night. And the bread we give here may be the only meal they get in a week." The flustered nymph scurried to the small round table near the marble bath to retrieve the fragrant herb.

"I'm sorry, Thea." When she turned, her eyes were wide, and her hands were shaking.

"Calm yourself," Athena said. "You'll trip and dump the lot."

"I don't mean to. It's just that I'm so nervous around you, my goddess." Karisa's eyes bugged out in horror to what she had let slip out of her mouth as her hand slapped over her lips.

It was times like these that Athena missed Medusa even more. At least she wasn't a frightened little bird or a clumsy cyclops. Karisa didn't have one ounce of grace in her body, not that it mattered, but she was much more like a bull than most men Athena knew. She preferred a softer touch with her priestesses, as did her visitors.

After the blooms were added to the bath, Athena held her hand out and took Karisa's to steady herself into the deep tub. As she sunk into the heat, the glow of the candles reflected on the ripples, and the scent of the dried herbs surrounded her like an aura.

"Will there be anything else for now?" Her assistant looked as if she were going to explode from her skin. Athena couldn't relax around someone like her. She would need to find a new caregiver. She shook her head and closed her eyes against the terror-stricken face of her priestess. She had gone through several of them in the past few months, with two in the last week. She was tired of breaking them in.

"You may go. I can get myself to bed from here."

"If you are sure..."

"Of course, I'm sure," Athena snapped. Her silvery eyes squinted at Karisa, causing her to take a few steps back. Athena realized it was the same look she gave most of her enemies before she gutted them. "I do know my own mind, Karisa, as well as yours." She really needed to tone down her resting goddess face.

"Yes, Thea. Of course, my goddess."

The young woman left too quickly for Athena to change her mind. She really would have liked a glass of wine, come to think of it.

She let the warmth of the bath and the soothing fragrance surround her with a sigh, allowing the water to lull her senses. Even with her eyes shut, she knew Hermes had arrived by the whir of his sandals. What could the Messenger of the Gods need at this time of night? Athena kept her head tipped back and eyes closed. She was too drained to do otherwise.

"The least you could have done was bring me a bottle of your latest vintage. What good is having a vineyard if you don't share the perks?"

Hermes's baritone laugh filled the room. "I've brought you two, actually. Would you like me to open one?"

Athena smiled. "Most assuredly, I would. The glasses are on my nightstand."

When the cork popped and he started filling glasses, she asked why he had come. After she didn't receive an immediate response, she opened her eyes and sat upright.

"Is everything alright with Hecate?" She searched his face for the answer, but he kept his expressions from her. He was one of the only gods who could. It was part of his divine purpose, the whole messenger function. It allowed him to relay information without emotion or bias. It was one of his most exasperating but useful qualities.

Hermes handed her a half-filled goblet and clinked his to hers before floating to the vanity and perching atop her cushioned seat. "Hecate is fine," he assured. "Better than fine, she's amazing. This is her blend by the way. She adds just the slightest hint of rosemary."

Athena nodded then took a sip. "Impressive. The flavor is incredible. You two make a good team."

The happiness radiating from him made her heart sing. "I agree.

I'm so glad she finally realized it."

Athena took another sip, the fruity tang filling her mouth. She was thrilled for them as well as herself. Her cellar had never been so full of quality wine. "I like the fruit. My compliments to the vintner."

"I'll let her know you liked it."

"So, if not for advice on how to keep a free spirit like Hecate happy, what exactly can I do for you, brother?" Athena was curious. She couldn't imagine what he could possibly need beside good council.

"I'm actually here for Father," Hermes sighed.

Surprising. Athena put her goblet down and leaned her head back. She would need to make the conversation quick; the water was cooling. Where was Hades when a quick warm-up was needed? Once again, Karisa hadn't drawn it hot enough to start with. She decided to pull every bit of comfort from the water she could.

"What on earth or in sky does he want?"

Hermes didn't respond, merely cleared his throat. It caused Athena to open her eyes once more and look at him. "Well?"

"It seems that Poseidon has requested control of Athens."

"My city?"

Hermes nodded slowly and took a cautious sip of his wine, barely containing a nervous grin.

"Precisely."

Athena's blood boiled. The water was no longer comfortable. "The city that was named after me? Full of people who adore me? Well, that is utter nonsense. I am the patron goddess after all. My temple is in the heart of its people."

"He is proposing a change to that. He wants the name changed to Posidia or something along that line. Anyway, Father knows how fond you are of Athens and wanted me to let you know what he finally proposed to Poseidon."

"Proposed?" Athena screeched like the owl she was connected to. She waved her hand at Hermes in a shooing motion. Enough was enough. "You need to turn your back, I'm getting out."

Hermes flew from his seat and hovered with his back turned. "Don't get mad at me. I'm only passing the message along—you know, divine purpose and all."

"Don't remind me about divine purpose. You know better than anyone I've had my share of that lot."

Athena rose from the tub and wrapped herself in a silk towel Karisa had left nearby. The magenta fabric with silver threads was breathtaking, but there was no time to fully enjoy it. It looked like another gift from Arachne and Thyia's shop. She wondered if perhaps they could create a silken gag and matching rope to tie Poseidon up in. Perhaps a duplicate set for her arrogant ass of a father.

"He can't give my city away," she said as she strode to the vanity. Her wet footprints trailed behind her, shimmering like mosaic in the candlelight.

"He isn't giving it away," Hermes countered.

"Well, that is what it seems like to me." Athena glanced again at Hermes to make sure his back was still turned then dropped her towel to put on her dressing gown. "Why does he owe that pompous blowfish anything at all? Poseidon has been a pain in the nether regions since day one. We all know it."

"Are you dressed?" Hermes asked quietly. He was trying to be patient, but she could tell from his tone he was stressed about the entire situation. He never liked to give her bad news. No one did.

"Yes. You may turn."

Hermes moved closer, picking up her wine glass on the way. "Here. You're going to need more of this."

Athena accepted the glass and drained the contents. She took his advice and made her way over to the bottle, pouring herself a hefty portion. After a few more sips and a deep breath, she looked at Hermes who was waiting patiently. "Okay, tell me."

"It's about Medusa."

"What about Medusa? Is she okay? The babies?" Her heart raced. There was no woman in the realm she cared about more.

"She's fine and so are the babies. But since you ruined his opportunity to get the bride of his choosing, Poseidon has requested retribution."

"Retribution?" Athena's thoughts started spinning. "Does he mean to fight me? Oh, trust me, it would be my pleasure. I have a new spear fashioned by Hephaestus I could skewer him with. And we all know my Aegis would…"

Hermes nodded. "Much as I wouldn't mind seeing that, he has only requested a battle of wits."

"Well, we both know who will win that also." Another sip of her wine and she felt the warmth spread to her belly. The drink was soothing her much like the lavender Karisa had added to her bath.

Hermes chuckled then straightened his face. He needed to remain as neutral as possible, but Athena liked it when the brother that adored her cracked through his serious facade.

"So, what exactly is he proposing?" Athena laughed. "Honestly, I would rather kick his ass."

"He is suggesting that the people decide who is the better choice of ruler. He has convinced Father that there should be a contest between the two of you. Whoever comes up with the best gift and is chosen by the people shall have their name forevermore associated with this city. He also stipulates that he will win Medusa's hand as part of his prize."

"She's already taken—married, in fact, to our half-brother."

"He said that could be rectified. Something about not minding making a widow his wife."

The wine turned sour in her stomach. How could he? There were several things she knew the people would love to have. Because she was already a part of the culture, she wasn't worried about the outcome, but she needed to be smart about the contest. Especially now that it involved the fate of Medusa and her new family, all of whom were an extension of hers. Poseidon was known to cheat. Who was she kidding, most of the gods and goddesses did.

"How long do I have?"

"You have until the next full moon, at which time the gifts will be presented, and the people will make their choice."

She slammed her empty glass down. "That's only two weeks from now." Athena was more irritated than ever. She was in the middle of a heated battle and didn't think it was a good idea to leave Ares alone for a minute. "This contest couldn't come at a worse time. Ares has things stirred up with Sparta, and if left to his own devices, we will all go to war before the month is up. Not to mention, Medusa will be having her babies any day now."

"Hades offered to keep an eye on Ares for you. And Hecate and I can check in with Medusa."

"Having the God of the Underworld sent to babysit the God of War is sort of dangerous, is it not?"

"You know Hades is way more level-headed than Ares. Besides, he and Persephone are spending more time above ground to make Demeter happy, so it works out. You know how he would rather do anything besides spend time with his mother-in-law."

"You both would do that for me?" Athena's heart warmed at Hermes's expression. His telltale smirk told her all she needed to know. He was helping her, but he and Hades had their own agendas. She nodded in agreement; the verbal contract acknowledged with a wider grin, this one accompanied by Hermes's signature twinkle glittering in his crystal blue eyes.

"We, of course, can't take sides, but you know who we are rooting for."

"Thanks, Hermes. I appreciate your help. Now to create the most incredible gift ever known to man to save my best friend from a fate worse than a second death."

"Sounds about right."

"No pressure whatsoever."

2

thena did her best thinking in the wilderness. She had packed a small bag with a few essentials and enough food for a few days then left the temple at dawn. She was happy to leave it in Karisa's care and wondered if her impatience with the nymph was due to her exhaustion. Perhaps a few days away would clear her mind and focus her attentions. Much as she had thought the timing was inconvenient, it was becoming more and more clear that the Universe knew exactly what she needed, as usual. The break would do her good.

She typically traveled on foot but decided to take her horse this time. It had been a while since they had been out together, and the mare needed to stretch her legs. The area around Athens was stunning in all seasons, but there was something special about the time right before the winter solstice. They walked at a leisurely pace, taking in the signs of the planet preparing to reset itself. The villagers readied themselves as well, and even though she dressed as a commoner, everyone knew who she was. Some asked for quick blessings by kneeling and bowing their heads as she moved past, which she did by holding her hand out and pushing her intentions through her fingertips. Some offered her loaves of bread or skins of water. Her people loved her, but it made her wonder if that would be enough when Poseidon came with his gift.

A just ruler, Athena spent a lot of time training both men and women equally. She could fight as well as any man and had a quick mind which served well in battle. For the women, she encouraged not only homecraft, but also supported their entrepreneurial spirit. She also held courses in sword and knife fighting for all who wished to defend themselves. She was a firm believer that every woman should know how to get out of a bad situation, which regretfully still happened in her beloved city. She couldn't be everywhere at all times even with the help of her Aegis.

There were a number of demi-goddesses and villagers that she had set up in business, in order to sell wares they were good at, which freed time up for others to pursue the crafts they were passionate about. Not everyone was a good weaver, so those who were did exceptionally well as it went for the potters and farmers. Arachne and Thyia's shop came to mind, and the goddess had to smile. There wasn't a god or goddess that hadn't purchased a piece of clothing or two from T.A. Creations, and their endeavor was a huge success. Athena was proud to have been part of it.

For all she had done for her people, she still worried that it hadn't been enough. What if Poseidon offered something more than she could? What if his gift was better, and the people chose him over her? What would happen to her temple and the nymphs who lived there? Worse, what would Medusa's fate be? How had Poseidon even learned she was still alive? She couldn't bear the thought of it and tried to shake the melancholy from her soul. It wouldn't do her any good to mope, she was a woman of action.

"This looks like a good spot to rest, Hippia." Athena led her horse to the stream and dismounted. "I'm sure you need a drink by now."

She let go of the reins and allowed the white Skyrian to find her own way to the water. While Hippia was not as large as some of the stallions she had seen in battle, Athena preferred the height of her small-bodied mare. It allowed her to stab opponents upward, slipping under the armor they wore and gifting them a quick death. Ares was not so thoughtful.

They had traveled almost every inch of Greece together and survived countless battles. They had an understanding, so much so that Athena almost didn't need to talk aloud. She did so anyway as it soothed them both.

As Hippia quenched her thirst, Athena sat on a nearby log with her back against a sturdy oak tree. The activity of tiny creatures in the nearby meadow calmed her soul. She wished that Ares would spend more time with her in places like this. Perhaps if he did, there would be less war.

"Hippia, what do you think Poseidon has planned?" Athena paused then added another question after no response. "What could he possibly be thinking to give to the people of Athens that they don't already get from me? The community is wealthy, the people are happy, and keeping Ares away from our city has made it peaceful."

Hippia snorted, shook her head, and then continued drinking.

"I realize what you're saying, there isn't much more he can provide. But you know me, I worry."

The mare looked at her mistress then took a few steps toward her in order to nuzzle her cheek. Athena reached up and stroked the bridge of her warm nose then pulled a carrot out of her sack and fed it to her.

"I never know if you're trying to comfort me or if you want a snack. Here you go."

As the horse munched, Athena closed her eyes and took in a deep breath of the crisp morning. She calmed her thoughts, enough that she could hear the song of the insects and birds around her tapping into their essences as they performed their talents. After her carrot, Hippia wandered into the sweet grass nearby to graze. It was as good of time as any for Athena to take a nap. It had been an age since she had done so, and she was looking at this next couple of weeks as a vacation. With the way Ares liked to cause issues, it would be perhaps her only chance to do so.

Her breath slowed, and her consciousness slipped away, then she registered whistling. Her eyes couldn't have been closed for more than a moment, but as she rubbed the sleep from them, she realized she had been out longer than she had thought. Morpheus had been busy. The amount of sand from the nearby pixies he sent was a telltale sign. She saw them giggling from behind a cypress tree and shooed them away with a wave.

The tune was louder now—whoever it was, was coming her way.

The song was happy and non-threatening. It sounded like a male from the length and tone of the whistle; although, her voice was often thought to be masculine. She didn't mind as it often gave her a bit more advantage over the men who thought women had their place. The length between breaths gave her the impression that the person was of large stature, certainly not a youth by any means. It would be wiser to meet them standing up.

She saw him then, just past the place where her mare was grazing. Hippia didn't seem disturbed by him and even allowed him to stroke her neck as he moved past. That was a good sign, her horse was an amazing judge of character.

He moved gracefully for his height and had the build of a fighter, but the demeanor was that of a scholar. His hair reached his shoulders and reminded her of the golden-bronze leaves that fell when Demeter missed her daughter. His face was clean-shaven, with skin as perfect as any statue she had commissioned for her temple. As his eyes met hers, he smiled, and what it did to her both frightened and delighted her. Never one for seeing a man for anything more than a fighting partner, his beautiful features appealed to her on a visceral level. She felt it in parts that had no business coming alive. He raised his hand in greeting, and his voice sent her over the edge.

"May the goddess Athena smile on you and your travels."

His tone was like music; she could listen to it all day. Interesting that he didn't recognize her. Perhaps he was someone that didn't get to town often? A farmer? Woodsman? That would explain the taunt muscles, although his shoulders were slight, almost delicate. The emerald, green toga looked as if it were made for him, and she wondered where he got it.

"My wish is she does the same for you," she responded as a commoner would. "Where are you traveling?" He was soft and approachable as well. Endearing. His beauty compared to one of her nymphs, and she found herself transfixed. He was stunning.

He pointed in the direction she was heading. "I live just beyond the hillside a few miles through the trees. I'm coming back from my daily walk." He pointed to a sack hanging from his belt. "I forage while I am on my hikes and found some sizeable mushrooms I'm going to work into my dinner."

He pulled one of the larger mushrooms from his sack, along with a sprig of wild thyme. His expression was filled with delight.

"I love to walk as well. Looks as though you made out pretty well, the area seems to have a lot to offer."

The man agreed with a nod. "It really does, much more so than Thebes. There, you need coin or must barter for everything, but here, it is much easier to live from the wealth of the land."

A sense of pride filled Athena's chest. She had worked hard to provide a rich land for her residents, and it seemed that, according to this newcomer, she had been successful. "What did you see on your travels today besides the mushrooms?"

He pointed to a log near the stream. "Mind if we sit? I've been on my feet all day."

"Not at all." Athena followed him and took her place on one end of the log. He removed his belt and placed the sack nearby. "I'm Tiresias, by the way."

There was no way she was giving her real name, she wanted to see where this was going without the intimidation of her power. "I go by Olivia."

He paused slightly, his head cocked as if trying to work out a puzzle, then let it pass. "Very nice to meet you, Olivia." He said her name as if he were tasting it on his tongue. It made her feel like a schoolgirl or at least what she imagined one would feel like. Since she had been born from her father's head fully grown, she had never known anything different than being a fully formed adult.

"It's nice to meet you as well, Tiresias."

"I prefer to be called Reese by my friends, if that is easier to remember."

Athena smiled. She liked the nickname. "Reese it is." With his humble demeanor, she decided he would be an excellent person to interview to determine what more she could offer her people. He seemed worldly enough to her to do so.

"So, what sorts of things do you look for on your travels? I find there is always something new to see even in the areas I frequent the most."

"I couldn't agree more." His smile lit his face like that of Apollo.

She was utterly engaged; this man was not like most she knew. He was much more amiable and less worried about showing his prowess. She liked that about him.

"This may sound odd, but I've been researching the mating habits of animals. It is a topic I am fascinated with. Through them, I hope to understand more about human nature."

"Understand what in particular?" Athena's interest was piqued. Not only didn't he recognize her, but he also seemed passionate about his interest, something she related to.

His face flushed, and it endeared him to her even more. "Well, I have this theory. I don't generally speak of it with anyone as it tends to scare people off."

Athena smiled. "Well, I'm not easily scared. If anything, I like conflict and resolution. It helps progress. Try me."

He looked into her eyes for a reaction and, after gauging her demeanor, nodded his head as if a decision was made. Most people looked at her stoic expression as displeasure or indifference. This was the first time it was received by someone the way it was intended… Honest interest.

"Okay, so I am fascinated with the differences between male and female versions of all species and why those differences exist."

"Well, there's procreation most importantly."

"Of course, that is important, but I argue not the most important. I have witnessed time and time again the female of a species selecting a male who perhaps isn't the strongest or most agile."

"So, you speak of love?"

"Perhaps, but I'm not sure it is that easy to explain when you are speaking of snakes, for instance."

"Snakes can't love?" Athena hadn't had this much fun in a discussion in a long time. Most of the conversations she had were about warfare or which linens to keep for the temple. Conversations like these hardly happened with humans, and she was excited to have the opportunity to do so.

Reese shifted his position to face her. "That's the thing—I don't know. That is what is so fascinating. Perhaps, they do love. Perhaps, there is loyalty or something in their psyche that connects them to a certain selection within the species. But there is the same sex coupling and cross-species selection which really doesn't add to the procreation argument."

"I can see your point." Athena nodded. Even though she was open-minded about all sorts of relationship types with humans, she hadn't really thought about it with animals. Love, as an emotion for gods and humans, was universal but how did that equate to the animal kingdom? Interesting.

He searched her face then smiled as if she had given him a great gift. She wondered about that and why such a delightful man was without a companion. Although if she were being honest, she more often than not preferred to be alone with her thoughts as well.

"You are really easy to talk to," Reese said. "I don't often get to chat to another person about my musings. I mostly chat to the animals I study."

Person? He honestly had no idea. That was truly refreshing. "Thank you. That is the first time I have ever heard that, although it isn't surprising considering my occupation."

"What do you do?"

Athena scrambled for a response. She couldn't believe she had let that comment slip. "I'm an investor," she replied. Yes, an investor, that would work. That wasn't a far stretch, since it was what she had done for Thyia and Arachne.

"That is exciting. What sorts of businesses are you involved in?"

"There is a dress shop not far from here that I helped with. It opened a little while ago."

"Not T.A. Creations? I love that place!" His face lit up at the mention of the shop she helped her friends open. "They have an amazing joint talent. That was a wise investment."

Athena warmed under his praise; it was so nice to hear that her support was appreciated. She wondered what other things would get the same sort of reaction. She decided spending some time with Reese was a good idea. His observation skills might be helpful to her in solving her dilemma with Poseidon and keeping Medusa and Perseus safe.

"Thank you. I'm really proud of what the ladies create together. Arachne has a special gift for weaving, her fabrics are the most beautiful I have ever seen."

"I would agree with that. Hopefully, Athena won't hear that though. I heard she can be pretty harsh on those who better her talent."

Athena was taken aback. She had heard rumors of her prior judgements being misconstrued as harsh. The tales of Medusa were a prime example. But Reese had given her the impression that he was much more open-minded and thoughtful than most, so his believing that about her was disturbing. Perhaps if he were given a chance to know her better?

"I believe that some of those stories are merely a facet of the truth. Sometimes you need to look at the entire jewel to appreciate its complex beauty."

Reese nodded in agreement. "That was beautifully put, and you are right. I should not be so quick to pass judgement on someone I haven't met." He rose and pointed toward the tree line. "I've loved our conversation and shouldn't delay your travel any longer, but would you be interested in joining me for lunch?"

Athena was delighted. "I would love to. I am presuming mushrooms are on the menu?"

Reese laughed and put his hand out to help her rise. She hesitated for a moment, fighting her nature that screamed to accept his help was a sign of weakness. His open and engaging face had her placing her hand in his and rising with his help. It was the first time in her existence that she had ever allowed a man to do so. The feel of her hand in his was electric, and as soon as he dropped her hand, she missed its warmth. She was glad she was joining him for lunch, she wanted to learn more about this enigma of a man.

"Shall we?" He started to walk up the path, and Athena whistled for Hippia. Once her reins were in hand, she waved in the direction he was heading.

"Lead the way."

Another first. Until now, she had always been the one to make way. It seemed that she would be learning a lot about herself, as well as her new friend, from this chance encounter.

3

Reese's home didn't take long to get to. It was in a secluded grove in the center of the forest straight back from a line of oak trees they had passed through. It was an ideal spot near a small stream, with an opening in the lush canopy that allowed light through. The garden was well-placed, dead center in the patch of sunlight that warmed the earth. It was filled with vegetables and herbs as well as some flower varieties she had never seen before. Prickly shrubs edged the gardens that seemed effective in keeping woodland animals from helping themselves to the colorful offerings.

"I've played around with cross pollination and blending seeds. It doesn't always work, but when it does, it's fun to see what comes up. I will show you around inside first so we can get lunch going. There is some sweet grass near the stream if you want to tether your horse there. I also have a lean-to with some hay which is where I keep Daisy."

"Who?"

Reese laughed at her expression. "Daisy, my goat."

"Makes a little more sense than what I thought originally." She smirked. "I'll meet you inside."

After tending to Hippia, Athena entered the small house. It was rustic but quaint, much smaller than the homes in the village adjacent to her temple. She looked around the expansive kitchen, which looked like a place he spent most of his time. There were bundles of herbs drying along the hearth as well as patterned fabrics that added a lovely touch to the windows. She looked around and noted other touches that one might consider more feminine, but he didn't act as if anyone else lived there. Perhaps not feminine, but romantic. Strings of glittering beads, bowls full of flowers, and the warm glow of candlelight. His home was filled with beauty and warmth, a welcome change from the cold marble of her temple.

He rummaged around in a cupboard and almost knocked over one of the glass vials that lined the counter. They were various shapes and sizes and were filled with liquids ranging from clear to cloudy in a rainbow of colors. He settled the bottle he had nearly knocked down and looked over his shoulder sheepishly.

"I never have company. Just trying to find us glasses. I have a wine that would go nicely with our lunch." He nodded his head toward one of the kitchen chairs. "Have a seat, it won't take me long to get this ready."

Once the wine was poured, Athena took the glass that was offered and watched as he moved around the small room and prepared their meal. She looked around once more for signs that he lived with anyone else but still couldn't tell. She decided to ask.

"How long have you lived here?"

"About five years. It was meant to be a stopping point on my way to Athens, but I soon found that everything I needed was right here. The man who built it had passed away, and the family just wanted to see it maintained. I agreed to take care of the property in exchange for living here."

"And you live here alone?"

Reese nodded. "I do. I find that I prefer it that way. I'm not comfortable around people."

Athena laughed, causing him to look at her with a question crinkling his brow. "I don't mean to laugh, but you seem to be doing just fine with me."

He shrugged. "Well, that's because you're different." He turned back to his task of preparing lunch as if his comment made complete sense.

Athena's defenses rose, and she tried not to let it bleed into her tone. "Different how?"

He turned and took two steps to the table. His hands were splayed in apology. "I meant that in a good way. Most women are only interested in sizing me up as a mate, and most men want to come to blows. I am happy to engage with either but fit with neither, if that makes sense. I find it is easier to be close enough to make my observations yet far enough that I'm left alone. You seem to be very much the same."

She nodded with a smile. "That I am," Athena agreed. "I have plenty of reasons to keep my distance, and most of the time, I'm too busy to make friends."

"Yet, here we are," Reese smiled.

Athena couldn't help but be excited about the potential.

"Yes, here we are."

He raised his glass to hers and clinked it on the side. "Here's to making new friends."

Athena nodded. "And expecting no more or less than friendship from them."

The delight of her comment lit Reese's face like the full moon. "Well put," he said quietly then turned back to the stove to cook. It made Athena wonder which additional reaction he kept hidden from her sight.

The conversation over lunch was pleasant, and Athena was delighted to learn several things about Reese that deepened her interest in him. He loved to cook, often using the vegetables and fruits he propagated in his garden. He was educated and had a mesmerizing speaking voice she could listen to for hours. Music was something he admired but was never able to master, so at an early age, he applied his talents into science. That was apparent with the amount of working experiments Athena saw scattered throughout the house.

He originated from Rome, and she asked questions about their culture which he readily answered. He didn't know much about the armies or their warfare but knew who was sleeping with whom and the nuances about the relationships more than anyone she had ever met. He explained that some pairings were only for sex, while others were a monogamous commitment. His words quickened and his voice lifted as he spoke about the wide array of human interactions he studied while he was there. He didn't seem to have participated, merely observed and weighed the benefits of all types of relationships as if he were a scholar. It was clear that he was least interested in the politics of the region, which fascinated her. That was typically a topic most people in her life discussed.

He seemed to be happy to fill the conversation with things he found interesting or where he found beauty in the world around him. When he asked questions about her life, she easily redirected the conversation by sharing enough so as to not to make him too suspicious. Nothing she shared would hint to her goddess status.

"Are you finished with that?" Reese pointed to the plate in front of her, which had been emptied entirely of the delicious meal he had prepared from the foraged mushrooms. There were salty fruits he served with it that she really enjoyed, and she made a mental note to ask him about them.

"I am, thank you." She passed the plate over. "The white sauce had a wonderful flavor."

"Something I learned when traveling in Parma," he said with a smile.

"What are the green fruits called that you served with it? They were delicious."

"I haven't named them yet. I'm experimenting with them. The pickling is just one thing I have been able to do with them, but I am finding other uses for them as well." He was excited by the topic and came to her side to help her out of her chair. "Come, I will show you."

Reese led her outside and around the building to the side yard. He walked to a row of trees on the back of the property. They were about the same size as an apple tree but with feathery foliage like a willow and a knotty, rough bark. She had never seen or smelled anything quite like them. The scent from the blooms reminded her of ripened apricots, with a slight hint of aniseed.

"I found some on my travels and saw the birds enjoying the fruit, so figured I would try them." He pulled one from the branch and held it out to her. "The fruit turns from green to black, so I've tried brining it at several different stages. They are too bitter when first picked from the tree. While I used the green for our meal, I am partial to the darker ones which ripen longer."

"I should like to try the darker ones as well."

Reese smiled, delighted at her request. "I have found also that they secrete a greasy substance. I've used it to coat some of my pots and pans, and it has given my food a nice flavor."

Athena squeezed a ripened fruit, and golden liquid coated her fingers. She licked the pad of her thumb and closed her eyes in delight. The taste was light and appealing. When she opened her eyes with a sigh, his intense gaze locked with hers.

She cleared her throat around the feeling that rose there. "It's good," she remarked. "I wonder how many things this could be used for. Have you tried burning it?"

His eyes lit up. "I haven't, but I have mixed it with oils I've distilled from other plants and attempted some perfumes."

"The blooms are fragrant. The scent is sweet but also carries an earthy tone."

"My thoughts exactly," he said. "Something for everyone."

"Promising," Athena mused.

"I could use an assistant," Reese suggested. "Would you be interested? I have an extra room in the house where you could stay."

Athena thought about the potential, of the fact that this could be the something she had been looking for. The fact it was something edible that could be used for other things intrigued her, as did spending more time with Reese. She wanted to see where it could all lead. Plus, she wouldn't mind getting to know him better. She enjoyed his company. Her mind was set.

"I would love to stay."

"Wonderful. We will start our experiments first thing in the morning."

"Perfect! So, what shall we do tonight?"

Reese smiled and rubbed his hands together. "How are you at latrones?"

"Games of strategy are something I've played my whole life."

"Excellent. Follow me."

With their glasses filled with wine, they settled next to the crackling fire and set the playing board. Athena watched Reese as he considered each move. He was a strong player, able to prevent her from taking his pieces easily. She was intrigued by that, considering he was a loner and didn't seem to be all that interested in warfare.

"You aren't making this easy," he murmured.

She looked up, just as his tongue swiped the glistening drop of crimson wine dotted on his lower lip. It was so unlike her to wonder how it would taste, but that was precisely where her mind went. The fact that she was sharing the same vintage didn't matter to her libido.

"I play this a lot," she responded.

"I can tell. It's been a while for me, but my father and I played every night when I was young. He said it would help me understand the ways of the world."

Athena nodded as she took a sip of her wine. "I understand that statement. Your father sounds as if he had your best interests at heart."

"How so?"

"Games of strategy are very much like society; each piece has a place and purpose within the overall world…or in this case, the playing board. Like the relationships that humans have with one another, there is a hierarchy within the pieces, and each represents strengths and weaknesses. Understanding one's place can help with finding one's purpose."

"I can see that," he mused. "However, even the most powerful pieces have limitations based on the location they find themselves in."

"True. And some pieces give the impression of greatness, only to fall by the abandonment of the pieces surrounding. Each piece is nothing without the other pieces. Like some rulers I know."

"Do you know many rulers?"

Athena's face flushed, and she hid it in the glow of the flames she faced as he considered his move. When she looked back, his head was bowed over the board, and she quietly sighed in relief. It was time to be honest, without being open.

"I have in my time," she said slowly. "However, most of my opinions are based on what I hear from others who spend time in that world."

He took one of her stones with his, leaving a key move exposed. It had her wondering what he had planned. She looked at the pieces on the board and started the moves in her mind. Why leave that one open?

"I believe other people's opinions are good enough to give you a general direction for your own. But they don't always include all the information, so it's best to do your own research. It's sometimes hard to filter out the deceit."

"In court especially," she agreed. "I have seen some vicious moves within the royalty who should honor their relationships a little better than they do. Family members fighting against each other for the right to call a territory their own. It's sad really."

"I agree, especially since the land isn't really ours to begin with."

Athena saw it then; the stone wasn't exposed at all, there was two more that stood nearby. She decided on another move. "Interesting concept. You believe there should be no leaders to help the people?"

He shook his head. "Not necessarily. I believe some leaders have the best interests of the community at heart, but some are ruthless. At the end of the day, the land will be here longer than any of us. It will see many rulers in its day, many of whom have no right to lay claim to it."

"So, who should care for it?"

"Those who nurture it will gain the best rewards. Rulers who are more worried about growth and coating the fields with the blood of their enemies aren't fit to lead. In my opinion, of course."

Athena thought about Ares and the most recent skirmish he had started. Perhaps Reese was right, although a world without guidance was chaos as she had seen in the past. Mortals didn't always see beyond their own experiences. Learning from their mistakes rarely happened.

"So, what is it that you feel would be the best for the world's people? What is needed that they don't get right now?"

"Peace," he said softly. He moved his piece over and captured hers. "No one would need to be in power if the world was at peace." As she reviewed the board, she knew she had lost. It was a number of moves in the future, but the outcome was apparent. She looked up into his eyes and saw the twinkle in their hazel depths she had come accustomed to.

"And what would be the best thing to represent it? More importantly, how would peace be obtained?" She moved her stone forward, making the only move she could. The move he had fully expected.

"In my world, a good glass of wine and full belly helps," he said with a smile. "A way to keep warm and a comfortable place to sleep as well. I believe a healthy understanding of what brings people happiness and those who have plenty providing it for those who lack it is a good start."

"And what brings happiness?"

He made his final move, taking her stone and leaving her last one cornered by several of his. "I have yet to find out," he said, lifting his glass to take a sip. "And I'm anxious to do so, especially in my current company."

Athena laughed and pushed her remaining stones to the center of the board, ending their game. "You don't seem too worried about happiness since you just beat me at one of my favorite games. That makes me unhappy."

"Then why are you smiling?"

"Perhaps, because it is the first time I've enjoyed the process of losing so thoroughly."

4

The first few days there went by quickly, and it didn't take long for Athena and Reese to fall into a routine. It was fascinating just how versatile the small fruits were from the tree that Reese had found on his travels. The pickling process for the fruit was time consuming, but the reward when she bit into the salty fruit he had processed weeks before was worth it. It made her wonder how they would taste with a small bit of garlic or pepper stuffed in them.

For his other experiments, Reese put her in charge of writing down the reactions of various animals he brought together and monitored. The animals chosen tended to be ones he knew would get along, however, he also paired a few that didn't, which was when it got interesting. The warrior in her loved watching the animals fight, and she paid special attention to the winner and what technique they used to beat their opponent. He walked up to her just as the viper took its last breath from the sting of a scorpion.

"I could have predicted how that one would go," Reese said.

Athena laughed. "Me too, although for a moment there it looked as though the scorpion was considering him."

"That would be a pairing, would it not?"

"No worse than the cat and mouse you put in the same box."

"I agree that pairing wasn't the smartest. At first, I thought they were getting along, but then I realized the cat was merely playing with its food."

"I found it interesting that she got along with the dog though."

"Me too, especially since he was so young and energetic. It was interesting to see how nurturing she was toward him."

Athena wiped her hands on her silken peplos then picked up the dead snake. The scorpion had already disappeared, most likely to find a more suitable mate. She looked down at her outfit and wondered if it would be worth trying to remove the stains. Perhaps it was time for a new one.

"I've made some progress in the kitchen. Are you finished here? I'd like to show you what I've come up with."

"Sure, just let me check on Hippia, and then I'll be in."

When she found the horse, she was cozied up to the goat with the cat watching from a nearby ledge. It was an unlikely trio, but she supposed some company was better than none. Or perhaps it was something more. Reese's experiments had her looking at the world in a new way. Perhaps some relationships were more than a necessity.

She checked Hippia's feed and water then stood at the entrance of the stall where she was laying. Daisy was curled up in the nook created by her neck, so Hippia merely looked up and blinked her large brown eyes at Athena.

"I can see it would be hard to move. Just checking on you." The horse let out a soft snort, which had the goat adjusting itself with a grunt. The cat looked on with interest but stayed seated. "I think we will be here a few more days. I am enjoying my experiments with Reese and believe he may have what I need for our quest."

Hippia gave another soft snort and closed her eyes. Athena backed out of the stall with a smile when the cat jumped down into the hay and started to inch her way over. It seemed that she wanted in on the nap; either that or Daisy would be disturbed soon.

On her way in, she stopped in the garden and pulled a few ripened tomatoes from the vine. They would be good with the lunch she was sure Reese was preparing. When she walked into the house, she was happy to find her assumptions were correct.

"I thought these better come in before the birds got them," she said as she settled herself at the table. There was nothing she liked better than to watch him work. He had a very graceful flow as he moved, almost as if he was dancing. It was captivating to watch.

"I wonder how they would be with some of the oil we made. Maybe include some of the dark vinegar I have?"

"What would you like me to do?"

"How about you chop them into small pieces and put them in this bowl. I'll come up with something."

"I rather like the things you come up with," Athena said softly. "The combinations are surprising and delicious. They are also things I would have never thought to pair together."

"Pairs that don't go together make the world a more interesting place, don't you agree?"

Athena found herself agreeing with most of the things he said. "I do indeed."

By the time she had finished chopping the tomatoes, Reese had given her some of the pickled fruits and green onions to cut as well. She chopped and added the onions to the bowl while popping the fruits in her mouth as she worked.

"There will be hardly any in the dish if you keep doing that."

"I can't help myself. They are so good."

"I shall forever think of you every time I eat one of those."

"That is one of the nicest things anyone has ever said to me. I like the idea of that."

Reese flushed as he placed a plate of sliced bread in front of her then turned quickly back to his task at the counter. "I can't imagine it is the nicest thing," he said quietly.

The comment warmed her, like the rays of a solstice sun. At the same time, she chose to pretend she didn't hear him, since she wasn't sure what to do about how she was feeling, if anything at all. It was clear they were mutually attracted to one another, there was no denying that. And they connected on an intellectual level as well, which allowed for them to spend countless hours in each other's company without irritating one another. But she had duties to the people that prohibited her from having a lengthy relationship with anyone.

It wasn't that she had never had sex, although some would argue that without penetration it didn't count as such. She knew from experience that was not the case, and she delighted in the freedom of expression that often came from her dalliances with anyone she trusted enough to share her passion with. Men, women, demi-gods, and goddesses, she had shared parts of her body with them all. It was the only time she felt truly seen.

She was careful with her partners, no one could know either on Mount Olympus or Earth that she had even been seen naked, but keeping secrets was something most people didn't want to do. Expressing love was natural, and once it was felt for another, most partners wanted to yell it from the mountaintops. She broke it off with most before that could happen, using a bit of potion from Hecate to eliminate her memory from their minds. It was hard for her to continue seeing them around after that, since the feelings were always unmatched as she continued to care for them in a way they no longer recalled. The price for using magick to erase her memory was the memories were replaced with unattractive narratives. For once, she wanted to have someone remember the beautiful moments she was part of, to see her as the person she was. She would give anything for a relationship like that.

Reese's voice broke through her musings. "I believe we will mix what you have there and add a bit of vinegar and oil and perhaps some salt and pepper." It seemed Reese was ignoring his last comment as well. "Then to make use of this older bread, we can put the tomato mixture on top with a little cheese and warm them on the skillet in the fire."

"That sounds good," she agreed. "I can get that done while you finish what you are doing." She lined the skillet over the fire and drizzled a little of the oil they had pressed the day before into the bottom of it. "I really like how this oil tastes."

"The last bit we pressed burns nicely. I have a lamp going in the next room. I really think we are on to something."

"I think you are on to something. I'm merely helping."

"Yes, but you are a great inspiration to me. I haven't had this much fun with my experiments in quite some time."

"I'm happy to help." Athena removed the bread from the skillet, which had cooked quicker than she had anticipated. "I think these may be done. Perhaps next time, I should toast the bread on the other side before adding the tomatoes."

Reese came over and examined the plate of relish-topped bread slices. "I think those look great. Maybe we can put a little more oil and vinegar on top to help soften the toasted part." They took them to the table and did just that. They took a bite together, and eyes met as the flavors coated their palettes and stunned them. For something so simple, the flavor was incredible.

"I love these," she said around bites.

"I do too," he responded with his shy smile.

Her heart raced over the double meaning of their phrases. The tension between them was pulled tighter as their eyes locked. She held her breath as his hand came up slowly.

"May I?"

She nodded before she even realized what he was asking. His hand cupped her face, and his thumb gently swiped the corner of her mouth. Her breath held as she watched him put the pad near his lips and kiss it.

"You had some vinegar just there." He pointed to her face with a blush. In that moment, Athena, the Goddess of War and heir to Olympus, silently promised Reese her heart no matter the cost. She only hoped that when she told him who she really was, the cost to their relationship wouldn't be the price she would pay. She wasn't sure she would survive the broken heart she would suffer for eternity.

He leaned back in his chair and took in a breath, pausing for a moment as if the words he wanted to say were stuck in his throat. "I have something to say, and I'm struggling with how it will sound."

"Go on," Athena said quietly. She gave him a slow nod as if to prompt him. The churning in her stomach was noticeable, and she wondered if he was as nervous as she felt. She glanced down at his neck and caught the wild pulsing of his heartbeat. He was anxious.

He took a deep breath, as if preparing himself for the worst, then slowly shared his thoughts. "I have never met anyone like you, and the fact that you are accepting of who I am and what I am interested in speaks to my heart in a way I never thought would happen. I'm interested in getting to know you better and love the idea of sharing a life with you. I know that with every fiber of my being I want to express it in ways I never was interested in until now, not because of how you look, but because of how you speak to my heart. If that makes sense."

Athena's eyes welled. "That makes complete sense. If it helps, I am feeling the same."

He turned in his seat and faced her, reached for her hands, and took them in his. They were warm, a little damp from the nerves that shook his voice. She soaked up every emotion that was coming to her, relishing the feeling of being loved for who she really was.

"I'm so glad to hear you say that. It does help me say this next thing." He squeezed her hands and finished his thoughts. "I have never been with anyone physically; I'm not comfortable in my own skin. It's also been awkward for me to get that close to someone when our minds didn't align. It's part of why I'm researching relationships and the various ways of expressing love both mentally and physically. I had hoped by studying how people show love, I would find it myself. That said, there is no reservation in my mind when it comes to sharing that part of myself with you. I imagine experiences with you that excite me, and I am ready to try them all, but I want to be sure that you want them as well. I would never do anything you didn't want to do."

His honesty spoke to her heart. The honor he was giving her by being his first was a gift.

"Reese, we haven't known each other long…"

"I know, I thought about that…"

"Let me finish," Athena said with a squeeze of his hands. He nodded in agreement. "I want to thank you for trusting your heart, mind, and body to me. I know what a big commitment that is, and I am honored. But I need to let you know I am a virgin as well, and for many reasons, I need to keep it that way."

His shoulders lowered and closed his eyes, nodding at the news. "I understand. Forget I said anything, I'm content with the friendship the way it is, if you are."

Athena couldn't take much more. She felt compelled to be honest with this man who had stolen her heart but was having a hard time finding a way out of the tangle of lies she had woven. Like one of her tapestries, she needed to pull some of the strings that weren't working and start again.

"What I meant to say is that I am open to the physical expressions of love in any way my partner chooses, but I need you to know that the last bit isn't something I can do. For now." She slipped her hands from his grip and placed them on his thighs. The toga he had on slid on one side, and she ran her hands along the soft hair that had been exposed.

He was motionless, and his chest unmoving. She had his attention.

"Does that sound agreeable?"

She glanced down at his arousal then back up into his smiling face. He cupped her cheek and leaned in toward her. "That sounds most agreeable. What do you want to experiment with first?"

Athena licked her lips, watching his pupils dilate at the motion. "A kiss would be a good start."

"I thought you would never ask."

5

The rooster crowed when the dawn came, but neither of them moved. They were still tangled up in each other, limbs and sheets twisted like some of the branches of the tree they were propagating. They had spent the night experimenting, shyly at first, but more demanding as they became comfortable with each other's bodies. Both were equally sated and completely boneless. Athena couldn't help but add things to her mental list of experiences she wanted to share with Reese when they were both a little more mobile.

His playful whisper tickled the top of her head. "I should like to experience last night all over again but in a woman's body. From a female's perspective."

She raised her head and looked into his clear but slightly worried expression. Her smile removed the doubt from his expression. "I would rather enjoy that. But I will have you know it's the person inside I'm making love to. That is where I find your beauty." Athena lowered her head and snuggled closer, the scent of apricot surrounding her from his warm skin. "I will also have you know experiencing last night from a female's perspective was completely satisfying for both my body and soul."

He tightened his embrace around her shoulders and sighed. His body was firm, as if carved from marble, yet soft and yielding in all the right places. She was comfortable, head pillowed on his chest, in a way she had never wanted before. She had always been one to avoid the awkward morning after routines, especially if she had an early morning session planned with her worshippers. She often left before her chosen partner ever opened their eyes. That she wanted to stay in the circle of Reese's arms was surprising and somewhat frightening to her. Especially since many of the things they experienced the night before had been a first for them both.

He was a generous and playful lover, willing to try anything Athena suggested, which suited her demanding nature. Reese's inexperience would work in her favor, for now, but she knew the time would come when she would want to share that final piece of herself. Reese was everything she could ask for in a partner, soft where she was hard, soothing where she was harsh, and his brilliant mind worked out solutions from all angles, which she appreciated as a leader. She was ready to consider the possibilities but not until things were settled with Poseidon. Losing the city to him would be devastating, so she refused to take any chances with her people.

Reese's stomach growled. He kissed the top of her head and drew her closer. "I could lay here all day, but I should look into finding us some breakfast."

"I don't need much. I often eat on the run."

"Toasted bread and jam it is." He started to move, and she slipped her head from the comfort he provided. She already missed the warmth on her cheek. "Don't move a muscle, I'll be right back."

He glanced back over his shoulder as he left the room and smiled. He had caught her admiring the view, his sun-kissed skin evenly toned unlike hers which was pale in the areas her clothing rested. It surprised and delighted her that he spent time outside in the nude; that was something she should like to try. Another experience added to the growing list.

After a few minutes in the kitchen, he returned. "I hope you like this. I used some of the oil after toasting the pita and added some fava and the fruits we have been working on. I also have a bit of the pastitsio left over from last night on the side here."

"That meal was so delicious." Athena's mouth watered. "This looks wonderful, thank you."

Reese rested the tray on the bed then climbed in beside her. There was an extra piece of pita that served as a wonderful spoon for the dips he had brought. They took turns feeding each other, another first for her and one of the most erotic things she had done with a partner that came to mind. She could watch Reese's mouth all day.

Athena cleared her throat. "What did you want to finish today? It appears you may have found as many uses for your new fruit as you will."

"I had thought about taking a trip into Thebes. I need some fabric for something I'm working on and wanted to go to T.A. Creations."

Athena's heart rose to her throat. She tried in vain to squelch the squeak in her voice. "Oh, well, that will take the better part of the day."

Reese's brows pinched together, and he tipped his head to the side. His mood grayed, like the sun going behind a cloud. She felt terrible, but there was no way she could be seen in Thebes with him until after the challenge.

Athena shrugged. "But if you really want to do that, I would be happy to stay here and get the last of the tests done." It clearly wasn't the response he was looking for, and Athena knew it from the stiffening of his body. Seconds later, he shifted further away from her and stood at the bedside.

"I'll just clear these dishes." His tone was deflated, she had hurt his feelings. Perhaps it was for the best. She needed to be on her way, having already lingered too long.

"Reese, I really should…"

He raised his hand to stop the flow of her words. "It's fine, Olivia." The name made her cringe. She had lied to him about more than that. She hoped when he learned the truth of her deceit, he wouldn't judge her too harshly. She was doing it for the good of her people, and he was included in that count—at the top of the list, if she were being honest.

"It will do me good to get out of the house for a bit."

She sensed he needed some separation from her, and while she was getting precisely what she wanted, her throat clogged with regret. Much as she would love to join him, it was much too risky. Everyone in the surrounding area knew her for her true self, and Thyia and Arachne both would address her as a goddess. She couldn't take the chance. Besides, she had a city to save.

"I'll can the last of the fruit we have curing." She looked up into his eyes, and his disappointment came to her in waves from across the room.

"At times like these, I truly wish I was a woman," he said softly. "Then I would know better what is going on in that mind of yours."

"What if it is nothing more than dividing our efforts so we can complete double the work and spend more time together later?"

"Seems to me that you don't want to be seen with me. Perhaps you are upset with me for some reason? Find me lacking perhaps?"

Athena jumped from the bed and closed the space between them in less than three steps. "I don't ever want you to say anything like that. No one, man, woman, or god for that matter, should ever make you question your worth." She took him into her arms, not worried about the fact that they were still both nude. It was important she at least got her point across on this.

He returned the embrace, and she thought about how perfectly they fit together in all the ways that mattered. His sweet temperament went a long way to smooth her volatile nature.

He gave a final embrace before releasing her with a sad smile. She lowered her eyes against the goodbye he knew she was giving but refused to acknowledge openly.

"I will be back after dinner, no need to stay up for me."

Athena felt the breakfast roil in her stomach; the guilt was eating a hole in her throat. The best she could offer was a quick nod.

He pulled on his toga, the one that highlighted the green flecks in his hazel eyes, then laced his sandals. His movements were efficient, as if he were in a hurry to be on his way. She hated herself for asking the next question, but she felt it was only proper that she keep something of him moving forward.

"By the way, did you ever decide what to call it? The fruit from the tree?"

His eyes shimmered; she had confirmed his suspicion, but he refused to let it stop him. He merely shrugged and answered as he left the room. "I had decided to call it an olive, named after the woman who captured my heart as we studied the tree."

She let herself cry after he had closed the front door behind him. It was the only time she had ever had any entity cause her to do so. After she had dried her tears and packed up a supply of fruit, oil, and dug up a tree, she left the only place she truly felt at home. A home she would most likely never be welcome to again.

Once back at the temple, Athena summoned Hermes, who brought another bottle of his latest vintage. He pointed to the tree with a question creasing the sides of his eyes. "Please tell me that isn't what you plan on saving your beloved city with?"

"And what if it is?" Her voice was strained from worry as well as the fact that Reese would have returned by now from his trip to the village. She hadn't left a note, but he would know she was gone.

"It's fine if it is, but I expected something a little more...I don't know...stately, I suppose."

"Perhaps that is precisely my plan. To be unpredictable."

"Well, I would say you have secured that without issue. What type of plant is that by the way?"

Her eyes welled as she repeated the name Reese had labeled it with. "It's an olive tree."

When Hermes shot her a questioning look, she elaborated. "The tree itself is beautiful, and the wood makes exquisite things such as a jewelry box or these bowls."

Hermes looked impressed, so she continued. "It also grows fruit, which is delicious when soaked in brine. Here, try one."

Hermes sniffed the black fruit she handed him and looked at her with suspicion. "Go on then but beware of the pit. It is hard like a peach."

He nodded then popped the fruit in his mouth. In quick order, he spit out the cleaned pit. He promptly pulled another from the bowl she had them in; this time, he selected a green one.

"They are tasty. I love the salty flavor. It's like the Mediterranean."

Athena pointed to the fruit he selected "The green have a bit different flavor, but I find I like them equally."

Hermes popped it in his mouth, and it was eaten as quick as the last. He pointed to the bottle sitting next to the bowl. "And what is this?"

"This is the best part," Athena said excitedly. "When you press the olives, you get this delicious oil. Here, let me show you."

6

thena spent the night tending to her own needs. She decided no priestess was better than having one that was a ceaseless disappointment. Besides, she was hours away from a battle for her beloved city, and she needed to keep the gift she was presenting a secret until the time came. The only one she could count on for that was Hermes. She heard his flutter echo in the halls long before she felt his presence.

"It's time, sister. Hades is outside with your ride."

Athena nodded then gave the bundle one last cinch before sliding it into the ornate purple sack she had waiting. "I'm ready. Where will we be meeting?"

"We have the crowds gathered in Thebes. Zeus thought it would be best to have this conversation in a neutral territory."

Athena's heart faltered, and she sent a small prayer to Olympus that Reese was done gathering his supplies. Running into him wouldn't be ideal.

"Any word on what Poseidon has planned?"

Hermes looked pained then lowered his eyes. Athena immediately regretted the question.

"I'm sorry, Hermes, I know you aren't able to say anything. I didn't mean to put you under any pressure to do so."

"No pressure at all. I just hate that you have to go through this."

"I'm sure it won't be the last time something like this will happen. It's like he's taking things out on Father through me, and it's getting old." They walked down the steps of the temple to the chariot Hades had waiting.

"That Uncle hasn't learned you are the more capable of the choices is getting old as well," Hermes quipped. "He would be better off fighting Father directly."

"Now that I would like to see," Athena laughed.

"I would like to see that as well," Hades piped in.

Athena went straight into Hades open arms, and his embrace brought tears to her eyes. This was how family was supposed to be, not like the dysfunction she had to deal with on Olympus.

Hades took the sack from Athena and loaded it in the back of the chariot before helping her into her seat. He gave her a wink and pointed to the reins. "You want to drive?"

"I'm too nervous but maybe after when we celebrate?"

"You're on."

"I'll see you both there," Hermes said before flying in the direction of the city.

"Shall we?" Hades reached over and gave Athena's hand a gentle squeeze.

She took a deep breath. "Ready when you are."

The four black stallions pulling Hades's chariot got them to the location in minutes, which was good considering that Athena was much too distracted to enjoy the flight. As they flew over the sage and gold fields, she saw her people gathered in small groups chatting to their neighbors. There were merchants taking advantage of the crowds, selling their wares, food, and drink to those who had been there the better part of the day. Her people… She wondered how long they would remain as such.

Athena started to worry that her gift wouldn't be adequate enough to impress them. Poseidon was known to be flamboyant, and his charisma was undeniable. She had seen him with men who were awed by his power and with women who fell at his feet with lust. What most didn't know was the trident he carried enchanted all who stood before it. In addition, although he was handsome, when he used the piece from Aphrodite's belt, his appeal couldn't be denied by any human. The worry snaked through her core and made her feel like she did the night before a battle. She had a hard time shaking the dread.

Hermes had arranged for a podium to be constructed in the center of town. She saw a few of her supporters on the left side of the stand, who greeted her with a wave when she arrived. Thyia and Arachne were both there, and she made it a point to stop and thank them for the beautiful sack they had created for her offering. She walked up onto the podium and took her seat on one of the two golden thrones they had ready. Poseidon had just arrived and was grandstanding his way to his seat.

"Just like him to make a spectacle of himself," Hermes muttered.

"Did we ever doubt he would? Where is Father?"

Hermes shook his head before responding. "He won't be coming, but he said he would confirm the vote of the people with a sign."

Her eyes welled, and she shook off the disappointment. Athena should have known she couldn't count on him for support. Staying out of it was conveniently political of him. "Let's get this over with. I don't want to be here longer than we have to be."

As Hermes crossed her view to gather Poseidon, she scanned the crowd, realizing that most of the women had congregated on her side of the podium and most of the men on Poseidon's. It was in the middle of the crowd where she caught a familiar set of hazel eyes looking at her with morbid curiosity. She had been right to worry about Reese being there. There was no hiding her identity from him now. Hermes's announcement startled her from looking at the question in Reese's gaze.

"Good People of Athens," Hermes announced. "Today, you have been summoned to make a choice which will guide the future of your fair city. Athena's governance over your livelihood has been called into question." Murmurs from the women were combined with each of them inching forward. The men on their side took an unconscious step back. Athena finally had the strength to look directly at Reese in the center of the crowds, who was staring back with mouth agape.

"Zeus has called this contest in order to determine once and for all who the patron god or goddess shall be over this land. Whoever provides the people with the most desirable gift, and who obtains majority vote of the people, shall have the city named after them for eternity."

Athena glanced up at Poseidon who sat tall and proud with a cocky grin, exuding all the confidence in the world she didn't feel for the first time in her existence. To have Reese witness this moment was something that made her want to crawl into a hole.

"We shall draw straws for the ability to present first. Shortest straw last." Hermes held out a fist full of dried wheat to Athena who made her selection. Poseidon then made his and held up his longer straw with a grin.

"Excellent," Poseidon said as he stood from his seat and directed his speech into the crowd.

"People of Athens, while I agree that Athena has been a just and fair patron, I believe you need someone who has the ability to bring commerce and trade into your fair city as well as fill your coffers." His followers nodded, as did many of hers, but Athena's attention was exclusively on one person. "You need a leader that can provide you access to the resources from the rest of the world, either by land or sea." He raised his trident and faced the back of the podium where barren and unfarmable land stretched as far as the eye could see. "My gift to you is life-giving water." He threw the trident from the podium into the center of the area, and the crowds gasped as a geyser of water sprayed up from the point where it landed. The earth quaked and rumbled, collapsing away from the trident, the water quickly filling in the gorge it left behind. In a matter of minutes, the podium was no longer on the edge of a barren landscape but bordering a rippling shoreline.

Much of the crowd went to the edge of the water body to investigate, marveling at the much-needed addition of water in their region. Athena's confidence dipped lower as the thinning crowds in front of her brought more focus on the man that still stood there shaking his head in disbelief. When he knew he had her attention, he mouthed, "why didn't you tell me?" With tears in her eyes, she mouthed back, "I should have."

"It's salty," a woman cried.

"Perhaps it has fish," said a hopeful voice.

"Won't be useful to us for crops," another added.

"We can travel by boat now to neighboring cities. I would imagine we could access the Mediterranean from here now," a man said. By then, the crowds at the shore had dissipated and returned to the podium.

Once the crowds settled back into their positions and the murmuring subsided, Hermes once again spoke to the crowd. "Now, for Athena's gift." He stepped back as Athena rose. She pulled the sack out from beside her seat and walked to the table at the front of the podium that had been set for her. The crowd of her loyal supporters gathered closer, curious to know what was in the beautiful silken bag she had brought with her.

"People of my fair city, I won't dictate to you what type of leader you need; you are all capable of choosing the best patron for yourselves. However, I will say that I will continue to work beside you to create solutions to enhance the life you choose to live. Whatever it takes, my people and their needs will always come first, no matter where their loyalties lie." Athena pulled a corked bottle from the sack, two sealed jars and a bowl, and then a small lamp. Lastly, she pulled a small tree with the root mass covered in the same silk her sack was made from. She kept her eyes focused on the horizon, far from the beautiful face that could break her concentration and bring her to her knees.

"I give to you this incredible tree, which not only provides wonderful wood to create artistic bowls such as this, but also produces amazing fruits that can be preserved and eaten. Those same fruits can also be pressed to make oil." She glanced over to Thyia and Arachne who nodded in support. She touched the tip of the lamp with her finger producing a flame which quickly lit the lamp. The murmurs from the crowd were favorable. "This oil can be eaten or burned, providing you with both a food and heat source." She opened one of the jars and poured the contents into the bowl before passing the bowl down to the crowd. "I welcome you to try the fruits, they are quite delicious."

The bowl was passed through the crowd as she filled another for the other side of the podium. When she finally had the courage to look into the center of the crowd, Reese was gone. She sat on her throne, no longer caring if she won her challenge.

"The fruits are amazing, and the oil light and flavorful," a woman said to another.

"I could create some boxes in my workshop," a man said as he examined the bowl Reese had made from the wood.

"The shrub looks sturdy, like it would stand up to the drier climate well," a farmer mentioned.

"The flame burns clean and true," a woman said to her neighbor.

The murmurs in the crowd came to a stop when Hermes raised his hands for attention.

"The voting shall commence now and will be allowed until sunset, after which a count of the lots will be made. There are bowls set up on either side of the podium which are carved with each of the patron's symbols, Medusa's head for Athena and a Trident for Poseidon. Each person is allowed one stone to place in the bowl of their choice. Voting begins now. Poseidon and Athena, you may return to your temples, and when Zeus calls the vote, I will bring word to you."

And with that, Athena's Challenge was at an end, along with any hope that she would ever be welcome in Reese's life again. She had Hades take her back home by way of the newly formed waterway that Poseidon had created. It did indeed provide access to both the Mediterranean and Ionian seas, and from a military standpoint, it also created a separation between Thebes and the other cities to the south, which were now on the other side of quite a substantial gulf of water.

"Poseidon gave the people a good gift, even if the water isn't drinkable," Athena said. "It makes the city more secure from invaders."

Hades pulled the reins to turn the chariot in the direction of Athena's temple. "Yes, I agree this is a benefit in more ways than one, but your gift is incredibly useful as well. The people will choose wisely. You should not let Poseidon's flamboyance make you feel inadequate."

Athena shrugged. "It isn't Poseidon that has me feeling that way."

"What then?"

"Something someone said to me about peace. Perhaps that is the only solution, and I'm not sure any of this will provide it."

"Peace does seem to be easier to obtain with fewer people. The most peace I have is when Persephone and I are alone doing nothing at all."

"That is the peace I should like to strive for."

"I hope you find it, my friend. In the meantime, getting you home will be a good start."

Athena teared up at the word. Hades had no idea that the only home she had ever truly realized had just turned his back on her. She might not ever know peace again, but finding a way for Reese to find his would bring her a small bit of comfort. How she would accomplish that would be the biggest challenge of all.

7

One vote decided the fate of Athens. The numbers were split equally between the sexes, with the men voting for Poseidon due to the gulf's commerce potential and the women for the versatile tree, which was dubbed the greatest thing to happen to homesteads since pita bread. The only vote Athena cared about was the one she lost before votes were cast.

Once Zeus confirmed the count, word was sent to the people of Athens. White doves flew to each homestead, leaving a small olive branch with each man, woman, and child to signify that Athena was the winner. When Hermes came to give her the news, she was sitting in the dark, twisting the tiny branch in between her fingers as her tears flowed freely. Hermes knew better than to ask. He lit a few lanterns then left a couple bottles of wine near her feet before flying into the dusk. He had been back nightly over the past few weeks, always leaving Athena in a similar state.

She could hardly function, sick over the fact that Reese not only caught her stealing his work, but also lying about her identity. How she wished she could go back to the day they met and tell him the truth. Perhaps had she done so, he would still be talking to her. She needed to apologize but couldn't see a way through. What was customary? Apologies weren't something a goddess needed to worry about, but she knew the guilt would eat her alive if she didn't find a way. The feelings of inadequacy were suffocating her.

In need of seeing a friendly face, she pulled out her Aegis with the image of Medusa and whispered the phrase that caused the eyes on the shield to open. When they did, the face on the shield came alive, and Medusa's soothing voice filled the room.

"Thea, it is so good to see you," Medusa said. "Congratulations on your victory. I heard about the challenge. I so wish I could have been there for you during that time."

"You had your hand's full," Athena smiled.

"I most definitely do now that the twins are here, although Perseus is a huge help with them both. We did finally settle on Chrysaor and Pegasus for names."

"Pegasus is a fine name. It means from a water spring, correct?"

"Yes, and you pretty much named Chrysaor by sending the golden sword to him as a gift. The golden wing necklace for Pegasus is also very much appreciated."

"Special gifts for special children," Athena said. "I will explain to them how to use them properly when they are older. I'm so glad you are all doing well."

"We are." The eyes on the shield narrowed, and the head tilted slightly to the side. Athena knew a question was coming before it was stated. "So, are you going to tell me what is going on with you, or are you going to continue to mope alone in your temple? Hermes says you haven't left there in weeks and only come out to gather tributes from the steps once a day. Why don't you have Karisa do that, by the way?"

"I relieved her of her duty," Athena shrugged. "I was doing her job anyway, fixing what she had messed up. And before you ask, there is no one I can find that is a suitable replacement for you, so I figured why even bother trying anymore?"

"As nice as that is to hear, I have to believe there is someone suitable to keep you company. Someone other than Hippia, that is."

"She isn't much of a conversationalist but is extremely good company, you know that."

"I meant no offense, my friend. I just worry about you."

Athena smiled at the hideous image on her shield, recounting all of the things she had to put Medusa and Perseus through, and regret wormed its way down into her chest. The choices she had made had benefited her beloved city, the Aegis allowed for her to have eyes everywhere and see all, but had it been worth it? She almost lost the love of two people she admired most in the world, and the thought of her making that same mistake again with Reese caused the tears to flow once more.

"I'm not sure why, I have only caused you misery."

The image of Medusa gasped, the snakes writhing from the sides of the shield. "Okay, what is going on? I have never seen you like this. You and I both know you had no choice. Having Perseus claim the gorgon head was the only way you could save us both. It made you a more effective protector to your people."

"Yes, but there could have been another way. Why did I have to lie and then take the thing he was most proud of? I could have found something else to challenge Poseidon with. Why did it have to be the one thing he named after the person he thought I was?"

"Apparently, we are not on the same subject," Medusa murmured. "Thea, who is the 'he' in this scenario?" The image on the shield smiled warmly, and the eyes softened. "Have you met someone?"

Athena nodded as the sobs shook her shoulders. Here was another first, the Warrior Goddess Athena crying her eyes out like a baby in front of a witness. As embarrassed as she was by it, she had to admit that it was also very cathartic.

The image on the shield beamed at her. "That is wonderful!"

"It's horrible," Athena countered. "He won't ever speak to me again!"

"Okay, pour yourself a glass of wine and start from the beginning. It seems that you and I have some catching up to do."

Half the bottle Hermes had left the night before was gone before Athena's tears had dried and the story of meeting Reese was shared. It felt good to have her friend to talk to again, and she realized there had been nothing preventing her from reaching out sooner. Pretty much any image of the gorgon head could be used as a link, and they were all over the land. Athena waited in silence for Medusa's council, which had always been sound. Another sip of her wine swallowed her sorrow once and for all. She was ready to act one way or the other.

"Thea, I always promised to be truthful to you even if it upset you, remember?"

"I do," Athena agreed.

"Even though your intentions were for the greater good, I believe he has a right to be upset, especially if he doesn't know you as well as I do. I also think that what you do in your private life is your business, and no one, god, human or goddess, should expect you to continue living as you do if you have found someone to give yourself body and soul to."

"But I feel an obligation to my people. What would they think?"

"Your people will love you no matter who you choose to share your body with. You are a fierce protectress and just ruler. Your people know that. Honestly, you have had relationships before, and there was no difference."

Athena looked at the shield with a frown. "There is definitely a difference this time. It was easy to always put my people first before. Now, all I can think about is giving him whatever he desires just to see him smile. I worry that putting him first will be a signal that I don't care about my city."

"I think you will find a way to take care of both. You have managed quite well until now with keeping your personal and public life separated. The question you need to ask yourself is, do you want to continue to keep them apart?"

"I'm not sure I do, I'm tired of the subterfuge. I feel like I've been lying not only to him, but to myself."

"Then I think the first step is to connect with Reese to see if he is willing to work things out. You owe him an apology at the very least. The next is to figure out what will make you both happy moving forward."

"I think having him in my life, no matter to what extent, will be a good start."

"Then that is where we will begin. I would suggest sending a letter and letting Reese know how you feel. That way, you can see if the path is clear to make amends."

"And what do I say?"

"That is up to you, my goddess. I would start by listing all the reasons why you don't want to continue on without him, then I think the letter will form from there. With or without him though, I believe you need to start being honest about what you want."

"Even with Father?"

"Especially with Zeus."

"I'm about to change my life drastically without the knowledge that it will work out in the end, aren't I?"

Medusa's image nodded. "Yes, and I can tell you from experience, it is the most frightening and exhilarating encounter you can ever have as a human."

"The trouble is I'm not human," Athena said.

"Yes, but you are in love with one, so it's time to start thinking like one."

After she and Medusa said their goodbyes, Athena worked on her letter long into the night. There were many iterations, and all included variations of apologies and explanations of why she had made the decisions she had. Most of those were wadded in a pile at her feet. As she pulled a new sheet of parchment out to start again, the next letter took on a different tone.

My Dearest Reese,

No words can express how sorry I am for what I did to you. While the goddess in me justifies lying about my identity, the woman in me is sickened that I hurt you. Stealing your research was unbelievably selfish, the crown to my deceit; I see that now, and I hope that you will find it in your heart to forgive me one day. If you can't, please know that I will always be here for you and will give you anything you ask for that is within my power.

Please accept the gift that accompanies this note as a token of my love, along with an offer that Hermes will relay to you privately. Choices about life and love should be made individually, and it is no one's business but your own what path you follow. I've tried to make adjustments in my own life and have you to thank for bringing my faults to light. This arrangement, should you desire it, is the one thing I felt I could help you with that might otherwise evade you. That, and it will allow for you to continue in your research, which I know means so much to you. I know your pursuit brings you joy, and I hope you accept the gift as it is intended, without strings, expectations, or judgement.

Your decision will be relayed in confidence by Hermes. He can be trusted, and I hope you find the answers you seek. I also hope beyond hope that one day our paths will cross again. You have my heart, Reese. Know that there will never be another person that holds the same place in my soul as you do.

May the light of Olympus forever shine on you.

With love eternal,

Athena

The fluttering of Hermes sandals came just as she finished signing it. She sealed the parchment then slid it into a package that a courier had dropped from Arachne earlier in the day.

"I felt your call. You have a message for me to relay?"

"I do."

"Does this have anything to do with the conversation you had with Father?" Hermes looked at her expectantly. She was trusting him with more than this package, and he sensed it.

"It does," she replied. "I was honest about what I wanted for myself as well as another moving forward. He agreed to help should the offer be desired."

"And you are sending me to the person in question to relay this offer?"

Athena's eyes brimmed with tears as she handled the parcel over to Hermes. "I am. His name is Tiresias. You will find him in a small cottage in the woods surrounded by a grove of olive trees, just east of Thebes."

"Who is this person who has stolen a goddess's heart?"

Athena shook her head and smiled. "He's stolen nothing, merely earned what I chose to give him as a woman." She leaned her forehead to Hermes's and closed her eyes, mentally relaying the terms of the offer she arranged with Zeus.

Once her thoughts were transferred, Hermes pulled her into an embrace. "I'm happy for you, Athena. I will take the utmost care with your message and will let you know the response."

"The response should go directly to Father. His decision is private, and I don't want him to feel obligated to me one way or another."

"You love him enough to let him go?"

"I love him enough to let him walk his own path. Whether that leads to me is something he has to come to on his own."

"I hope your paths meet again. I will take good care of your message."

"Thank you, Hermes. I know you will."

The winter turned to spring, and more priestesses came and went. Athena was edgier than ever and still couldn't find anyone that didn't annoy her. She tried to be as patient as possible, but with no word from Reese, she had fallen into despair. Her thoughts of him were endless, and she decided it might be better for everyone if she spent some time alone.

She spent time planting new fields of olive trees in the temple gardens and showing her people how to grow and harvest the versatile fruits. At the end of each day, she would draw herself a bath, settle with a glass of wine, and try to banish his memory. It was no use. She longed for the comfort of his arms and the warmth of his smile. Most of all, she missed the conversations.

With the last worshipper gone and the steps cleared, she lit the final set of lanterns for the night. A shadow in the entry near the porch caught her eye.

"Tributes may be left on the steps. The temple is closed for the evening."

The shadow stepped forward, the steps light and steady on the marble floor. Athena squinted her eyes and took a few steps forward, straining to see the visage in the haze. The figure was that of a woman, she was sure of it, and found she was right when she held the candle high, and the Nymph-like beauty came before her.

"I've heard you're in need of a priestess," the woman's voice was familiar in a way that spoke to Athena's gut, but she couldn't place her.

Perhaps she was a friend of Medusa's?

"I am," she said cautiously. Athena was close enough now for the flame from her candle to illuminate the shimmering fabric the woman wore. Was that a dove on the shoulder? The workmanship was undeniable, the robe had to have been crafted by Thyia. "Who did you say you were again?"

The bronze-haired beauty turned in place with her graceful arms held high as if leading a dance, and Athena caught an embroidered image of an olive tree on the woman's back before her turn was complete. She could better see the fabric now; the doves were all there, placed at her request as a symbol of the peace that Reese had wished for. There was only one person that would have that robe. Athena's breath caught in her throat, and her heart paused. Her eyes were already brimming with unshed tears as she looked into Reese's warm hazel eyes.

"Am I so unrecognizable then?"

Athena shook her head. "It took me a moment," she croaked. "I didn't think I would ever see you again. Do you still go by Reese?"

"I do. And I wasn't sure about that either," she said truthfully. "It was hard to know what to believe. But the gift you arranged through Zeus has taught me a lot so far, and I decided I wasn't ready to give up on you so quickly."

"I'm so relieved to hear you say that." Athena bent down to put the candle on the floor then splayed her arms as she rose. "May I?"

Reese stepped into Athena's embrace and wrapped her delicate arms around the back of her neck. Athena was home. She nuzzled into the embrace and pulled the familiar scent of olive blossoms into her lungs. She melted into the comfort it brought her senses.

"I fear you will crack a rib," Reese whispered. "But don't let go. Not yet."

They stood for several moments in the silence of the temple, bathed in the moonlight that shone down only for them. Hands started to move, first Reese's then Athena's, sliding over the changes both in form and perspective. The attraction was still palpable for them both, nothing had changed. Athena pulled back with a questioning look.

"Please tell me you are here to stay. I dare not start anything that will make either of us regret our actions. But I have to let you know, I'm fighting every impulse to scoop you up, take you to my chamber, and worship you like a god."

Reese took Athena's hand and led her to one of the marble benches lining the entry.

"Worship me like a goddess," she said with a grin. "Or at least for now. And I have a few things to say before I respond to the first part." After they were both seated, she took Athena's hands in hers and turned to face her. The ambient light from the candles made Reese so captivating, Athena feared she would die from rapture. She tried to concentrate on the words, but the lips forming them were luscious and smiling so sweetly. It was as if they would bestow her every wish. It made it hard to concentrate.

Reese gave Athena's hands a gentle squeeze then took a breath to organize her ideas. Athena knew the thoughts would be clear and well-formulated, just like everything Reese did. She pulled as much patience as she could from the recesses of her mind and gave Reese her complete attention. No matter what carnal thoughts she was having about seeing her beautiful soul naked before her, it ultimately had to be Reese's choice to act on them.

"First, I want to thank you." That had Athena's attention. "I know it seems strange that I should say that, especially after the way we parted, but I've had time in this new body and mindset to realize a few things. You did what you did out of love."

"That was no excuse for my…"

"Let me finish."

"Of course," Athena nodded.

"It is apparent to me that you love your people. You have built a thriving community with a robust commerce, and the women, as well as a large number of the men, would do anything for you. I have had opportunities for discussions I would have never been welcome to as a man, and what I found is that you have built a warm welcoming community of brilliant people who adore you."

"None of that matters to me."

Reese sat up straight and squeezed Athena's hands. "It should matter. What you have built is something to be proud of, and it should be guarded at all costs. You have built a safe community for all and have empowered those who seek it out. I learned the hard way that Poseidon is a pig, and everything he does is self-serving."

Athena's hackles rose. "He didn't touch you? I will gut him like a fish…"

"No need," Reese soothed. "I don't think he will be coming around me anytime soon. I managed to slip some hemlock into his tea, and he had a rather embarrassing episode of stomach issues in front of several nymphs."

Athena smiled but made a mental note that Poseidon would be getting a visit from her. It was time she started reminding the gods what the Aegis could truly do.

"Anyway, I saw first-hand what he was capable of, and I know that you did what you felt best for your people. I also understand why you would have held back from telling me who you really were. I would imagine that it gets tiresome being asked all day to do things for others. I understand needing a sense of normalcy."

"In a way, yes." Athena agreed. "And I didn't expect us to get along so well. And then when we… Well, when we…"

"Fell in love?"

Athena closed her eyes and relished the sound of the phrase coming from Reese's lips. "Yes, fell in love," she sighed. "It made it even harder, since by then you had already named your plant after me, and I knew I couldn't stay."

"I knew deep down you wouldn't be staying, but I hoped for more time to change your mind. Your letter explained what I already knew. I want you to know that I appreciate what you have done for me, and your father has agreed to allow me to live as a woman for seven years in order to conduct my research and make my observations. He agreed to revisit the agreement after that time as he has taken an interest in my studies. What I need to know from you is do you want me here with you as I am or would you rather wait…"

Athena put a finger across Reese's lips to stop the flow of words. "Hear this now: you are captivating to me as a man, stunning as a woman, and I would love you as a monster or demi-god. When I look at you, I only see the person I fell in love with. I adore you Reese, and if you will have me, I want to spend as long as the Universe grants us, learning more about each other as the days grow old."

Reese leaned forward, close enough for Athena to feel the tickle of her soft breath. "That is what I needed to hear." She closed the distance, and Athena tasted the sweetness of her then. Athena pulled Reese into her lap to deepen the kiss and let one hand explore her thick tresses as the other ran over the satin fabric adorning her firm breasts. Reese was already exploring as well, which caused Athena to stand with Reese straddling her waist as she strode toward the bed chamber.

"So, am I hired then?" Reese said with a grin as Athena walked her over to her bed and tossed her on it. Athena's robes came off with lightning speed.

"Oh, you are hired all right, and your training starts now."

Reese leaned up on her elbows and tossed her head, tempting Athena with her sass. "And what will be the first lesson?"

Athena kneeled before her, with hands sliding up her smooth legs and opening the silky orange fabric to reveal the beauty underneath. "First lesson, Reese, my love, my goddess, is to instruct me line by line what I must do to make you happy."

Athena's thumbs circled either side of the place she wanted to be, her eyes taking it all in as Reese's hands wound through her hair. She then cupped her face and brought Athena's gaze to hers.

"And if you already have? Made me happy?"

Athena continued the circles with one thumb and firmly pressed the other against Reese's core. "I have some ideas for lesson number two." Reese tipped her head back and pushed against the hand that was giving her so much pleasure. Between pants and groans, she asked her next question.

"How many lessons are there again?"

Athena's heart swelled. "Oh, my darling. There are more things to show you than there are stars in the sky. You are in really good hands."

"So, I see. Show me what they can do, my love."

EPILOGUE

Athena couldn't think of a better way to introduce Reese to the people she loved than to attend the belated birth celebration at Medusa and Perseus's home. The party was small, but everyone that Athena thought of as true family was there. Along with Medusa's sisters, Hecate and Hermes were in attendance as well as Persephone and Hades. Medusa had also invited her friends, Cleodora, Melia, and Thyia, who in turn brought her business partner, Arachne. Perseus's mother was watching the babies when Medusa pulled Athena aside and congratulated her on finding such a wonderful partner.

"My goddess, I am so happy for you," she said after having spent the better part of the afternoon fielding questions that Reese had about the pregnancy as well as the birth. "Reese is delightful, and I can tell you care for one another very much."

"I can't imagine being with anyone else," Athena agreed. "Reese is the one person in this Universe other than you, and perhaps Hermes, who sees me at my core."

Medusa hugged her friend and gave her a warm smile. She noticed her mother-in-law making her way over and took Pegasus from her.

"He's fed, and now I have to see to Chrysaor."

"Thank you, Danae."

"It's my pleasure," she said wistfully. "It gives me a little more cuddle time with them. They are getting bigger by the day." She walked up the hillside into the small home Perseus had finished just before the birth, and Medusa watched as she disappeared through the door. Perseus walked over and kissed Medusa on the cheek before taking the baby from her arms. He walked over to his guests who proceeded to play pass the baby.

"She's been an amazing help."

"You've made a wonderful life here, my friend. I'm happy for you," Athena said. "Before I forget, I need to explain the gifts I gave you." She waved to Reese, who had been looking for her. "I wanted to be sure that your boys always had a choice over who they would become. I know that was always important for you, and I knew their gorgon heritage might be used against them when they get older."

Medusa's eyes widened. "What do you mean? Are they in danger?"

"Of course they aren't, but there are those who would go after the people that mean the most to me. Those gifts will ensure that no matter what they are turned into, by choice or by fate, that they can turn back easily. I don't ever want them to have to go through something like you did."

Medusa pulled Athena into an embrace. "Thank you, Thea. Their gifts will be kept safe until they are old enough to understand their power. You couldn't have given us anything more thoughtful and meaningful." She nodded knowingly at her best friend and goddess, then Medusa joined her husband in opening the other gifts that guests had brought.

Reese took Athena's hand, and they walked slowly to the back of the house, stopping on the edge of a cliff that overlooked the water. "They have a beautiful home here," Reese acknowledged. "Filled with love. You can tell Medusa and her sisters are close."

"They are," Athena agreed. "They have been through more than any family should have to bear. It's good that they are able to enjoy their lives here in peace."

"So why the frown?"

Athena shrugged then leaned over and gave Reese a kiss. She pulled Reese down to sit at the base of a nearby tree. Their hands remained linked as Athena gathered her thoughts.

"I suppose it's because I know what the gods are capable of, and with the babies' gorgon blood, it is highly likely that they will be shape shifters. I don't ever want them to think of it as a curse or to have any god or goddess use it against them. It should be their choice who they want to be, always."

"I like that thought," Reese said. "And the gifts allow for that?"

"They do," Athena nodded. "As long as they have those items on their person, they will be able to shift back and forth at will. I had them blessed by someone with a great power to harness and direct curses."

"I believe you have done all you can for now. The choice will be theirs as they learn their own mind."

"I suppose that is true. Perhaps all of my worry will be for naught."

"I certainly hope that is the case. In the meantime, we should probably get back to the party. We aren't being very social."

Athena stood up and put her hand out to help Reese rise. "You're right. Let's go, my love. The sooner we finish up with the chatting, the sooner we can go home."

Reese laughed. "Like I said, anti-social."

"Can I help it if I want you all to myself?"

They were too absorbed in their playful whisperings to notice the slim shadow slip out from behind the house and walk slowly behind them toward the group. Arachne had been horrified to realize that she was eavesdropping on a private conversation, but it was impossible to move from her location until the couple moved from beneath the large oak. No matter how she received the information though, she was glad she had overheard it. Perhaps Athena's mystery conjuror had the answers she needed to control her own curse.

Thyia walked up to her with a smile. "I wondered where you had disappeared to."

"Sorry to worry you, my friend."

"Not worried, since you tend to do that, just wanted to make sure you were okay. You've seemed preoccupied lately."

Arachne nodded. "Preoccupied is a good word for it. I'll be okay though, just a lot on my mind."

Thyia handed her a glass of wine. "Okay then, let's go chat with

Euryale. Her boyfriend has some friends she would like us to meet."

"Not sure that is a good idea. Remember what happened with the last date you tried to set me up on?" Thyia's pretty pout made her laugh. "Okay, you win. Lead the way."

"Excellent! And if they turn out to be duds, we can always drop by that party in town on the way back to the shop."

"Why do I let you talk me into these things?"

"Why do you let me?"

"Good point."

"Come on, it's time you stepped out of your dream world and into reality. You are missing out on a whole lot of living."

"And what if I'm okay with that? Staying in a dream world?"

Thyia draped her arm over her shoulder and paused for effect. "Then you are way worse off than I realized, my friend. These guys are really cute. Seriously, what have you got to lose?"

Before she had a chance to respond, Thyia ran to join her new friends. Arachne shook her head slowly then took a deep breath. Her whispered response was heard only by the sun starting its journey down to the horizon.

"Just myself."

To all those
who have touched my heart
and then moved through the veil.
My regret is that we
couldn't say goodbye.

Goddesses in Love 4

WEB OF LIES

CONTROLLING HER CURSE IS THE EASIEST THING ABOUT THEIR RELATIONSHIP.

1

It's not every morning that you're snapped out of your musings with a blood curdling scream. Thyia had found him again. Arachne's dark, brooding visitor who snuck in while she worked and lurked through the magical hours of dawn. He wasn't bothering anyone. If anything, it was the opposite. The tiny creature had kept Arachne company over the past several years while she finished the orders she couldn't get to during the day. Or worse, messed up.

Thyia's hurried footsteps echoed toward the back corner of the building, causing Arachne to lower the fabric she was folding.

"Why does that thing keep coming back?" Her business partner screeched through the doorway to the adjacent room.

Arachne didn't respond but quickened the steps she was already taking. By the time she got back to their shared workspace, Thyia was already swishing the broom toward the corner that stood directly over Arachne's loom.

"Thyia, he really doesn't bother me. Leave the poor thing alone."

"Well, he bothers me." She took another swipe at the corner this time, brushing the black furry creature and causing him to spread his leathery wings and flap around the room.

"Now look what you've done, he's upset."

Thyia's scream filled the small room, and Arachne jumped at the shrill of it. If that didn't make him leave, nothing would. The sound practically made her want to do the same.

The tiny bat made one more circle around the room, brushing by

Arachne's cheek as he slipped past her. The touch was soft, like a lover's apology, although Arachne thought Thyia should be the one to say sorry. She couldn't help the small grin on her face when he buzzed by Thyia's head, prompting one more screech. The bat flew out the open window and into the pinkened morning sky with a squeak.

Arachne's grin turned into a belly laugh watching Thyia dance a full-bodied shudder as she allowed fear to flow through her body.

"It's not funny! I've chased that thing out of here every day this week! I can't stand those things!"

"He isn't a thing," Arachne responded. "He's really quite smart and makes an amazing companion once you get to know him."

"Please tell me you aren't considering keeping it."

Arachne shook her head. "He is his own master and can come and go as he pleases. I would never do that to him. But he's nice to have around."

Thyia shook her head. "I love you, but you're a little strange sometimes."

"There was never a truer statement, my friend." She took the broom from Thyia's hand and put it back into the corner. Changing the subject was the best way to handle her friend's moods. "I managed to finish the fabrics for the rush order you have for that wedding. I stacked them by your worktable."

Thyia moved to her space then ran her hand over the shimmery blue fabric that topped the pile. "I'm not sure how you managed to get all of this done in such a short amount of time. You didn't have any of this started before I went to bed last night."

Arachne shrugged. "I've always been able to manage on just a couple of hours of sleep. Besides, I like what I do."

"Well, the customers do as well. You outdid yourself on this, my friend. It's simply stunning." The glittering piece of dark blue fabric fell open in front of her into an ombré scene of the night sky. "The detail makes me feel as if I could wrap myself up in midnight."

"That is one of the nicest compliments I've ever received. Thank you. That was just what I had in mind when I wove it. I'm excited to see the dresses when you are done."

"Me too," laughed Thyia. "I'd better get to it."

Arachne nodded with a yawn. "And I'm heading off to get a few hours of sleep. I'll see you after lunch."

Thyia called out as Arachne left the room. "Sweet dreams."

Arachne waved before walking out the back door of their shop, T.A. Creations. The birds were stirring, and the corner of Thebes where they lived started to hum. She crossed the short distance to her cottage and looked up into the branches of the olive tree that stood right outside her bedroom window. He was there waiting. Folded up on himself and hanging upside down on the lowest branch of the tree. The small animal unfurled its wings as if to wave, similar to what it had done for several mornings in a row. The routine had become one of the bright spots in her day.

She waved back then watched the bat drop from the branch, spread its wings, and flutter away. It disappeared into the rising sun, and it made her wonder where it went each day when it left her. When he left her. She had the distinct impression the bat was a "he," though she wasn't sure why. Entering her small kitchen, she closed the door behind her and moved toward the fireplace. Another log and a stoke brought the fire from a glow to a small flame. The house was small but comfortable, big enough for a single woman with no intentions of marrying. Perfect for her.

She walked her weary bones into the bedroom and pulled down the thick fabric she had created to darken the room for sleep during the day. With the fabric covering both her window and the door to the rest of the house, she could hardly see her hand before her face. She stripped her clothes, leaving them in a pile near her bedside, and slipped naked into her silken sheets. It was the one luxury she allowed herself in order to attract the sweet dreams that Thyia had wished her. She hoped she would have them; she was running out of ideas for the pieces she created.

In her dreams, her lover gave her much more than satisfaction and beauty, he was integral to her ability to weave exquisite fabrics. Most people thought she had amazing skill and talent, but only she, and perhaps now the bat, was aware of the web of lies she had woven. Her only escape was to wrap herself in the arms of the man who came to her in her dreams and wove the images into her mind each night.

With her eyes closed, she tried to slow her mind to no avail. Sleep would evade her once more, as would her dreams. Even the brilliant red flowers that heralded his approach were nowhere to be found in her imagination. Prayers to Athena that she would see him once more filled the space that sleep once ruled. Even they didn't soothe her restless soul this morn.

Morpheus took the long way home; he needed to think. For him, the long way was remaining in bat form as he traveled. Smaller wings caused trips to take much longer than the wings of his personification. Not that he would be able to take his true form in the Earth realm. He could have chosen a larger winged form, a griffin or perhaps a harpy, but the bat gave him time to think. Besides, she liked him that way.

That led to his next thought… He was spending too much time with one human. But there was something about her that was intriguing. He doubted, however, that his siblings would see the wisdom in his obsession. They would remind him that he was the God of Dreams and was charged with providing all humans with equal opportunity to chase their desires or obtain the answers they sought. But his heart told him otherwise. So did all his other parts.

Of late, it was impossible to lull her to sleep. It had been easier before to control her dreams and be with her in a form she desired. But something had changed. He wondered if it was because she was something more than a human. That he was able to reach her dreams at all had been a miracle in his mind. Whatever the case, they hadn't been together in dream-state in weeks, and he was getting edgy. It wasn't a good look. He was starting to act like Hades had before he met Persephone. That was a dark time, and he couldn't ask his subjects to deal with that.

He was weighed with remorse. He had never been happier than

to be with the lonely weaver in her dreams, yet he knew that was not something he could ever have as part of his existence. Ignoring his duties, and ultimately the creatures that he had designed, was not something he could continue doing. He knew from past experiences that it would catch up to him. The humans he cared for would suffer. Toxins would build from the stress they endured without the release found in sleep. Perhaps his inability to reach her was for the best.

The two halves of his psyche fought with his heart, and he came back to the realization that this woman was very similar in nature to the dreams that he wove and the creatures he created from the ether. Not entirely human and yet not entirely the monster that some would call her. When in her true form, he only saw beauty, and in her hands, either two or eight, she wove fabric like he wove dreams. It was there where their kindred spirits met. Perhaps they were meant to be, yet he couldn't see a path to the place where it could happen. He couldn't be in his true form on Earth, and only the dead and immortals were allowed to visit him in his realm.

Transferring to the form he was most comfortable in, he landed in the throne room, a dark empty hall of ancient marble and towering black pillars. His historian was waiting.

"Lord Morpheus, I hope your travels went well and your mission was successful."

"You hope that each time I return, and it is appreciated. Thank you, Ash. What's the report?"

As Morpheus made his way to the obsidian throne, he received updates for the nightmares and dreams that Ash monitored for him. Much like the tree he was made from, his barked skin reflected a rough exterior and his core was hidden with the rings of time. But Morpheus knew him better than anyone. He had created him after all.

Ash rambled, and Morpheus's mind wandered, touching on her once more. Arachne. Beauty personified and much like the creations she wove… Magick. The tapestries above his head to the left hung in the expanse, flapping with each manufactured breeze. He had five of them so far and took great pleasure in revisiting the scenes in his mind they had been born from. Each one, more beautiful than the next, depicted a dream he had shared with her. A vision where their experiences were immortalized in each delicate thread of the fabric she had created. The more he looked, the more he longed to return to the memories which had borne them.

"Lord Morpheus, an answer?"

Realizing his name had been called, he snapped to attention. "Answer?"

Ash squinted, the creases on his ancient face becoming more prominent and tightening around the knots he used for eyes. "Yes, my lord. The satyrs?"

Morpheus tipped his head, attempting to recall what Ash could possibly be speaking of. He didn't need to wait long before his assistant prompted him yet again. He could hear the disappointment reflected in his voice.

"They are asking if they may be released from their punishment and join the Samhain festivities on Earth this year."

Ah yes, now he remembered. "I'm not sure I can trust that what happened last time won't happen again."

"That was a hundred years ago, my lord. And little harm was done."

Morpheus laughed. "Not sure I would call it little harm. I had to alter the memories of an entire continent to imagine that what they had seen was only a dream. Now their descendants believe either that their ancestors were right and there is a conspiracy or that they were crazed and belonged in the temples that they were committed to serve. Either way, I have no interest in letting swarms of bored satyrs go up for a night of fun. They can find something to do down here."

"Very well. I will let them know. Perhaps Hades will have some ideas." Ash paused then shifted slightly. He took a breath, held it, then released it slowly.

"What is it?" Morpheus wasn't one to hesitate. If Ash had bad news, he wanted to hear it now and take care of it.

"It's nothing, really. It's just that I worry about you. It is apparent you have something on your mind, and I wouldn't be any sort of an assistant if I didn't ask you if I could help."

Morpheus paused, letting the weight of Ash's words sink in. He hadn't been an effective leader, and it was starting to show. Filling his lungs, he rose from his seat toward Ash and placed his hand on his rough shoulder to get his point across.

"Thank you, my friend. It isn't anything you can help with, but I appreciate your concern. Please know I will do better. I realize I've been unfocused."

The gap in Ash's face split wider which was his equivalent of a smile. Morpheus nodded, indicating their business was done, and lowered his hand from Ash's shoulder. "So, what should we do first? I have a few hours before I need to weave some complicated prophecies."

They walked through the center of the throne room toward the back where the library was located. It held tomes of the past, present, and future and was where Ash spent most of his days. Other than Morpheus, he was the most knowledgeable about their contents.

"Religious leaders?"

Morpheus shook his head. "No. Politicians."

"It seems to me they are about the same."

"They can be," Morpheus mused. "I don't direct them, merely pass the message along. However, their interpretation of the true meaning continues to get twisted. I believe it is time I am a little more direct."

Ash stopped his stride and looked over at Morpheus, knots wide and the leaves he had as hair as still as the dawn. "Are you sure that is what you want to do?"

"I don't see an alternative," Morpheus countered. "If I allow the current course, it could mean devastation for the planet."

Ash nodded then proceeded to the library door and opened it.

"Where do we need to start?"

"I need to refresh my memory on the rulers of Persia."

"Excellent," Ash grinned. "I have some new materials you may be interested in which just came in."

2

Arachne woke unrested and edgy. She wasn't sure how long her creativity would last without new dream experiences so focused instead on what she did have. Even with the curse, her life was incredible. As head weaver to one of the most powerful entities on Olympus, she lived a simple life in a comfortable home. Athena had been the goddess who had made it all happen, and for that, she would be forever grateful.

They were a natural fit—Arachne wove, and Thyia created the clothing that kept customers coming from miles around. Arachne was in charge of the fabric inventory, easy enough for a spider but, at the same time, a secret that needed to be kept from all who knew her. The "how" behind her skill and the inability to control her curse was a secret she bore alone. It was that secret which had left her single and longing for someone to share her dreams with. To love.

As she made herself some cinnamon tea, she thought about the shift in her creativity and how it had paralleled meeting the man in her dreams. When had the inspiration stopped flowing? Was it when the dreams stopped? Thinking back, it coincided with the longer hours as a spider, which was getting more impossible to hide as time went on. Unable to stop her head from mulling over her predicament, she took her tea to the porch in an attempt to lift her mood. The change in scenery didn't help.

At first, the shifts were an hour or two at night. But with the demands on her fabric and a shift in the curse, she spent practically dusk until dawn as a creature with eight legs and superior weaving skills. No one ever saw the hideous monster she became. The only living being that witnessed her true form was the bat that Thyia shooed out with a broom each morning. Arachne feared it was only a matter of time before the shift became permanent.

The curse had fallen upon her shoulders, one that she had taken willingly at the time. But her regrets increased with time, much like the threads she added to the tapestries she wove. When she met the stranger in her dreams, things changed. But if she couldn't be with him as a woman, if she had to hide what she truly was, it would be more of a curse than changing into the creature that fed her artist's soul. It was days like these she wished she hadn't sacrificed for the sister she no longer had. Perhaps she, too, could have found love.

Dreams didn't find her anymore, and the comfort she had found in them was all but a distant memory. The solace of illusions was meant for humans, and as the days went on, she was becoming less and less like one. Her past was catching up to her, and the lack of sleep Arachne had suffered over the last several months was debilitating.

Weaving day and night, from a drying well of inspiration, wasn't something she would be able to maintain. She needed to find a solution, a balance or possible removal of the curse. But could a spider that wasn't a spider still weave? Did it matter if her inspiration had all but left her? If she didn't find a way to sleep, she might never see him again, and she was pretty sure it would break her heart in both forms. That was her worst fear of all. But an overheard conversation at a friend's gathering had given her an idea.

Perhaps if she could find the witch she had heard Athena speak of, she could lessen her curse. Ideally, to be able to control the time she spent in spider form was the goal. Magick had a cost, and she had saved every drachma she could in anticipation of the price she would be expected to pay. She hoped she had saved enough to change her destiny.

The tea was cold and had lost its soothing qualities. Knowing she wasn't going to get any more rest, she went inside and snuffed the dying fire, before heading back to the shop. Perhaps they would be busy enough that she wouldn't have to pretend to be weaving the fabrics she could no longer create as a human. The illusion she was forced to live was taking its toll.

3

The God of Dreams wasn't sure what to do. His spells only worked on humans, and the woman that held his interest was becoming less so by the day. Spiders didn't dream. They didn't sleep either, or at least if they did, he wasn't able to slip inside their minds. He was created to oversee the dreams of humans and to pass along divine messages between gods and their mortals in order for their commands to be carried out. But he grew weary of his role. He wanted more. He wanted her.

A stunning creature in both forms, he longed for her in a way that could not be reached without a restful slumber. Neither of them had slept properly in weeks. He watched over her in other forms, but she didn't recognize her devoted dream lover in the bat perched in the corner of her room.

He was finally back in his domain after a long night of dream weaving. Located in the far corner of the Underworld, the Land of Dreams was a place very few entered. Those that did aided Morpheus in keeping his creations alive and well. He also cared for the souls who lived between life and death, existing in a constant dream state. Those souls were kept comfortable on beds and surrounded by sensory objects that would aid their healing process on Earth. Some had been put in that state unwillingly, captured and held between the two worlds until their destiny could be resolved. For some, a resolution wasn't to be had, and they were sent on to Hades for judgment.

There was one who had been there the longest. Epimetheus wasn't human and had been the first to embrace perpetual slumber as a way to aid the woman he loved. At the time, Morpheus agreed to it, the challenge the couple had before them seemed obtainable. But as the centuries wore on, Morpheus pitied their task. Out of all the gods, Morpheus was the most capable of seeing inside the hearts of men and knowing their minds as they pursued their dreams. He feared that Epimetheus would never be reunited with his love.

The winding steps were narrow as Morpheus wound his way down to the cavern where Epimetheus lay. The floral scent of rosemary came to him before he stepped into the room. The fragrance was as strong as the day his ward had been lain atop the scented cushions, hand-sewn lovingly by his wife. A wife who hadn't seen him since the day he arrived. Morpheus felt obligated to visit since he had been the only creature able to do so for over a millennium.

He sat near his bedside in the chair intended for that purpose and started a one-sided conversation as he had done from the start. Epimetheus would have no recollection of the conversations they had, but Morpheus felt better including him in what was happening in the world. Sadly, the only reality Epimetheus knew was the dream that had played on repeat from the day he took on his burden.

"Sorry, I haven't been here lately, my friend. My own desires are the only excuse."

Strangely, even with the lack of response each time he came, Epimetheus had become one of Morpheus's dearest friends. He had unknowingly heard all of his secrets, something no other living being had.

"I'm spending too much time with her again, but I knew you would understand. What it was like for you to connect instantly and love so deeply. In a mere matter of seconds. Your heart knowing before your head that she was the path you should be on."

Epimetheus lay there with a small smile stirring on his face.

Knowing the dream that he wove for him as well as he did, he knew the smile wasn't for him, but he took it just the same as a sign that his comment was received.

I knew you'd understand, but I struggle with my purpose. I was not designed for the life I desire; that emotion is my sibling's job entirely. However, longing has taken hold of me in a way that I'm just starting to be able to articulate. We have more in common than I've ever had with any being in this world or the next, and there's an incredible sense of completeness when I'm around her. However, I've been blocked from her dream state. The plans we made and the experiences we shared have stopped."

Epimetheus's smile widened as tears streamed from his eyes. Morpheus knew the part of the dream he was now experiencing and decided to give him some privacy. He took in the height of the candles illuminating the small room and made note to direct Ash to replenish them.

"I will leave you two alone," he said to the prone figure. "Let me be the first to congratulate you." The echo of his footsteps followed him out the door. The whispered phrase of a man in love, from a reality that played in his mind alone, was the last thing Morpheus heard.

"I love you, my darling. What a gift you are."

Morpheus paused at the entrance, digesting the words he had heard whispered countless times before and looked at the jar which stood at the opposite end of the bed. The vessel was covered with more of them now, the tiny black swirls that indicated progress was being made. It seemed to him that the curse should have been lifted long ago. But the markings were only made by those who sought an answer and who were brave enough to seek it out. His heart broke every time he came here.

He left Epimetheus's chamber with his soul weighted by melancholy, even more than it had been before he entered which he found astounding. However, if Epimetheus could wait an eternity to be with the woman he loved, then Morpheus could as well. What the prone god symbolized, without even being aware of it, was the one thing that every god and human alike faced at one point in their lifetime.

A hopelessness so overwhelming it crippled to the point of inaction. At the same time, he represented resilience in the direst of situations, which was more powerful than any magick that Morpheus could weave in a dream. It was that tiny kernel of hope that he clung to when it came to the dreams of his beautiful distraction.

Imagining his life with her was the only way his heart found peace.

4

The shop was busy and they were behind in their orders. Thyia and Arachne had hardly spoken two words to one another by the time sunset came. The weaving came slowly. Arachne was hesitant to start anything she'd have to fix after close, so instead, she helped Thyia pack up the customer orders.

Thyia finished the piece she was working on, folded it neatly, and placed it on the table beside her. "I'm done for the day," she said with a yawn. "I'm completely wiped."

Arachne stepped over to her corner of the workshop and sat at her loom. The tapestry she was working on was a bit drab, perhaps a splash of red?

Thyia shook her head in disbelief. "I can't believe you're going to stay. You are always working. If I tried your schedule without at least six hours of sleep, I would probably sew my finger to a peplos. How do you do it?"

Arachne shrugged. "I've always had a hard time sleeping, so it's just something I've learned to live with. Besides, I do my best work at night when the Earth is still and the world is at rest. There is much less distraction."

"Makes sense." Thyia pointed over her shoulder to the showroom. "I'll go lock up. Thanks for your help today, by the way. I was starting to get overwhelmed."

"Not a problem," Arachne answered. "I was ahead on the fabric and thought it was more important that we get some of the orders

bundled. My part goes quickly once I get going."

"Well, I appreciate it. Do you need anything before I go?"

"No, thank you." Thyia glanced up in the corner over Arachne's head as though she expected to see something there. The corner was bare, but Arachne knew it wouldn't be for long. Thyia gave her a small smile, turned, then left the room. Arachne was alone with her thoughts for the first time that day.

Minutes later, the noises quieted with the snick of the front door. The house, which served as their storefront, breathed a sigh of relief. Thyia was an amazing person, but when she was stressed, she was hard to be around. Arachne helping her had more to do with making it easier on herself than it did helping Thyia get ahead on her work.

She was an hour into her weaving when her visitor arrived. The small creature fluttered in and took its place in the corner using the end of the curtain rod as a perch. She acknowledged him with a quick glance.

"I'm sorry that Thyia keeps chasing you out. You upset her."

Gathering threads of indigo and turquoise, she recalled the night sky from her dream. With the colors of her pallet selected, the set up was next. As had happened each time since the curse found her, the change began with a stirring in her stomach. There wasn't much time, so she finished her set up quickly. After the final knot, the tingles moved to her fingers, and she sat up in her seat to await the inevitable.

Each time it happened, the change started the same. Her fingers elongated as her thumb and pinky finger disappeared into her hand. Simultaneously, her arms shrank into her shoulders. There was no pain anymore. As her legs thinned out and elongated to match the width of her thickening fingers, her torso shrank then pinched, making her already slim waist much tinier. As she shrunk into her new form, she adjusted herself on the backless seat. Her once shapely thighs were now long and jointed, clinging to the legs of the seat to keep her from tipping.

As always, the bat watched silently from the corner as the transition took place. She hadn't known that she could speak aloud in this form until he had started visiting. Never having held a conversation, she still struggled with the raspy and hollow quality of the sound her bulbous face now made. She spoke without turning to face him, for fear of frightening the tiny creature hanging behind her. The company he provided was most welcome, especially in her current form. She couldn't afford to frighten him off.

"It's a good thing that Thyia isn't here," she said conversationally. "It's really not as bad as it looks." The rasp in her voice filled the room as did the whisper of her fingers, now spindly legs pulling out the threads.

"I've actually gotten quite used to it; my fingers work better as arms, especially for a piece with this much detail." She watched as the base of her tapestry came to life. Her finger-legs already knew what her mind envisioned. She hardly had to think at all, merely sat back and watched the scene unfold.

Her long legs wove in a frenzy. She was mesmerized by their speed and accuracy as the tapestry formed. It looked like a mosaic as each of her eight eyes picked up a different vantage point and focus. When the curse first happened, the view had been disjointing, but as the years went on, she found that she could see the finest of details more clearly. As the six upper arms worked, the lower two worked the treadles and take up handle. Focusing on her work helped her avoid the reality of what she had become. The artist in her appreciated her new form, even if the woman in her didn't.

"I looked at myself once," she said softly. "Then I cried for a week. The tears stopped soon after." She finished the row then started the next. "It was all for my sister." In her mind, she wondered if she should continue the thought. She had talked to the bat about a great many things, also shared secrets with the man in her dreams, but she had never broached the subject of her sister with either of them. For whatever reason, her heart needed to put it to rest at this moment. The fluttering behind her let her know that she had his attention.

"I didn't always look like this," she whispered. She cleared her throat of the apologizing tone and took a deep breath. "And I realize that in a lot of ways I've been given a great gift." The tapestry included some of the water now, the reflections on the ripples light and silvery as they were that night in the moonlight.

She glanced behind her, and the bat was still in the corner, with its head peeking out of its wings. It seemed to her as though it was listening. "I loved my sister, always looked up to her even though we were precisely the same age. We were twins, you see. As we grew up, she was always chasing love, and I was content to stay at home. One day, her free spirit got her into trouble, and she upset the wrong person. A goddess, to be precise. She was given one day to get her affairs in order, which is when she came home and told me the whole story. She had fallen in love with the goddess's son, a demi-god who she had been carrying on with. He loved her in return and wanted to marry her, against the wishes of his mother who had other plans for him. But they had been found out, and the goddess said that she would let her live but only as a monster that no one would ever want to be with."

Arachne heard a flutter then felt a puff of air touch her cheek as the bat flew by. He settled on the rafter above her loom in her direct line of sight. She wasn't as comfortable speaking now, but she was too far into the story to let it go. She needed to get it off her chest. The scene was bigger now, the grassy berm where the entwined lovers laid was forming.

"I honestly don't know why I'm telling you this," she said, ignoring the discomfort. "My sister and her lover were married, with the hopes that his mother would soften toward her in time. But it didn't work, and the goddess gave her new daughter-in-law twenty-four hours to say her goodbyes. She begged me to help her, and the best we could come up with was that I would take her place."

The bat fluttered its wings, its tiny head shaking as if in disbelief.

"I know. It was reckless. Perhaps the most I've been in real life," Arachne said. "However, I loved my sister, and I would have done anything for her. Besides, she wanted to be out in the world, while I was content to stay alone. I didn't think a curse would be that much of a burden for me. And she had promised to come back with her husband and make things right as soon as they had children." Arachne shook her head. "You're right, by the way. It was a terrible idea, but one we proceeded with, nonetheless. So, I dressed in her clothes, met the goddess the following morning, and she gave me my sister's curse."

The scene on the tapestry drew a sigh. What a gift that night had been. Glittery threads dotted the midnight blue sky, like dewdrops on delphinium. Reliving the scene through her art soothed her soul enough to continue with her story. "The first time I transformed hurt the most, but after so many centuries of changing, I hardly feel it now. The changes started as a few minutes a night but now are much longer. I've learned to live with it and much prefer to design in this form, if I'm honest. I'm much quicker and less likely to make a mistake."

The bat dropped down to a nearby chair and clung to the thin rung that crossed the back. He was so close now that she could see his eyes, and for the first time while in this form, she didn't hide from another creature but turned and faced its reaction. She ached to take a deep breath but was unable to in her current form. It didn't prevent her from finishing the story for the first time in her long life.

"They moved to another land and had eight children, one for every leg I have in my cursed form. I watched them from afar, heard of their accomplishments as the years went on. She never came back. I went to her funeral, a grand affair put on by the man who had taken her out of my life. I'm not sure he even knew that I existed. Cloaked and distant, I watched her family mourn. As her children had children of their own and as their descendants had families, I lost track of where they all were. There are times I wished that the curse didn't come with an immortal life, but when I think about the family I now have, through the friendships I've made, I realize how fortunate I am to have this gift. Even if it is not in my control and I will need to reinvent myself all over again one day."

The final threads were put into place as she finished her story. She stared at it, taking in the beauty of the scene before her. She could almost smell the salt of the sea and the musty fragrance of the moss they had lounged on. The woman was wrapped in his arms with her head back in the hollow space just below his shoulder and turned into his chest, hiding her pinkened cheeks from the love they had shared just minutes before. With his chin resting atop her head, his strong black wings were cocooning them, providing warmth in places where they lacked clothing.

Arachne's pulse raced as if she were there once more. "This is one of my favorite memories," she whispered. "It's the last one I have of him. My well has run dry." She finished the seams and removed the completed piece from the loom, pinning it on a nearby wall in order for it to rest. "I hope it brings me enough. I need to be on my way. The curse gets worse by the day."

The bat flew from the chair and circled her head three times, before flying through the window. It was then that Arachne noticed the sliver of yellow, orange, and pink that heralded the sunrise. Before she could worry that this had been the longest that she had stayed in her spider form, her legs started to shrink back into her body and fatten into human limbs. She had just slipped her dress back on when Thyia came through the front door.

"Good morning, Arachne."

"Good morning, my friend," she said with a stretch.

Thyia walked toward the tapestry Arachne had pinned to the wall and ran an admiring hand over the image. "This is stunning," she said with awe. "The detail is incredible."

"Thank you," she said in a choked response. "I'm proud of how it came out." As much as she didn't want to sell her last memory of him, she knew she had to. "How much do you think I can get?"

"At least double your last price. This is flawless."

Arachne helped Thyia straighten up and open the blinds. If she was right, she would have enough to travel to the witch and ask that the curse be removed. The first step would be to ask Athena about the witch's identity, which she wasn't sure she would share, but she was out of options. Not having a choice of the form that she took for the rest of eternity would truly be the worse curse she could ever imagine for herself, especially after having a taste of love as a human.

It was time to take hold of her future.

5

Morpheus knew he was going to help her before she had finished her story. Just as he had known he was going to purchase the tapestry before she completed it. The emotion she put into each layer nearly broke him. He longed to take her into his arms, to promise to make things right, no matter the cost. No one, no matter what they had done in their lives, ever deserved to live under someone else's curse. And she had done nothing to warrant the destiny that had been placed upon her.

In a way, the curse had been a blessing to him, so he was thankful. Humans' lives were short, so he never really got to know them before they were moving on to the next plane of existence. With her, it was different. He knew she had lived several lifetimes, and he was still uncovering her true nature dream by dream. Perhaps she was immortal, in which case she was perfect for him. He needed to find a way for her to be in his reality.

The curse caused her to be in spider form much longer as the years went on. He understood her lack of control over her ability, but if the curse were removed, what would she become? Would she still be able to meet him in his dreams? He worried about her changing and if she would long for him the same. The moments they had shared, memorialized in the tapestries she lovingly created, were magical…but he wanted more. As much of a risk as it was to his desires, he was compelled to give her anything in his power in order to see her happy.

He was going to give her whatever amount of money she decided she needed for that tapestry. The scene was burned in his mind. He thought of it practically every time he, himself, slipped into a dream state. It had been the last night that they had been together, and the spell she wove around his senses had been addictive, like the delicate red flowers he could no longer function without. He needed to find a way to return to her dreams and give her new memories to blend into the art she created. Her expression of the dreams that they'd shared together made him feel alive. Real.

In a nearby cove, he shifted from his bat form into a beautiful woman, one of the personas he had disguised himself with when making purchases from their shop. He could mimic human form but only those humans that didn't resemble his personification. Animals were something he was still practicing. He waved his hand and filled his empty bag with more gold drachmas than he knew she would ever ask for and made his way to the shop he had just left. He walked into the doorway as the two owners were laughing, and his heart filled with the sound of it. He longed to know her in reality as her friend did.

Arachne looked up as the familiar customer entered the shop. "Hello," she smiled. "I was just wondering when we would see you again."

"How nice," he said in a melodious voice. "I've been traveling and couldn't make it in. I'm only just back and had to see if you had anything new."

"As a matter of fact, I just finished something last night. I can go get it if you would like."

"Wonderful." Morpheus nodded as the delicate woman. "I can't wait to see it."

"It's a little more sensuous than the others," Arachne explained. "But the colors are divine."

"I think you will love it," Thyia whispered as Arachne went to fetch the piece. "It's her finest work. She should be right back. If you'll excuse me, I have some supplies to shop for."

Arachne came back into the room, waving to Thyia as she left the shop. She held the tapestry to her chest then allowed it to unroll in front of her. "What do you think?"

Morpheus was stunned by the sight of it in the daylight. There wasn't any way he would leave without it; he couldn't imagine it going home with anyone else. His response was heavy with emotion in the feminine voice he now had. "It's a masterpiece. I can feel how much he cares for her." He ran his delicate hand over the textured wings in the tapestry. "The quill of each feather."

"That detail is my favorite part of that piece," Arachne said softly. "His wings are so powerful and strong but so soft and loving in this moment. Always actually." There was something in her voice that caused him to pause. She was gazing at the tapestry as she responded to the conversation, with a look of longing and sadness. With a wistful intake of breath, she centered herself.

"I can see how much this piece means to you."

Arachne nodded then looked up and gave a small smile. "This was a beautiful dream, one that is near and dear to my heart."

"I will take extra special care of it," he promised. The delicate hand he wore settled on her arm to make the point. He relished the touch of her skin; doing it with a hand that wasn't truly his own would have to do for now.

"Thank you, that means a lot. It will be one of the last pieces I do for a while as I will be heading out of town to take care of some business."

Curious to know what she meant but needing to remain in character, he simply nodded as Arachne rolled up his purchase for his journey. He handed her the bag of gold as she passed him the bundled hanging. When she attempted to pass some of the gold back, he shook his head.

"Take it. I was charged far too little for the first pieces you sold me, and they bring me more pleasure than you could ever imagine. It's worth it to me to know that I'm helping you with whatever you need to sort out. May the goddess keep you safe on your travels."

"Thank you. I appreciate everything you've done for me, I really do."

"I'll check in from time to time. I hope your travels don't keep you away too long."

Arachne excused herself as her eyes welled with tears. She didn't know where the journey would take her, only that she needed to make it. The sound of the door closing let her know that Cassandra had left, and she wondered if the woman even noticed that they had never been formally introduced. Arachne had only just learned her customer's name from Thyia the week before but felt strange addressing her by name. It had become part of her habit to keep her friendships superficial, another thing she hoped to change once the curse was removed.

Thyia was always gone for at least an hour when shopping for supplies. It would be just enough time for her to slip out of town. After putting a sign on the door that they were closed for lunch, she wrote a quick note. It would be better this way, just in case things didn't work out and she never returned, since she couldn't bear to say goodbye. She left the note on her table near the stacks of fabric she had completed for orders. There was extra as well, which would be enough to keep Thyia in business for quite some time.

She peeked into the bag which was filled to the top with gold and pulled out a handful of pieces. The remainder was more than enough for her to take the next step of her journey, so she didn't hesitate to leave several pieces on top of the fabric stack for Thyia. She pulled the small bundle of supplies that she had packed that morning from behind her workspace then walked out of her shop without looking back. She had to believe she'd return. It was the only thing keeping her moving forward.

6

Luckily, Arachne found a merchant traveling to Athens, and the gold she had saved covered her fare. She had the remaining gold she received for her tapestry buried deep in her bag. The merchant was happy with the opportunity to make some extra coins for travels that he would have had to make anyway. He made a space in the back of his wagon for Arachne to ride in, and when they stopped to rest, he was so tired from traveling that he would sleep the night through, unaware that his traveling companion was changing into a hideous monster.

She regretted leaving her threads and loom behind to travel light so spent the hours in her spider form spinning delicate webs between low hanging branches and shrubs. The activity kept her fingers nimble and her creative soul happy. Some mornings, as they loaded up to go, she spied some woodland fairies gathering the intricate webs she had left behind, excitedly discussing what they planned to do with the fabric. It thrilled her that her art had found a new audience.

The journey took several days, and when Arachne finally arrived at Athena's temple, her head priestess, Reese, was there to greet her. Stunning in emerald, which brought out the mossy tones in their eyes, Reese already looked relaxed and at home after being at the temple only a few months. They had met several times at the shop, with and without Athena present, and were on friendly terms.

"Don't take this personally, but you look like something that the temple cat dragged in."

"I don't take that personally at all," Arachne laughed. "That's precisely how I feel."

"Well, you can't talk to Athena looking like that. Come back this way, and I'll get you somewhere where you can clean up. She's out right now anyway, so you have some time."

Reese walked her through the marble temple then to the left and down a hallway where there were living quarters. Arachne presumed this was where the priestesses stayed when they were here. Thyia had been in Athena's service to start when Medusa was the head priestess, but Arachne didn't know her then, so this was her first time at the temple. Reese ushered her into a small but serviceable room with a bed and more importantly a pitcher and bowl. There was a small fire already warming the room as if Reese had expected her.

"I'll get you some fruit and hot water. I just heated a pot for tea. You have plenty of time to relax. She plans to be back for dinner."

"Thank you, Reese. I appreciate it." She stifled a yawn. "A nap sounds good."

Reese returned in a matter of minutes with a tray and a pitcher of warmed water which was poured into the waiting bowl, then they pointed to the small cupboard next to the bed.

"Towels are in there. Make yourself at home. I'll be in the kitchen if you need me. I have some experiments brewing, so if you will excuse me."

"Of course."

The days of traveling and hiding her identity from the merchant had caught up to her. She had hardly taken her first bite of an apple before falling into a deep restful sleep. For the first time in weeks, Arachne slipped firmly into a dream state.

She would hardly have known it was a dream at all as the setting was in the palace she was in now. The only thing that gave it away was that she was still in human form, and it was in the middle of the night. In reality, she remembered that she had arrived at the temple at midday.

Hollow footsteps echoed, and as her eyes adjusted to the inky darkness, she sensed she was not alone. Her gasp caused the shadow to move toward her with hands splayed in apology. The voice she had longed to hear again brought a smile to her face. The rumbling tone of his deep bass affected her in ways she couldn't hide. His sexy smile let her know that her reaction to him didn't go unnoticed.

"I didn't mean to startle you. It's been so long since I've been able to see you. When I realized you were finally dreaming, I came right away."

"I'm glad you did." Her voice cracked with emotion. "I've had a lot on my mind, and sleep evades me."

"If I could control it, I would make your respite soothing. Always." He took a step closer within arm's reach of where she stood. She could see his strong wings, black as the night that surrounded them. It was the form she had seen him in last, although not a form she saw him in always. In her dreams, he was fully human, just as she longed to be when she was with him.

Endearments were all they knew each other by, it never occurred to her to ask for anything more. She wasn't sure what he was, didn't even know his true name, but longed for him, nonetheless. He moved closer still, and her breath paused in anticipation of his touch. She ached for him like no other before.

"I've missed you," he said as his hand caressed her cheek. No other words could be filled with more longing and desire.

She leaned her flushed cheek into his palm, and her eyes welled with unshed tears as he warmed her from the inside out. "I don't know how much time we'll have."

His hand slipped from her face as she took the final step that brought them chest to chest. Sliding her arms around his neck, she couldn't help but think they fit perfectly together as he wrapped his arm around her slim waist and drew her tight against him. The familiar scent of smoke and musk with a hint of something more filled her senses as she closed her eyes and pulled in a deep breath. He was more relaxing than the lavender pouches they made and sold at the store.

His response came out in a sigh. "We should make the most of our time while we can, don't you agree?"

She had hardly agreed with him before his lips were crushing hers. It was like coming home. If only he would scoop her up and fly back to the land that he came from. A land he had explained in such general descriptions, it could have been anywhere on Earth. She had no idea where it was or what it looked like—all she knew in that moment was that she wanted to be wherever he was. Even if it meant she would never return to the life she had created for herself.

The sound of a throat clearing caused him to break the embrace and push back. His expression was one of apology as he evaporated into a wisp of smoke.

The muffled voice repeated itself as she hadn't caught what it said the first time. "Arachne, she's back. Are you awake?" Pulling herself from the deep sleep she was enjoying and irritated that that might be her last chance to see her dream lover, she sat up in the bed and adjusted her clothes. Reese was standing outside the doorway respecting her privacy, but she could hear the urgency in their tone. It made her wonder how long Reese had been outside her door.

"She's only here for one night while she resupplies her bags. I hate to wake you, but she's in somewhat of a hurry to hear your concerns."

"I completely understand, "Arachne said. "I appreciate the few hours of sleep you gave me. It was time that I woke. By the way, how close are we to sunset?"

"I would say a couple of hours. Thea has requested your presence at dinner, so I hope you can stay."

"Absolutely, thank you. I'll be out shortly. Just give me a moment."

As she readied herself, the familiar scent of musk and sage caused her to pause. Had he truly been with her or were her desires starting to play tricks on her desperate mind? Her choices were limited, and time was trickling. She had to stay on task. His ill-timed presence slid from her shoulders like the fabric that she donned for dinner. It was time to take hold of her destiny.

It didn't take long to make herself presentable. Arachne was happy to hear she had some time before she'd have to worry about morphing into the hideous creature that she changed into each night. She had a feeling that the time had come to be honest with Athena. Which was fine—she was tired of hiding her nature, and out of anyone she knew, the goddess would be the most likely to understand. Athena's best friend, next to Reese, was a gorgon after all.

By the time she entered the throne room, the line of visitors was filing out. It was the first time Arachne saw Athena in her goddess state, complete with a halo of gold light surrounding her robes of pure white. She was proud to have spun the intricate gown that Athena wore to greet her worshippers. The endless layers of fabric pooled around the base of her throne very much like a cloud.

Arachne stood in the back of the temple as Athena finished up with the last couple offering tribute. They were young and didn't have much in the way of material wealth as was apparent by their offerings. Athena accepted the basket of baked bread just as graciously as she would have a stack of gold.

"Thank you, goddess, for your great many blessings on our marriage. We ask that you honor us with a family."

"May you be blessed with many healthy children and long lives to enjoy them in as well as abundant prosperity."

"Thank you, goddess. And may we add that we are both thankful that it was you who won the challenge against Poseidon, although we were prepared to follow you to whatever city you reigned over."

Athena's smile was radiant. "Thank you, and I'm glad it didn't come to that. I am honored by your faith in me."

"Also, the olives are one of our favorite things to eat."

Reese and Athena shared a look, then she nodded to the couple. "Then I suspect you will be starting that family in no time."

The couple bowed, leaving the basket of bread on the steps before they walked from the temple hand in hand. Athena rose and disappeared through an archway behind her throne. Reese picked up the basket of bread and tipped their head toward the doorway.

"We're having dinner in her private quarters," Reese explained. "Less likely to be overheard."

Arachne couldn't help but be curious. "So, what was that all about?"

"You mean the olive comment?" Arachne nodded, and Reese gave a small shrug. "We noticed almost right away that they act as an aphrodisiac."

"That makes so much sense."

"I take from your expression that you understand what I'm saying," Reese laughed. "When couples come in about fertility issues, it is one of the first things we give them. They are honestly one of our best discoveries." Reese led her up a narrow hallway and into a marble foyer. Athena was already changed into a silk robe and seated at an enormous wooden table with a glass of wine.

"Come join me, my friend."

Arachne sat where Athena indicated then took the glass Reese offered her.

"This is the latest vintage from Hermes and Hecate. Let me know what you think. They're always looking for testers so they can perfect their blends."

Arachne took a sip, and the flavor burst on her tongue. She was instantly calmed. "I feel so relaxed all of a sudden. Like there is something in it?"

"A little magick is all she will tell me," Athena laughed. "I say whatever works. I have a glass every night."

"Sometimes two," Reese chimed in. A third glass was poured, then Athena's was filled once more.

"Well, if you had to deal with my war-mongering brother or my philandering father, you would drink too."

Reese soothed Athena's shoulders then leaned over to kiss her on the cheek. Athena beamed as Reese settled in the seat beside her. They sliced one of the loaves and placed the pieces on the table, pouring some olive oil in a shallow dish and adding some dried seasonings.

Arachne watched as Athena tore a piece of bread and dipped it into the golden liquid. "Try some, it is delicious. Reese's own recipe."

"Athena should be given just as much credit for it, she helped perfect the blend of herbs."

Reese glowed under Athena's attention. That they were in love was more than apparent. Arachne was happy for them and tried not to let her unfulfilled desires darken the mood. Athena turned her attention back to her guest.

"Reese said you wanted to talk to me. I thought it must be important since you came all this way and left Thyia to work in the shop alone."

"You're most perceptive, my goddess. Although I did leave her fully stocked with fabric to use in my absence."

Athena squinted her eyes, and Arachne squirmed under the observation. "What's troubling you, Arachne?"

Between her worried tone, Reese's understanding look, and the wine, Arachne's eyes watered. Warm tears tracked down her face as she tried to keep the emotion from thickening her voice. The story needed to be told, even if she had the desire to hold it back. It was time to share it with more than the bat in the corner.

"I've lived my life under a curse. The curse isn't something I necessarily want to undo, but it is becoming more of a burden as the years go on. It is my hope that you can help me find a way to control it."

"I don't have the power to undo curses," Athena said. "Even goddesses and gods have limits."

"I was hoping that perhaps you know someone who could? Perhaps someone who could offer a charm or a token to help control it?"

Athena and Reese glanced at one another, and a conversation occurred in a look. Reese moved in the direction of the throne room. They were alone. Athena took another sip of wine then a deep breath before speaking. "If you aren't comfortable telling me specifics, I will do my best to work around that. However, the more I know, the better I can help you to get to the right person. Magick is a tricky thing, and certain beings have certain skill sets. There is also the fact that some are better at harnessing magick than others, such as Hecate."

"I understand," Arachne said. "If I stay much longer this evening, you will see the effects of the curse for yourself. It does not matter how I got it, only what it does to me. I shift into something else, mostly when the night falls, but of late, it has been unpredictable, and I worry it will start happening during the day."

"And what is it you turn into?"

"A living nightmare," Arachne whispered. "Or something similar to that, at least in most people's opinion. I change into an eight-legged creature, a spider of sorts, but never on demand. As of late, it has been much longer periods of time that I remain in my cursed form."

Athena nodded, her lips pursed. "Your affinity to weaving makes much more sense now. I feel better knowing I would have only lost in a match against you because of your advantage. Four sets of arms to one is hard to beat."

Arachne laughed. The joke settled her nerves. "I would have never beat you in any form, my goddess, but yes, it is much easier to do the intricate work as this creature. My ability has increased over the years, and I found that weaving in spider form creates the art that I've become known for. So even though I was cursed originally, it's become part of who I am, and I've learned to embrace it. But I fear one day I will remain in that form permanently. I'm not sure I'd be happy with that."

"There's no shame in who you are or what you've become. You could live as you are surrounded by the people who love you."

"I understand, but like Medusa, I want to live in human form with the people who know me as such. I would like to one day have a chance to love and be loved. And while he would have to accept some uncomfortable things about me, I hope that I would be able to have that choice to live a life with someone who could love me for who I am and whoever I'm most comfortable being."

Athena took another sip of wine. "I understand more than you know. I do know someone who can help you. It's the same person to help me with Medusa and her children. She specializes in curses, but she isn't easy to get to. As a matter of fact, it requires you going to a place where humans generally can't go."

"What do you mean by generally?"

"There are those that have gone there and have been able to return to the Earth realm, but the sacrifices were great. It's easier if you have a guide. If you trust me, I can send a message to a friend and ask him to help. But you will need to be honest with him, and he will need to know more about you than you've shared here with me. I will also let you know he is not someone you want to trifle with. His ability is unequaled, even for a god."

Arachne didn't hesitate. "Agreed. What do I need to do?"

"Give me a moment." Athena closed her eyes and took in a deep breath almost as if she were meditating. In the next moment, Hermes arrived at her side, his sandals fluttering, causing him to float beside her. He glanced to Arachne, clearly curious, but turned his attention quickly back to Athena.

"What do you need, my sister?"

"Please take a message to the God of Dreams. Tell him the honor of his presence is requested here this evening. Ideally, within the half hour."

Arachne glanced out the window. The colors bled onto the horizon as Apollo pulled his chariot downward. She hoped their visitor was someone who didn't startle easily. She wasn't quite sure how long she would remain human.

Hermes glanced her way then confirmed with Athena he would do her bidding before disappearing in a wink. Reese came back with trays of food and placed the dishes in the middle of the table, pointing to the plate in front of Arachne. "We're pretty informal around here, please help yourself to anything you'd like."

"The olives are especially good right now," Athena added. "We should have enough time to eat before Lord Morpheus arrives."

Arachne wondered how this person could possibly help but had no other recourse but to put her faith in her goddess, who up until now had only ever had her best interest at heart. She loaded her plate as if it were the last meal she would ever have as a human, especially since it could be precisely that.

7

The dinner conversation was enjoyable, mainly art and creativity, which kept the mood light throughout the entire meal. It helped Arachne squelch the niggling feeling that she was making the wrong choice. What if her request caused her to lose her dreams? To lose him? It was a thought she couldn't fathom so forced her attention to the present.

Reese had a lot to offer. They were adept at creating new species of plants and flowers and were passionate about their work. A tour of the garden was planned, and when the meal was done, Reese cleared up the plates and said goodnight, leaving Arachne and Athena to welcome their visitor alone.

The god's arrival was heralded by swirling black smoke which filled the corner of the room by the fireplace. After a few seconds of that effect, there was a flash of lightning that split the room with its electric glow. If she didn't know better, she would have thought it was Hades himself. When the smoke cleared, a dark moody presence and impressive wingspan filled the room. It was as if he had just flown a thousand miles to be with them, pulling in oxygen without trying to show that he was winded. His head was lowered as he caught his breath, and then he raised the red glow of his eyes to meet hers.

Arachne gasped, causing Athena to look between them. He tipped his head as he took a step forward, his powerful arms reaching toward the table for a split second before he caught himself and lowered them. His eyes, no longer red, glanced at Athena in confusion then back at

Arachne. His voice was low and raspy and cracked ever so slightly. "What are you doing here?"

"I could ask the same of you," she answered. "I'm only just wrapping my head around the possibilities as impossible as they seem."

He took another step forward, lowering his wings and snapping them behind him in a blink. In a matter of seconds, they were gone, and he stood before them as the man she had made love to in her dreams. The man who had been immortalized in the tapestries that she had sold to get to the goddess's temple. "Athena, what is going on?"

"I take it you two know one another," she said with a delighted tone. Her look with a single raised eyebrow was sent to him across the table as she waved to the seat at the end and invited him to sit. "Well, that should make this conversation a bit easier."

"Easier for whom?" He was moody and somewhat embarrassed. Arachne wasn't sure what she had done wrong, but this wasn't the same man with the melodious laugh and heart-twisting smile that she had been with in her dreams. The same being who tried to kiss her in the temple not hours before dinner. "Hermes didn't explain there would be anyone else here, only that you needed my presence."

"Well, I suppose he was half right then. There is someone else here."

"I can see that."

Arachne had had enough. "That someone else has a name, sir. It is Arachne. What is yours?"

"Surely he's introduced himself properly?" Athena's teasing tone flustered him. Arachne wouldn't let him out of explanation. Her gaze locked on his.

His eyes softened, and the glow she was used to seeing returned to their depths. The man she knew was returning as he calmed himself. He kept his eyes locked on Arachne's as he responded to Athena's question. "There were more important things to discuss. My name has no bearing on who I am or what I do for that matter." His voice was a purr, deep in his chest. A chest she had just had her hands on. The thought of it all was bringing heat to her face. She was starting to regret the extra handful of olives she ate with her dinner.

Athena's voice broke into their moment, bringing them back to reality. "Well, I believe there is power in a name, as well as respect. Our guest deserves to know them both from you. Arachne, I would like you to meet Lord Morpheus, God of Dreams and Nightmares, Master of the Ether. Morpheus, this is my dear friend, Arachne."

His eyes looked to Athena then straight back, as if the term, friend, was something he had only just learned. He cleared his throat then nodded his head down in greeting. "The pleasure is mine, Arachne."

She breathed in the feeling of hearing her name come from his lips. She was having a hard time holding herself together. "Lord Morpheus." The name tasted sweet on her tongue, and his reaction to hearing her say it caused his nostrils to flare and eyes to widen. Presumably, she wasn't the only one struggling.

"Wonderful," Athena said. "Now that we all know one another, let's get down to business."

"As you wish," Morpheus responded quietly as he lowered his smoldering eyes and gave Athena his full attention. "What can I do for you, my goddess."

"It's not what you can do for me, it's what you can do for Arachne. I want you to take her to the Underworld with you."

The look on his face mirrored the emotion Arachne was feeling. Confusion at its finest, inconvenience at its core. "Excuse me?"

Athena smirked, she was enjoying his reaction all too much. It was like watching a cat play with a mouse. If Arachne wasn't so worried about the time of night and her impending change, she would have enjoyed it a little more. He had played enough pranks on her in her dreams; she would rather like seeing someone get the best of him.

"You heard me. She has a situation she needs corrected, and the only one that can help her is Pandora."

"The cost for seeing Pandora is high," he warned.

"I have gold…" he shook his head effectively cutting off her comment. "Gold isn't what you need, you need a guide."

"Which is precisely why you are here," Athena said. "I need you to take my friend to the Underworld to speak with Pandora and to ensure her safety there and back. Think of it as a personal favor to me."

Morpheus stood then paced between the table and the fireplace.

"You know I am unable to say no to an Olympian."

"Precisely." she smiled. Athena rose then looked directly at Arachne. "I will leave you now to get to know one another better. You can take as much time as you need in here, I won't be returning this evening." She glanced over at Morpheus with an expression that Arachne couldn't quite see, but his reaction caused him to look into Arachne's eyes. "I know you are busy but do me this favor, my friend. This woman is under my special care."

He nodded without looking at her. "Consider her under mine now as well."

Satisfied, Athena left the room by way of the entrance to the temple where Reese had gone. Arachne watched her exit then turned her attention back to the brooding man standing near the fire. "I'm sorry to be a burden," she said to him quietly.

He took the few steps to her side before lowering himself to one knee so she was eye level from her seated position. His hands took hers, and the warmth of them was a contradiction from the dreams they had shared. This was not a figment of her imagination, a specter that shared dreams and experiences with her. No, this was a flesh and blood man who made her body react in ways that she had already experienced emotionally, but now her physical body was taking and making its own.

"You are never to call yourself a burden," he said. "I'm sorry for the way I reacted. You surprised me, and it is rare that that ever happens in my experience." His thumb rubbed the back of her hand, soothing her jangled nerves. "Your skin. It's soft like a petal."

The rhythmic caresses were scattering her brain. She was having a hard time concentrating so pulled her hand out of his and pointed to the seat beside her. "Please sit down."

"Of course," he said as he sat. He placed his elbows on the table in front of him and steepled his hands. "I'm sensing you have questions." His words said one thing, but his body was having a different conversation with her. When he lowered one hand and slipped it across the table to reach for her, she sat back in her seat.

"I do. But I also feel that we should take some time to learn more about one another."

The comment brought a wicked grin to his face. Her movement had him relaxing back in his seat. "I'm pretty sure you already know more about me than anyone in this world or the next. About my thoughts, my dreams, and most importantly…my desires."

"The time that we shared together was a dream," she argued. "How can I believe any of it?"

His intense stare rattled her, she had never seen him so serious. "Know this now—anything you experienced with me, anything I said or did, was more real than anything you will ever know in this life. I am the God of Dreams, but what I shared with you was not created or manipulated in any way."

Her face flushed with the memory of some of the things that they had shared. His eyes lowered to the pulse beating in her neck, and his boyish smile was back. She cleared her throat and shifted in her seat. "So, what we shared…"

"Was real," he answered. "I don't understand how. I only know that when I realized our connection was something more than my obligation to you, god to human, I needed to spend more time with you. One thing led to another, and soon I was coming…"

"Every night," she finished. "And when the dreams stopped because I was restless…"

"I wasn't able to reach you." He lowered his eyes and took a deep breath. When he raised them and looked into hers, he slid his hands across the table palms upward. She placed her hands in his and he squeezed, thumbs soothing once more. This time, she allowed it without hesitation. "I came in the only way I could," he said quietly.

"I don't remember seeing you."

He looked sheepishly at her, and he glanced over his shoulder then back into her eyes.

Remembering his arrival, the strong black wings, the idea formed in her mind. Once it did, the realization flooded her to the pit of her stomach. "The bat," she whispered.

He squeezed her hands and nodded. Embarrassment colored his cheeks as she pulled her hands back into her lap. "Oh, my goddess, the bat."

"Arachne, I can explain."

She pushed the chair back and stood in order to pace the floor near the table. She was working herself up, she realized, but she couldn't help it. She felt as though she had been lied to. "I thought you were, well, a bat!"

"I was," he tried to explain. She cut him off with a wave of her arms.

"Morpheus, you heard things about me I have never told another soul. Private and personal things never intended for anyone else's ears!"

He rose to his feet and walked to her, taking her into his arms. She welcomed the embrace but was still embarrassed, so she hid her face in his chest to hide the uncontrolled tears.

"You have every right to be angry with me, but I had no way of telling you the truth. By all accounts, we would have never met in reality."

"So, you already know about me. What I am." She looked up into his eyes and allowed her brimming tears to fall.

He raised his hand to cup her cheek, his thumb wiping a tear from her face. "I know that you are an amazing person, that took on a burden that wasn't your own because you have the heart of a heroine. I know that you are extremely talented and can move me to tears with the scenes you create with mere threads. And I know that I will never forgive myself if I don't help you with whatever you feel you need to accomplish."

Why the Universe had allowed them to meet and connect may never be understood by either of them. Arachne realized this chance was a gift, and it was one more reason she needed to find a solution. Morpheus was looking into her eyes, his thumb rubbing back and forth on her cheek, and the love in his eyes washing over her as the change happened. Her vision split as her body morphed, but his gaze didn't falter. He kept his hand on her throughout the entire transformation, and at the end of it, he still looked at her with admiration in his eyes.

Her voice came out in a rasp. "And what if I can't accomplish what I set out to do? What if I stay this way forever?"

His warm smile soothed her worries. "Then I shall take you to my palace, and my home will be yours. You can spend your days weaving tapestries as I weave dreams."

"And if I'm able to control the curse and live as a human?"

Morpheus shrugged and winked. "I'll love you anyway. How do you feel about having a pet bat?"

She didn't recall a time when she had laughed in the spider form, but she did now. "You are by far the strangest person I have ever met."

"That is because I'm not a person and neither are you. We are both something more. It's time we learn more about our destinies, don't you think? Now, tell me more about this sister of yours."

8

Arachne woke the next afternoon fully rested from a dreamless sleep. Morpheus had made it so. She had never been so happy to have a full night of deep sleep in her life. During the conversations that they'd had the night before, they made plans to meet in the Underworld.

Hermes relayed a message to Hades to request that he deliver Arachne to the entrance. When she asked why she couldn't travel with him, Morpheus explained that his powers were tied to the god realm. He was limited to a dream state on Earth, and he was only able to be in his true physical form on Olympus or extensions of it. Temples or other godly worlds were examples.

Because she could shift at any given time, and because he wasn't able to carry her in bat form through the night skies on Earth, they decided it would be best for her to travel with someone who had the ability to get her to the Underworld quickly. If Hades could pick her up and bring her to the House of Judgement, Morpheus would meet her there. With everything arranged, they said their goodnights, and he put her in a trance-like slumber in his arms.

She slipped on a shawl and padded over to the window where the sun was starting its downward climb. She had slept the day away. Hades had confirmed he would pick her up at 8:00 PM, so she washed up, gathered her few belongings, and then went out to find Reese.

The temple was empty, the bustle of the day already done, so she walked across to the archway that led to the gardens to look there. She found Reese just outside the doorway pruning some shrubs.

"Good evening. You look rested. You must have needed the sleep."

"I did," Arachne replied. "I haven't slept like that in months."

"I'm glad you were able to relax. Hermes stopped by and mentioned that Hades would be coming by to get you in about an hour. Did you need anything for your journey?"

Arachne thought about it for a moment before responding. "I think I'll be good. Morpheus is supposed to be meeting me there. My guess is that he will have anything we end up needing."

"How long is it that you've known one another? Athena mentioned that you were, well…friendly."

Arachne hoped that the light of the setting sun hid the pink of her cheeks. "I only just found out that he was real. He's been in and out of my dreams for some time, but it's only been in the last few years that we've gotten to know one another better."

"I don't know him very well, but Athena thinks very highly of him, and she's an extremely good judge of character." Reese turned from the shrub that they were trimming and looked pointedly at Arachne. "She thinks very highly of you as well. She wishes that she was here to see you off and hopes that you will find the answers you seek."

"Please tell her that I appreciate everything she's done for me. I also want to say that in the short time I've known her I've never seen her so happy."

Reese beamed. "Thank you, Arachne, that's sweet of you to say. Now, I had better wash up and prepare for our guest. He should be arriving shortly to collect you."

At eight o'clock, Arachne was on the front steps of the temple awaiting Hades. There was an orange glow in the distance, which at first looked like a building on fire. When she saw it get bigger and move toward her, she realized it was her ride.

The chariot was impressive, much larger than she had expected, black as night and trimmed with gold. The breath of the four horses who strained to pull it created visible flames. While she expected something flamboyant from Hades, what she didn't expect was that it wouldn't be him at all getting her. The petite blonde woman pulled on the reins, and the horses stomped down onto the drive, bringing the chariot screeching to a halt, long before the bouncing ringlets framing her delicate face did.

"You must be Arachne," she said. "I'm Persephone. Hades sent me to get you… Well, actually, I offered. There was no way I was going to let him pick up the first woman who has ever come to the Underworld to visit Morpheus, that I know of. Especially not alone. It ended up that he was pretty busy dealing with a huge influx of soldiers. Ares has been at it again. Anyways, I thought it would be fun to get to know one another since I don't have very many friends down there."

She had rattled on so fast that Arachne had hardly caught most of it. But she had the gist.

"Nice to meet you, I'm Arachne. I need some help with something that's becoming an issue, and Morpheus was kind enough to offer his services."

"His services? Really?" Her grin and the wicked little gleam in her eyes told Arachne that perhaps she wasn't as sweet and innocent as she looked. Now that she thought of it, of course she wouldn't be. Being married to somebody like Hades had most likely influenced it. Of course, from what she had heard about Demeter, she didn't blame her for wanting to get away. She reigned in her judgement; she wouldn't want anyone to do the same with her.

Persephone's face was open and genuine.

"Climb in so we can get going. I thought we could take the long way home. More time to chat."

Arachne didn't have very many friends either, and the notion that she would be making a new one intrigued her. "That sounds great. I'm looking forward to it." She tossed her small bag into the carriage and pulled herself in. The horses were off before she had a chance to sit down.

"How long is it that you've known Morpheus?"

Here we go again. Why was everybody so interested in Morpheus? It seemed to her that there was a lot more about him that she needed to learn.

"Not very long," she said with a shrug. "He only just told me who he really was. I honestly thought he was a figment of my imagination."

"For almost everyone, he is," Persephone answered. "It is interesting to me that he chose to be himself with you. You must be someone special."

"Not sure I would call it that, as much as he is doing Athena a favor."

"We'll see about that," she said knowingly. She changed the subject before Arachne could question the tone. "So, where are you from?"

Arachne paused slightly before giving the response that she tailored for polite conversation. "I have a dress shop in Thebes. Athena helped Thyia and I…"

"Not T.A. Creations? I adore your fabrics! It's like wearing nothing at all, which drives Hades mad with lust. He will hardly let me out of the bed chamber in my midnight blue. The sparkles are so strategically placed!"

Arachne remembered the piece. At the time, she thought that she was designing it for Aphrodite. She would have never pictured it on the innocent Goddess of Spring. All she could do was nod, which Persephone took as a sign to continue.

"I bet your wardrobe is stunning. With your long black hair, you would look amazing in red. Perhaps Morpheus would lighten up a little if you wore something sheer like that. Who am I kidding, he would never let you out of his sight. I do like the color you have on as well, that is a beautiful shade of emerald. Reminds me of the leaf on a jasmine. You have such a good eye for that kind of thing. Oh, but listen to me rattle on, of course you know how amazing your creations are."

"I'm not sure about all that, but it is always nice to hear."

"Well, I will tell you firsthand that if I want my husband's attention, all I need to do is slip on that dress. I don't think I've worn it longer than a few minutes at a time since I've owned it. I'm surprised he hasn't torn it yet, with as impatient as he can get at times."

Arachne was glad the chariot was moving so fast, as it cooled her blush. She was delighted to find that her impression of Persephone all these years had been entirely wrong, although she was not quite as much of a sharer.

Persephone directed the horses to start their downward climb. She pointed her finger to the right of the chariot. "The entrance is just there."

"That didn't take long to get to," Arachne remarked. She was thankful for the reprieve Persephone had given her, but now worries were slipping back into her mind. What had she gotten herself into?

"These horses are much faster than Apollo's," Persephone said as a way of explaining. "Hades breeds his horses for speed. He generally doesn't like to leave his realm if he can help it, so when he does, he wants to be quick about it. Although he misses me terribly in the summertime, so he has been coming up more frequently. He still won't stay at my mother's for more than a few hours. That suits me—she doesn't care for him, so I would rather not deal with the stress of them being in the same room."

Arachne didn't know how to respond, so she kept her thoughts to herself while she put the view to memory. Perhaps one day, she would have the chance to weave it. Soon they were at ground level, skimming over lush forests and crystal streams. It looked like they were heading straight for a mountain, but after a second look, Arachne saw the opening wide enough to be an entrance. At least that was what she hoped it was since they were heading straight for it.

Persephone pointed to the split in the mountain. "There is the opening," she explained. "It's the one we use most since we typically have the chariot and not too many people know about it, so there is less likely to be a crowd of souls waiting to get in. I will drop you off once we enter the cave, and you will need to walk from there. If you stay to the right, you will find Charon. You have a coin, right?"

Arachne nodded. "Yes, Reese gave me one from Athena before I left."

"Okay, good. You won't get very far without one. You will need to get on the ferry, and he will collect the coin, which will take you past Cerberus. The ferry will take you directly to the House of Judgement, which is the first stop for all incoming visitors. Morpheus will be able to take you from there."

"Thank you, Persephone, I really appreciate all you have done for me."

"You're welcome," she said with a dismissive wave. "I'll be seeing you soon since all visitors are brought to the palace to meet us first before traveling on to wherever they are going. It's tradition. Anyway, I'm glad to have gotten to know you better. I'm sure we will be fast friends."

Arachne was surprised by the attack hug but couldn't help but lean into it. Persephone was a force, talked a mile a minute, but was a sweet and loving person. She was right—they would be friends, if she could remain in human form. Only time would tell.

No sooner had she stepped off the chariot and collected her belongings than it left in a puff of smoke. Arachne was left alone to start the next leg of her journey. She pulled in a breath, her lungs filling with stale and acrid air which she longed to spit from her mouth as she walked toward the ferry landing. Arachne wasn't the only one there, and there was a line that formed at the side of the platform. There were people from all walks of life there, standing together and chatting about how they had each met their demise. It wasn't lost on her that in the end death was what everyone had in common, no matter who they were or how they lived their lives.

She kept away from the crowd, holding back just in case she felt the change coming and needed to find a dark corner to hide in. There were a few souls that noticed her, but for the most part, she was ignored.

The cavern was dark with the only visible light coming from the glowing lanterns which lined the path. There were torches on the pier as well, and the glow reflected on the ripples of the River of Woes, or Acheron as it was known. Charon traversed the waterways in the Underworld four hours a day, taking souls to their final destination. When the silhouette of his ferry was visible in the distance, the chattering in the crowd ceased. It was finally sinking in… Their journey was truly coming to an end, and not one person on the pier knew what to expect. Fate loomed for them all.

It brought tears to Arachne's eyes, the thought that one day she, too, might stand on the pier and consider where she would end up. Things weren't always equal in the world, and from her understanding, the Underworld wasn't much different. There was a hierarchy, and there was judgment, and the people in the crowd who silently watched as the ferry came to gather them grew more tense as they considered the reality of their situation.

Charon pulled the ferry alongside the pier and tied it off, securing it to the posts intended for that purpose. Arachne stepped out of her shadows and lined up at the back, waiting her turn to hand Charon the coin that he would require for passage. Almost all of the passengers were loaded, and as she placed her drachma into his skeletal hand, she made the mistake of looking up—the only thing she saw peeking out of the hood he wore were two glowing red dots she presumed were his eyes. He said nothing, merely pointing his bony finger at the ferry. She stepped on and slid behind the crowd waiting while he untied the ferry and pushed them off.

The light from the pier faded fast in the recesses of the caves that they traveled through. Just when she thought she'd never see light again, the room was filled with it. The narrow pathway opened into a large cavern, and tiny pinpoints of light were dotted all over like stars in a midnight sky. The hushed passengers gasped, taking in the beauty completely awestruck. Soon they came to another pier, this one more illuminated than the last. There was a path in the distance leading straight to an enormous structure which she presumed was the House of Judgment.

After the crowd disembarked, they proceeded up the path and passed an enormous statue of Themis standing on one side, with a likeness of Hades on the other. As she followed the silent passengers that she had ridden with into the hall, she heard a familiar male voice call to her from the shadows.

"You made it," Morpheus said. He sounded relieved as if something could have happened on her way to him. He embraced her long enough for her to feel relief but quickly enough so as not to be improper. She leaned into his warmth, her arms naturally gravitating around his neck and her hands wrapping up in his shoulder-length ebony locks.

"Persephone took good care of me," Arachne explained. "She told me what to expect at the pier."

Morpheus tilted his head. "Persephone?" he questioned. "I wonder what Hades is up to. I suppose we'll soon find out since that's our first stop. Since you're new to the Underworld, we need to go pay our respects first."

"She mentioned that. Something about tradition."

"Yes, we have quite a few we can't seem to move past. Although, I don't mind this one. It allows Hades to keep track of everyone who enters his realm and, by extension, mine. It keeps everyone safe."

Morpheus took a step back and looked to each side. Seconds later, his great and powerful wings unfurled behind him. "If you don't mind, we can travel quicker this way." He held out his hand toward her, and she put her hand in his. He guided her arm around his neck then bent to scoop her up in his powerful arms. She put her other arm up and around, snuggling closer into his chest.

"Hold on," he said softly. "I've got you."

Before she had a chance to respond, he had pulled them into the heights above the marble building and was soaring effortlessly toward a large building in the distance up on a hill. It was surrounded on all sides by a moat of flames. Her reaction was to pull in closer to his body, and his arms tightened around her.

"It looks more intimidating than it really is," he said. She could hardly hear his voice over the thrust of his wings. "Most of the flames you see are an illusion meant to keep unwanted visitors out. Hades is busy, he oversees quite a bit down here."

"Do all the souls come here?" She was curious about the process.

"The souls don't come here. Once they travel to the House of Judgment and receive their verdict, Charon takes them to their final destination. The luckiest go to the Elysian Fields, and the less fortunate end up in Tartarus. And there are those who choose to live in limbo, who are the ones I spend the most time with. Some dream of resolution, others a chance to make things right. Some desire to make sense of their lives, only to realize an existence without purpose nullifies their legacy, and they are already much too late."

Arachne nodded her head; it was a lot to take in. "These people in limbo that went to the House of Judgment? Why was a decision not made one way or the other?"

He landed on the great marble steps of Hades's palace and lowered her feet to the hard surface. He shook his wings, ruffling them before snapping them into place where they disappeared from her sight. He swept his hand toward the doorway, indicating she should walk up the final few steps. He followed behind her, his hand on the small of her back guiding her and offering support.

"Mostly free will—even in the Underworld it matters—and at times, sentences can't be made for one reason or another. Most of the time, it's because they have unresolved issues in their lives, and they choose to stay. We'll be flying over the area where these souls congregate later. It's interesting to me that some people would willingly choose a meaningless existence in the hope that they would be given the opportunity to resolve it."

"Resolve it how?"

Morpheus stopped and looked over, his expression reaching a small smile. He seemed delighted to be answering her questions. It made her wonder if anybody ever asked him about his world or if he was merely used as a way to fulfill their desires. He was happy to have company, she could tell.

"Resolution comes in a number of ways, the most significant of which is facing the wrongs that they caused in life and asking forgiveness. There are very few who actually accomplish this since most of the people who were mistreated are sent to a place much better than what they experienced in life. The wronged rarely choose limbo before moving on to the place they're meant to go."

"Makes sense," she said.

Morpheus considered her murmured response then ushered her into the great palace of Hades and Persephone. Arachne wasn't sure what she expected, but she certainly wasn't prepared for the beauty and splendor of the home of two of the greatest gods of Olympus, especially since the illusion on the outside gave an expectation of something darker and foreboding. The reality was the complete opposite.

There were flames, torches, and lamps everywhere, although used primarily for light. The aisle was lined with marble planters filled to the brim with ivy and colorful bulbs, such as hyacinth and daffodils. Every container that could hold dirt was filled with a colorful reminder that the new queen was also the Goddess of Spring.

Dotted in their path along the side of the room were trees bursting from the floor, deciduous in varying shades of foliage. There was a steady drone from the bees busy pollinating the blossoms of the fruit trees, and as they got further into the building, the song of the goldfinch was unmistakable. Arachne was proud to see fabric that she herself had made hanging behind the thrones that they were walking toward. Persephone was seated in the smaller of the two. The man seated next to her dwarfed her, and Arachne imagined he was at least a foot and a half taller than her when standing. When Persephone saw her, a grin flashed across her face, and she hopped up from her seat. She practically ran down the steps toward them.

"I'm so glad you made it! Nice to see you, Morpheus."

"And you as well, my queen. I see you've met Arachne?"

Persephone nodded. "Yes. I had the pleasure of escorting her to the pier."

Hades walked up behind her, and Arachne found that she was wrong. He was at least two feet taller, dark, imposing, but uncharacteristically friendly as well. She felt instantly welcome. Persephone indicated to him with her hand. "Arachne, I'd like you to meet my husband, Hades, Lord of the Underworld and supreme Judger of the Departed.

Honey, this is Arachne, Morpheus's friend."

His eyebrow raised without a word, then he took Arachne's hand and bowed over it. "It's very nice to meet you." He gave it a squeeze before releasing it and glancing at Morpheus.

"Nice to meet you as well. Thank you for allowing me to come here and settle my business."

"You're welcome," he said. "And although your business is your own, I am curious what areas of the Underworld you may need to travel to."

Morpheus answered him. "I'll be taking her to the Fields of Mourning."

"Pandora's realm?"

"Precisely. And I hate to cut our visit short, but time is of the essence."

He shook Morpheus's hand and gave a quick bow to Arachne. "Of course. I hope your meeting is successful and that you find what you are looking for. Be sure to get a coin from her for Charon, otherwise you'll never get out of here. Lastly, just a reminder—don't eat anything while you're here, and whatever you do, no matter how thirsty you are, do not drink out of any of the rivers."

"I'll keep her safe," Morpheus said.

"Safe travels, my friend."

"I hope to see you again soon, Arachne," Persephone said. She gave her a hug. "I wish you the best of luck for whatever it is you're seeking. Please know you have a friend to call on should you need it."

As they left, there were other visitors being ushered in who apparently had been held back to give her and Morpheus privacy. Morpheus let her out to the outer platform where he once again spread his wings. As he picked her up, she stifled a yawn, and he looked at her with concern. "It's been a long day of travel for you. We can go somewhere to rest if you need it."

Arachne shook her head. "I would rather get it over with," she said.

"I don't blame you. If you're sure..."

He waited for her nod then slipped his hand in hers. The warmth of his touch made her simultaneously calm and anxious. It wasn't lost on her that, until now, she had only imagined the warmth of his skin. That her mind had conjured the magnificent creature that now stood beside her. How his physical form felt, the salt of his skin, as they learned about each other in the leisure of her dreams. Even as an immortal, she wasn't sure she would ever get enough of his electric touch. That she could change what they had by continuing her chosen path was something she refused to consider.

But she needed to make a choice. Soon.

9

Arachne had never put much thought into what the Underworld looked like. She was somewhat surprised to realize that it was an entire world that paralleled the land of the living. It made complete sense, considering that each birth on Earth would equate into a death and a move into the Underworld. Or at least that was what she assumed. Morpheus's wings made travel quick, with hardly a strain in his physical form.

"So, what am I to expect?" she asked. "Have you met Pandora?"

"I have." His voice was hushed. Mulling over the question for a few moments, he continued with a sigh. "I will say that I don't always agree with the ways of the gods, especially in the beginning when our purpose was designed and distributed. We didn't get to choose who we are or what we do, but every one of us takes their purpose very seriously. Over the millennia, we have each perfected our gifts to serve the purpose but have also found ways to create a better life for ourselves. Pandora is no different. However, her very existence was doomed from the start."

"Because the gods gifted her all the ills of the world which she was unable to contain?"

"Not so much that as much as it's her purpose to teach mankind a lesson that they have long since forgotten. So now, she's had to reinvent herself in order to survive."

"I believe that's something to admire," Arachne said. "Taking no matter what life throws at you and still finding a way to make your dreams come true. It's what life's all about. Once fear is removed and purpose is established, I find that the passion follows."

"And makes for a life worth living, I would add. But for some, that journey takes longer than expected. That gives doubt, fear, and foreboding a foothold in your psyche. In Pandora's case, she doesn't doubt her purpose, only the time it's taking to resolve it."

"And her purpose was to release evils into the world?"

Morpheus shook his head. "No. Her purpose is to gather them back."

The land beneath them, once lush and green, had changed to a barren wasteland. Morpheus's grip on her was tighter, and she snuggled into his warmth, purposely avoiding looking down at the thousands of souls trying to get their attention as they passed. Arms reached up beckoning, the moans and wails barely heard over the flapping of his wings.

"The lost souls," he explained. "They're neither damned nor sent to paradise and spend their time here reliving the choices they made in life that sent them there."

"And do any of them ever leave?"

"Very few, since the evils or ills that they would need to repent for are typically against another person who may have long since gone to the place that they were meant for. Even if they were forgiven, they would need to travel to Charon and would need a coin for the journey. Most of these souls will never have the opportunity to resolve the thing that keeps them here, and even if they did, they would never get past the ferryman."

Arachne thought about her own life and where she might end up. She looked down on the fields below, desolate and meaningless, and hoped that her fate would not lead her there.

"Your heart's too pure," he said softly. "This would not be your fate, Arachne. I promise you."

He changed the subject as they started to get lower in the sky. Arachne feared they'd be landing, swarmed by the desperate souls that they had just flown over. He nudged his head forward, indicating that she should look which is when she saw the great peak they were heading toward.

"She's in that mountain, so we will be landing just there on that ledge. I already sent word that we're coming. She'll be expecting you."

They landed just within the cave entrance, and he lowered her feet to the ground as his wings folded in on themselves. He left his arms circling her as she gained her footing, and she gripped his arms for support.

"Are you alright?"

She nodded and slipped her hands from his arms. "I'm good, thank you. I'm ready when you are."

"You can still turn back. We could find a way." He held out his hand with a questioning look. She didn't hesitate to take his hand in hers.

"I need to do this. For me."

"Understood. Come with me." Together, they walked into the arched stone. It was the point of no return.

The glow of torches lining the walls in the entrance swayed as they moved past. There were small doorways along the main corridor that were cut into stone, presumably leading down to other areas of the cave. Just when it was hard for Arachne to catch her breath, they entered an enormous space. Darkness, with no end in sight, filled the void above them. The walls on either side were worn smooth, covered with symbols from a language she wasn't familiar with.

The torches came up from the floor in waist-high pillars of stone that had been hollowed out as pits. The flames danced orange, blue, and green, without the familiar crack and pop you would hear with wood. Almost as if the flames survived without fuel to fire them.

As they walked further into the room, she spied a large platform with steps leading up to an immense clay jar covered with the same symbols she saw on the walls. Other than the jar and two fire pits on either side, there was nothing else on the platform. There was a table and chairs at the base of the stairs, which is where they stopped. A stunning woman sat on an ornate golden chair centered at a long rect-angular table. As they reached her, she spread her hands and indicated that they should take the seats across from her.

"Welcome, my friend," she said to Morpheus. "Please have a seat and help yourself to refreshment."

Morpheus pulled a chair out for Arachne and helped her to settle before taking his own seat. "It's nice to see you again, Pandora. I would like you to meet Arachne. She's a dear friend, has been granted passage by Hades, and is under my protection during her visit here."

"Well now that we have that out of the way, it's very nice to meet you Arachne." The stunning redhead nodded gracefully then shifted in her seat, attempting to hide the discomfort the movement caused her. The smile was genuine, but Arachne saw something else in her eyes. A weariness that she was fiercely attempting to hide. "The greeting traditions are archaic. Old habits die hard, with the Titans especially. I'm sure you've been warned not to eat or drink anything while you're here."

She looked pointedly at Morpheus, waiting for his confirming nod. Sufficiently convinced that the rules had been explained to her new guest, she addressed her once more. "We don't all agree with trick-ing souls into staying in the Underworld, but we aren't able to get away without offering things that would cause you to stay. Having everyone go to Hades first and get the warning is our workaround. Now…what brings you here?"

Arachne glanced over to Morpheus who gave her an encouraging nod. She could trust Pandora. "Years ago, I was cursed by someone who mistook me for my twin. The curse was not intended for me, but I took it willingly at the time. Out of love for my sister."

"So, you wish to remove this curse?" Pandora asked.

Arachne shook her head. "Not so much remove it as learn to con-trol it. This curse has become a large part of who I am, and I fear losing that piece of myself. Along with this curse came immortality." Arachne caught Morpheus's intake of breath and his shift in his seat out of the corner of her eye but kept her focus on Pandora. "The cost of immor-tality was that I was to spend it changing into a hideous beast each night. The spider I become sees the world differently and has the ability to create things in fabric that, prior to the curse, I had only dreamed of. Over the centuries, I learned to embrace my curse as a gift."

Pandora listened intently, her eyes shining bright with emotion. "But the curse wasn't yours."

"No, it wasn't," Arachne responded. "And I think because of that and perhaps because of my acceptance of what I've become, the curse is changing. I fear it was designed that way to mimic a cruel twist in fate. Just when I get comfortable with one situation, it seems to give me something else to work with."

"I can completely relate," Pandora said with a small smile. "So, what is it you hope that I can do for you, Arachne?"

"I'm aware of some charmed gifts you gave Athena for the purpose of helping Medusa's children with their shifting abilities. I thought you might be able to give me something similar. I want to be able to choose when I become a spider and how long I remain in that form. I no longer want to live at the whim of fate. I want to be able to control my own destiny."

"I can relate to that as well. Curses are not easily broken or manipulated. They are woven by a magick that I have only started to understand through Hecate's teaching. However, the one thing I do know is that they are generally unbreakable when made against the person they were intended for. In this case, this fate was intended for your sister, so we have a bit of an advantage. The gifts I gave Athena for Pegasus and Chrysador were reinforced with an intention that the power is within the self."

"Do you think you can do the same for me? Give me something imbued with your blessing that allows me to focus on one form or the other? Right now, it's impossible for me to change back on my own. I don't mind the fate that I've been given, but there are times that I wonder if I'll ever change back. And the thought of living in that form for eternity frightens me because I love both lives equally, and each of them are a part of who I am."

"My divine purpose started out as one thing and is now entirely different." Pandora pushed her chair back and rose at her seat, causing

Morpheus to get up and go around the table to help her. She smiled at his assistance and waved him off, placing her hand on her enormous belly while rubbing the small of her back with the other.

"I was under the impression that the gods and goddesses on Mount Olympus we're giving me life in order to be happy with my husband. He was a gift to me as was the jar behind us which we didn't know until our wedding night was filled with every ill and evil imaginable. We were blamed for releasing things into the world from a jar we didn't even touch because we were too busy creating the young lady who now lives inside of me. I don't know who opened the lid and released the evils into the world. I do have my suspicions. But I do know that I'm going to gather every last one of them in order to help those who have been given a fate that they didn't deserve."

Arachne rose and went over to her with tears in her eyes. She went into Pandora's open arms and allowed her tears to flow freely as they embraced.

"Arachne, I can't promise you that my ability will have any effect on the outcome, nor can I promise that what I do won't take the curse away entirely. You have to be sure that whatever the outcome you'll be able to live with it, or I won't even attempt to mess with it." She pulled back, making eye contact with Arachne, and placed her hands on either shoulder to get her point across. "My ability will only take you so far, and it will be up to you to do the rest."

"I understand. What do we do first?"

"Come with me," Pandora answered. "It's up to you if you would like Morpheus present."

Nervous about being alone with a stranger and unsure about what she had planned to do with her, Arachne made her choice. She looked at Morpheus who was seated with his hands folded in front of him with a tightened grasp. She understood from his body language what he would choose. "I should like it if Morpheus came with us," she said decidedly.

"Very well. This way."

Morpheus immediately came to Arachne's side and took her hand. They followed Pandora up the steps to the platform where her jar set.

As they got closer, Arachne realized that the jar was enormous, and she wondered how it was ever carried as a wedding gift. It was several feet over Morpheus's head, and he dwarfed her. It was a simple design, a plain rose-colored clay with no ornamentation other than the symbols that had been carved into it. There was a flat stone lid that fit on top and two rounded handles on either side which were also covered with symbols.

Pandora pointed to it as they got closer. "It wasn't always this big nor did it have all the carvings. But each curse or evil I take back adds a symbol, some larger than others. The size of the jar changes also as I make my collections."

She led them around the side of the jar down a few stairs and to a platform where there was a small archway. Arachne looked behind her at the jar once more and realized the symbols not only covered the jar but also the platform it was on and trailed to the walls surrounding the cave.

The enormity of Pandora's situation sank in as they traveled into her living quarters. Every effort had been made to see to her comfort in this room. The room was neat and serviceable with beautiful art and silky fabrics adorning the stone walls. She walked to a large table filled with all manner of herbs, oils, and crystals and a large book with handwritten notes. She pointed to a large chair to the right of the table.

"Arachne, you sit here. Morpheus, if you don't mind giving us some space and sitting over by the fireplace."

"Of course," he said. He looked at Arachne and bowed his head. "Let me know if you need me."

Arachne nodded then looked back to Pandora who was preparing some items on her table. "I think it's going to be best imbibing something you always have with you. The items I gave Athena were meant for young children as a temporary solution until they grow into adults and can choose for themselves what they want their lives to look like. But since you already know that, it might be best to give you a sigil."

"Which is?"

"Basically, a symbol made just for you that signifies your intent. You wish to regain balance in your life between the two sides of yourself, and that is where we'll start." Pandora mixed a few things in a mortar from the bottles in front of her and crushed them with her pestle, which released a calming fragrance of lavender and sage. Once candles were lit, she pulled a chair up in front of her and took Arachne's hands. "I'm going to need you to close your eyes and concentrate. Focus on what I'm telling you. Envision it in your mind. When the symbol finds you, you may notice some discomfort depending on the area of your body it gravitates to. Once the sigil is placed on you, I will absorb the negative aspects of your curse, and then we will take it to the jar. Are you ready?"

"I think so. I mean, what is the worst that could happen?"

Pandora shot a pointed look at Morpheus then moved her questioning gaze to Arachne. "Do you really want me to answer that question?"

Morpheus's calm voice interrupted Pandora before she could continue. "What she means to say is that no matter what happens, you will have a place here if you choose it, should things not go as planned."

"And what Morpheus meant to say was that you can plan things all you want, but sometimes the Fates get involved and like to stir things up for us. The gods and goddesses all have their so called 'plans' which don't always align with what a person wants or needs. So yes, he is right to say that you would have a home here if you chose it. However, I want you to focus on something more powerful than any magick ever was or could be."

"What is that?"

"Hope." She looked down at her stomach and smoothed her hands over it. "Hope for how things could be. Hope for a world without pain and suffering. Hope that you can live the life you want without judgement or persecution. Hope will get you through everything that life can throw at you, Arachne. Don't ever lose sight of yours. It is the most powerful magick this world will be gifted with and that you will ever wield. Let's begin."

10

Arachne had spent her life struggling with a curse that caused her agony and had lived through it thus far. But not knowing what type of pain to expect, if any, bothered her in a much more profound way now. Perhaps the sign of weakness had more to do with the fact that she now had someone in her life to watch over her. She didn't care what it was or what it looked like to anyone; she wanted the comfort of his touch.

She pulled her hands from Pandora's. "Would it be alright if I had Morpheus behind me? I think it would help me to feel his support when we do this."

Pandora nodded. "Of course."

Morpheus didn't need to be asked twice. He moved behind Arachne and placed his hands on her shoulders. His thumbs moved rhythmically along the sides and back of her neck, instantly relaxing her. It would make whatever happened to her much more bearable.

"Okay, I'm ready now." Arachne took Pandora's hands once more, completing the circle between them.

"Close your eyes, Arachne. Envision the life you seek. In this life, you control your power as well as your destiny. It completes you. Through this control, you find happiness and joy."

Arachne took what Pandora was saying to heart and focused on what it would feel like to control her powers and to change at will. She let the feeling of empowerment move through her body and jolted when she realized her change was coming.

"Don't worry about changing, it is often part of the process," Pandora said. "I've seen all manner of creature, so you won't upset or disgust me."

Arachne nodded then felt Morpheus's gentle squeeze on her shoulders. As the change occurred, their hands shifted to accommodate her body turning into the spider, never breaking the circle they had formed in front and behind her. The pain was easier to bear with them giving her strength, and she concentrated on the words that Pandora recited.

"Both of your forms are beautiful in their own way, and both serve a purpose to you and others. It's time to balance the two sides of yourself and bring them together into one soul. When in the form of one, the other is always connected and present. Each takes its turn when called upon, and when one is drained, the other will take over to carry you throughout your immortal life."

Images flickered in her mind behind her eyes as she focused on something mundane. Her eyelids were gone now, and Arachne could feel the pressure and warmth of Morpheus standing behind her, his hands on the place where her spindly legs attached to the upper part of her body where her shoulders used to be. Pandora had a hold of the ends of her upper legs, continuing with her meditation as if nothing had changed.

"Welcome the magick, Arachne. Allow it to come to you whenever you desire to channel your gift. The symbol your heart chooses will represent balance and connection between the two halves. Once you realize the shape, it will find the best place to connect with you."

Without her eyes closed and the panoramic vision she had of the space, it was hard to find a spot in the room without items that her mind naturally focused on. There was the orange flame in the fireplace swaying as it popped and the stunning red satin on the bed where Pandora slept. There were tapestries on the wall, one of which she recognized as something she designed, and the calm, serene face of her hostess as she meditated with her. Her mind continued to wander; she needed something to aid her focus.

Looking over to the table where Pandora had her supplies, she focused on the largest thing present and allowed her mind to blur.

It didn't take long once she was no longer distracted. "It's starting," Arachne's raspy voice filled the room. Another squeeze from both Pandora and Morpheus filled her heart with joy. She had found her people. Others who could share her life, no matter which personification she happened to be in. Friends that could balance her, no matter the form she took. She felt it to her core, that she was in the right place.

The burning started out as a tickling sensation then warmed like a muscle that had been overworked. She kept all her eyes focused on the item on the table even as the pain was excruciating, to the point where it felt as if a brand was searing her tender skin. The pain was limited to her abdomen, and while it was hard to sense in this form, she felt as if the placement would be from her upper stomach to the top part of her pelvis. The outline of the shape had come first, then it was as if it were being filled in, like one of the figures on her tapestries. Just as the pain was to the point where it would bring tears to her eyes in human form, it ebbed. She felt the pressure on the upper and lower parts of her leg lighten, realizing that both Pandora and Morpheus had been squeezing to balance out the pain. Balance… That is what she had focused on. That is what she hoped she had received.

Her body was changing back, but it felt different to her. The change was smoother, less chaotic. Legs and arms slid back into place without as much as a thought, and when she looked at Pandora with human eyes, she saw tears streaming down her face. When Pandora opened her eyes, her pupils had separated into smaller circles of green, mimicking the eyes Arachne had in spider form.

"I will need help getting to the jar," she said calmly. "I can't see very clearly right now."

"It takes some getting used to," Arachne said as she rose to take her arm. Morpheus went to the other side, and they walked toward the jar room with Pandora between them.

"I'm glad I don't have to keep it long," she said. "I don't know how you did it. If you could guide me to the front of the jar, I can open my eyes there."

They led her to the front of the vessel, and she placed her hands on the surface of the jar, with her forehead touching as well. She recited some lines in an ancient dialect that was familiar to Arachne but that she didn't fully understand. A rumbling came from the jar, a churning sound as Pandora hugged it. The symbols etched on its surface lit up and flashed in either direction with a powerful and stomach-dropping pulse. There was a tinkling sound, and Arachne looked down where two gold coins lay at Pandora's feet.

Pandora's shoulders drooped, and she pulled in a deep breath. Stepping back, she looked at Pandora with her corneas, now single circles of green and smiled. "The transfer was made. Did you feel the sigil being formed?"

Arachne nodded. "I believe so. With her back turned to Morpheus, she pulled her peplos open and pulled it aside, revealing one half of the symbol in bold red on her stomach. She would have to get a better look at it later, but from what she could see and what she felt when it burned into her, the image reached from below her breasts to the top of her pelvis.

"The shape has a point, perhaps a star," Pandora mused. "I like the color that was added, that doesn't usually happen."

"I didn't have eyelids to close, so I needed to focus on things in the room during the process. Perhaps that has something to do with it."

Morpheus bent down to pick up the coins then handed them to Pandora. She held one up and spoke pointedly to Arachne. "This one is for your trip back. You will need to give it to Charon, and without it, you won't be able to leave here. These coins can't be duplicated, and there is no one else in the Underworld who is allowed to distribute them. The process we just went through is the only way they are created, do you understand?"

Arachne nodded and accepted the coin in her open palm. Pandora held up the second coin.

"This coin is identical to its partner and is meant to be placed in a jar that looks similar to this one. The lid can be removed from that jar and the coin dropped in before putting it back in place. Think of it as payment for services rendered. It is yours to do with as you wish, however, I would be forever grateful if you would see the quest through and place it where it belongs."

"Of course I will," Arachne said. "Tell me where I need to go."

Pandora hugged her, turning slightly to the side so she could get closer to Arachne with her huge belly. "Thank you so much, you have no idea what this means to me. Morpheus can show you the way, he is familiar with where you need to go."

"I appreciate you doing what you could, Pandora."

"It was my pleasure. Remember, the way you harness your power and how you use it is up to you. Like with anything, it will take practice to see exactly what changes have been made. Anytime you want to change to one form or the other, use the symbol as a starting point for your meditation."

Arachne nodded then turned to Morpheus and placed her hand in his.

"Are you ready?"

"I am," she answered. Ready as she would ever be. She worried about this next step in her adventure. What if she still couldn't control her power? What if the changes that came were something that made things worse for her? After walking back through the corridor and out into the cave opening, Morpheus's wings spread without a thought, and she wondered if one day she would be able to make the conversion in the same way. If her immortality was still intact, she at least would have the time to find out. But after so long of knowing her limitations and working with them, the change in them was unnerving.

He pulled her into his arms and took to flight, far over the heads of the lost. She couldn't help but stare in pity at the countless numbers of souls living out this part of their existence without purpose or passion. For as much loneliness as she had suffered at the hands of her curse, it was a far better alternative than living a life without her art. She couldn't even imagine it.

The symbol on her stomach started to burn, and the sense that she was being pulled down to the ground was present. It was as if a string was tied to her waist and being pulled upon. She looked down to the ground, to an oasis among the wastelands. A small pool of water with a single tree was present, along with a lone figure sitting beneath it. The sensation of being pulled heightened, and she looked down once more on the figure.

She could see long dark hair, but it was the dress that caught her eye. A favorite shade of plum to match the fruit they grew on their farm. The similarity in size and stature was hard to determine with the woman seated, but the tugging was insistent. She made her choice.

"Morpheus, I should like to speak to that woman."

11

At first, Morpheus looked confused, then worry crossed his brow. "I would advise against that. The souls can be desperate and do harm, even if they don't intend to."

"I understand, but I feel compelled to have a word with her. I think she's my sister."

Tears filled her eyes at the thought. After all the years and after all she had been through at the hands of her twin, she could finally make peace. Morpheus circled back and lowered in order to get a better look. Arachne's tears flowed in earnest. She didn't care what had been done in the past, she could hug her sister again.

"People change in this place. Please don't be hopeful that she will be the same person. That is an exercise in futility."

They landed on the outer edge of the pool. Arachne looked around, but there was no one else in sight. The woman was alone.

She stood from her sitting position at the tree then took a hesitant step forward. "Arachne? Is that you?"

Arachne ran like the child she had once been into the arms of a woman who had been her mirror image so many years before. The dress that had been her sister's favorite hung from a bony frame that was weakened with age. Her long raven hair was sprinkled with silvery gray, similar to the shimmering threads that Arachne used in her tapestries. But it was her. And when she embraced her, she drew in the long lost scent of jasmine, something she always avoided in the centuries that she lived without her. The scent was no longer of loss and pain; it was as if she had come home.

"Oh Ana, I thought I would never see you again," Arachne cried. As much as she had been wronged, the next sentence was genuine. "I've missed you."

Ana pulled back from the embrace, putting her spotted hands on either side of Arachne's face. "You haven't aged a day." The tears tracked down her wrinkled cheeks, making Arachne cry all the harder. Morpheus, who had kept a watchful eye on the exchange, took a few more steps away to give them privacy. Ana glanced up and acknowledged him with a nod then looked back into Arachne's eyes. Dropping her forehead to Arachne's, she said the words that Arachne had been waiting centuries to hear.

"I'm so sorry. What I did to you, how it hurt our family. The pain." The tears flowed anew, and the sisters embraced while the sobs wracked their bodies. When they had both calmed themselves enough, they walked to the tree hand in hand and lowered to a seated position. Ana had her back against the tree as Arachne sat cross-legged in front of her. They kept their hands clasped and eyes locked.

"I watched what it did to you, heard the screams at night before I left to live with my husband. I made you a promise, but I felt that it would be easier just to move on. I was wrong. How do you move on without the other half of yourself? The other part of your soul?"

"Anastasia, I took the curse willingly."

Ana shook her head. "You took it willingly because you thought I would be back to help you remove it. I left and didn't look back. I abandoned my own sister!" She was sobbing uncontrollably, the tears from them both washing the pain of the centuries of hurt away. Arachne had always assumed she was the one that lived with the curse, but she was wrong. She adapted, she survived. She embraced and worked with the changes. For the most part, she had been happy. She saw now that her sister had a worse curse than she could have ever imagined. Living your eternal life out in solitude, ruminating over regrets that could never be resolved, was something that she wouldn't wish on her worst enemy. Arachne leaned forward and hugged her then sat back down.

"Ana, it's okay. I'm okay." Arachne squeezed her hands for emphasis.

"The curse is part of who I am, and I've learned to accept it. I've taken steps to gain more confidence in my ability, and I'm in a good place. But I always regretted not being able to say goodbye. I came to your funeral but stood in the shadows, as I did for all the members of your family."

Her sister's surprise was evident. It was as if she hadn't thought of that. Leaving behind a legacy, but spending eternity focused on the one thing you should have changed, had to be the worst thing a soul could go through. For whatever her sister did to her, she didn't deserve this fate. Arachne stood up, pulling on Ana's hands and helping her to rise.

"I'm getting you out of here," Arachne said. "Ana, I realize now I forgave you long ago. You didn't need to stay here and do this to yourself. It's time you move on and reunite with your family."

"Family?" Ana acted as if a fog had lifted. "My beautiful children and grandchildren."

"You have generations beyond them," Arachne smiled. "So many beautiful families, Ana. And I see your essence in all of them, which makes me so proud."

"You've watched over them? My family?"

Arachne nodded. "I have, and I will continue to. But I couldn't live with myself if I allowed you to languish here when I had the power to do something about it." Arachne looked over to Morpheus then waved him over to where they stood. When he came up beside them, Arachne made the introductions. "Ana, I would like you to meet Lord Morpheus, God of Dreams. Morpheus, this is my sister, Anastasia."

He took Ana's hand and bowed over it. "It's a pleasure to meet you."

Arachne placed one of the coins given to her by Pandora into Morpheus's hand. "I would like for you to take this and my sister to the ferryman so she can continue her journey."

Morpheus glanced over with a tilt of his head but said nothing.

She continued. "She doesn't belong here. The reasons she remained here were a misunderstanding, and I can't live my life knowing that she is here."

"That leaves one coin…" His eyes were filled with worry, and his jaw was clenched.

She placed her hand on his arm to calm him. "I realize that, but it's the right thing for me. If you could do me this favor, I would be forever grateful. I can wait here while you make the trip."

Morpheus nodded. "Because it is your wish. I'm doing this for you, only for you."

Arachne turned from him and took a step toward her sister. Ana had watched the exchange with curiosity then leaned into Arachne's open arms.

"Morpheus will take good care of you. Once you get to the pier, he will give you the coin that will take you back to the House of Judgement. You will be able to be judged now with a lighter heart knowing that we have resolved things."

"Thank you for everything you have done for me, Arachne. Now and in the past."

"Safe travels, my sister. Give my love to your family."

Morpheus picked Ana up with care and then looked over to Arachne. "I'll be back soon, and then we are going to talk."

Arachne smiled. "I knew that was coming."

Morpheus shook his head, trying and failing to hold back his exasperation. He flew off with Ana waving to her as they left, which made Arachne smile all the more. Why she was smiling when faced with being stuck in the Underworld forever was beyond her, but at this moment in time, she felt as if a great weight had been lifted. Forgiving her sister was the right thing to do, even if she paid for it for eternity.

12

Arachne sat at Ana's tree, staring into the waters of the pond and watching the scenes from her life reflect in the ripples. She was sure each person that sat there must see something else entirely since the images were those of her own past experiences. In the time that she was there, no other souls came near, and she was left to her introspection. Having your faults play over in your mind, with no other soul to commiserate with, was a special kind of torture. She understood if left there for any length of time, just what it might do to her mind. What it probably did to her sister's.

Morpheus was impressive to watch from this distance. Much like an eagle, he soared in the ashy skies above. He came straight for her and landed smoothly within feet of where she sat. He took a few steps forward and held out his hand for hers. The electricity between them was hard to deny as he helped her to rise.

"I waited until the ferry left with her," he said. "Her head was clearer when she made way, and she wanted to let you know how much she appreciated everything you've done for her. She also said I should tell you to 'remember the pond.'"

Arachne smiled at the reference. Morpheus tilted his head then glanced over to the pond they stood by. It was an exact replica of the one she and her sister spent hours near when growing up, but her message had more to do with Morpheus, strange as that was. Her sister was referencing the day they both caught trout when fishing. Ana's was a beautiful rainbow, while Arachne's was dull and brown. Arachne had wanted to throw hers back, but Ana persuaded her against it, insisting that it was a "fine catch." She would never forget her words—that it didn't matter what the fish looked like, it was what was inside that counted.

Their fish were gushed over equally by their mother. Once cooked, you couldn't tell the difference between, and from that day on, they used the phrase "remember the pond" as a reference to giving people a chance. Ana was letting her know that she thought Morpheus was someone worth keeping in her life. With all she had seen in her dreams as well as all he had done for her in the Underworld, she would have to agree.

"I do remember the pond," Arachne said quietly. "I suppose that is why she chose this place. But I certainly wouldn't want to stay here anywhere near as long as she did."

"It's best to resolve regret before your soul moves to the next phase," Morpheus said quietly. "I have a feeling that had your sister known what was at stake for you by giving her that coin, she would have told you to leave her here."

"Yes, but then regret would have been mine to bear. I'm glad I had this chance to resolve this. I'd have it no other way." Arachne yawned and rubbed her eyes. She was having a hard time keeping them open.

"I'm glad you feel that way." His face held an emotion that she was having a hard time grasping. She yawned once more. "By the looks of it, I should get you somewhere a little more comfortable."

"What of the final coin? The quest Pandora would have me complete?"

"There is time for her quest, and most decisions are better made after a night of rest. The answers will come to you in your sleep."

"You're sure?"

He suppressed a laugh and shook his head. "I believe I am the most qualified to make such a statement. I am the God of Slumber and Dreams, after all."

Heat pinkened her cheeks as she readied herself to be pulled into his arms once more. "Well, since that is the case, some rest does sound good. Is there a place nearby we can go?"

"There are any number of places we could go, but while you are here, it would mean a lot to me to show you my realm."

The opportunity to see where he lived was too good to pass up. She slid her arm around his neck nestling closer into his chest. "I would be honored to see it. I'm ready when you are."

He pulled her in with a sigh, moving the hairs on the top of her head ever so slightly. Was that the touch of his lips she felt? She dared not breathe, lest she break the spell he had woven that tied her to his side. If she could remain in his arms, she might be tempted to stay an eternity. If anyone could cause her to turn her back on her responsibilities, it would be this god that had crept into her soul and stolen her heart. It made her wonder if once seeing his home she would ever want to leave.

The journey was quick as the land of lost souls was on the outskirts of his domain. At first, she wasn't sure about postponing Pandora's quest, but the more she thought about it, the more she realized Morpheus was right. She was exhausted, and bad things always happened when she was tired. There was also the likelihood that he needed to follow up on things that he had pushed aside to help her. Knowing the benefits of dreams and the tranquility that could be obtained from them, she felt sheepish keeping him away from his duties. But she couldn't help herself, she was curious about him. Seeing where he lived would be a way to get to know him better. Perhaps the walls he kept up, in all but their dreams, would be lowered when he was home.

His entrance accommodated his wingspan, and he flew directly between the towering black pillars and beyond the pristine marble floors. There were low-lying fire pits that gave both heat and light, but reflections stayed close to the ground. Flapping backward, he slowed their speed and landed near a shimmering black throne that looked as though it was carved from the darkness itself. When he placed her feet on the ground, she stepped toward it and ran her hands over the ornate carvings that covered it.

"It's incredible, I've never seen anything quite like it."

"It's obsidian," Morpheus replied. "Formed when molten lava cools quickly. We use it for several things down here. The ceiling, in fact, is made from it. High enough that you can hardly see it and dark enough to give you the illusion it's the open night sky. The diamonds were added after, and I keep those aglow with magick." He slid his hand in hers and led her through an enormous door made of the same material. It opened with a wave of his hand.

"I didn't want you to leave without seeing my home," he said softly. "I never bring anyone here, other than the creatures I create of course. In fact, you're the first from the Earth realm to see it."

Arachne smiled, unsure about how she felt about his admission. The plan was always that she would do what it took to get her life back, but she wasn't sure anymore if that was truly what she wanted. Knowing he was real and not just a figment of her imagination had complicated things for her. He ushered her through the entryway and closed the door behind them.

"My library is this way," he said with pride. "This is where I do all my research. I started it when Hecate and I were looking into how to help Pandora and Epimetheus, and now goddesses and gods I'm friendly with help keep it stocked. I house books from each decade to use as references for the dreams that people have. Some of them get quite elaborate."

"I would imagine they could." The thought made the heat rise to her cheeks and upset her in a way that was surprising. Remembering things that they had done in her dreams bothered her in a way it hadn't before. If she lived out her fantasies with him, sexual or otherwise, what was stopping any other person on the planet from doing it as well? The possibilities flustered her in a way she couldn't articulate. The knowing smirk on his face almost upset her more. He knew what she was thinking.

"While dreams do sometimes include sex or the act of making love, those acts have never involved me, except with you. You're the only person, god, monster, human, or otherwise who has seen me in my true form in a dream." He moved closer and tilted his head lower. His warm breath tickled her ear as he whispered. "The only person who has felt my body above and below her. Inside her."

Arachne closed her eyes. Her pulse quickened. Images flooded into her mind as she relived their experiences. Kissing recklessly in a waterfall. Laughing as they cooked a meal together. Both of them naked and her riding him with wild abandon on a bed of clover.

The tone and cadence of his voice filled every cell in her body. "You are the only person who shall ever do so. Everyone else sees an illusion comfortable to their mind alone. There is never anything physical with them."

She was still processing the meaning of his words. He grasped her chin lightly and tipped her head until their eyes locked. "They don't see me as I am, that is important to me. It's easy enough for me to conjure an illusion to take my place once I know where the dream is going. That is how I am able to spend time with you and still do my job. Others get an illusion, but you have always been with me in reality."

She released her breath, satisfied with his explanation, and reached for him. Her body slipped easily into his embrace, and she tucked smoothly beneath his cheek which he then rested on the top of her head. Even though she was in the most feared place in the Universe, she felt at peace with him, like nothing could touch her. The Morpheus she knew would never let any harm come to her. She knew that as well as her own name.

"I have another place to show you, but if I take you there, we won't be leaving until the morning." His voice had lowered an octave, and the deep notes of it connected to her soul. He affected her in ways she was only beginning to understand, but she knew what he was implying.

She took a deep breath, centering herself and searching for the spider form that typically showed itself by this late hour. She could feel it inside, but there wasn't the same sense of urgency or restlessness. It was as if the form was finally comfortable in the realization that it wasn't going anywhere, that it was no longer part of a curse but of a choice. Staying quiet was based on mutual trust and understanding that it wouldn't be purged. Arachne felt equally sure that it wouldn't show itself until it was called upon, so for the first time in her life, she knew that she would start and end the night in the form of her choosing.

The idea that this would be the first time they were together in true physical form wasn't lost on her. They had done things in their dreams that removed all ideas of modesty, but she was still excited and nervous to know his true touch. She was ready to see if her curse could truly be controlled, even when she wasn't in complete control of her senses. Her response was husky and laced with desire. She was beyond ready.

"I hope the place you want to show me involves a bed and taking these clothes off."

The laugh that erupted from him surprised and delighted her. His smile couldn't possibly be bigger. It would be her mission from now on to make him do it more often.

"It's as if you read my mind."

They couldn't walk fast enough. He pulled her down the hall, laughing as they went through a black door trimmed with red which he opened with a wave. Every inch of space was red with dots of black, and it took her a moment to realize that the rugs they were walking on were flower blooms.

"Poppies," he said. "They are the only thing that aids my sleep."

The recognizable fragrance came to her then, earth and smoke, just as her eyes focused on the brilliant flowers that covered the floors. He carried their fragrance with him to the dreams he touched, and she now understood their power. The simplicity of the black furniture surrounded by the blooms left no other distractions to the senses. She could spend days here in quiet solitude. "It's completely relaxing. I should like to weave this one day." Her hand cupped his cheek, and his gravitated to her waist. "Thank you for sharing this space with me. For helping me."

"Anything for you, Arachne," he whispered. He lowered his head, his lips hovering over hers. "What's mine is yours. Anything I have or can obtain, including my heart. I truly mean that."

She lost herself in his embrace as he carried her to the large poster bed centered in the room. The silken red fabric was cool to her touch as he laid her across the top all the while keeping eye contact with her. "I've been with you countless times. Both in your dreams and my imagination, yet nothing has prepared me for this moment." The nervous crack in his voice endeared him to her even more. "Please tell me you desire me as much as I do you. That you are ready for this."

Her answer was not much more than an exhale. "Beyond ready, my love."

Relief washed over him, relaxing his stance. His hands caressed skin and fingers slipped beneath her shoulder strap, as he lowered the fabric with a whisper to her hips. He traced the pads of his fingertips on the outline of the sigil Pandora had placed on her body. The warmth of his touch extended far up under her breasts then low against the top of her thighs, which was when she realized it was much larger than she had originally thought.

"The color is perfect," he whispered. "It's as if the poppies were redesigned and placed here. I should like to spend some time in this garden."

She was mesmerized by his touch, her upper body pressing into the bed beneath her by the weight of his gaze. She lifted her hips, allowing him to pull the remainder of her dress from her body. It was then that she was able to see what had been placed on her stomach.

"It's so big." She pulled in a breath as the tears welled. It was important that her voice not reflect any disappointment. She had chosen this.

His fingertips continued to trace the lines on the symbol, worshiping her body with his hands and placing kisses along the image he admired. He looked for her reaction in between each caress. "Does it hurt? Tender at all?"

She shook her head. "No, if anything more sensitive. Your touch… It feels good." Her admission brought heat to her face and fire to his eyes. His smile was barely perceivable as his fingers continued their journey.

"It looks like an hourglass."

She laid back and allowed his fingers to soothe her worries. "That was what I was focused on when the change started." He continued to trace around the edge, the kisses now replaced with flicks of his tongue sending warmth throughout her body. The electricity of it was bringing things to attention, things which were new and exciting for her. Stilling his hand, she savored the moment.

"I think before this goes any further, you have some things to take off."

One moment he was looking at her with hooded eyes, the next he was gloriously naked.

"Better?" His hand started its pattern once more as he leaned in closer to kiss her abdomen.

"Much. That is some talent."

His lips lowered, traveling nearer to the places that she touched when she dreamed of him. So lost in the feeling, she almost missed what he said next.

"We each have our abilities. I've only just begun to show you mine, my bloom."

Sliding along her length and pushing her deeper into the layers of fabric piled on his bed, he kissed her fully for the first time in their true physical form. The cool satin texture of the linens beneath her and the warmth of his firm body above her had her wishing she could stop time like the hourglass she now had on her body. It was a sensory delight, heightened by her new symbol that he was now rubbing as he moved against her. The stirrings of passion were being stoked. Her deepest desires, woven by the god who had stolen her heart, were coming true. That the dreams alone would never be enough moving forward would be a worry for another time. One more look into his eyes and she was lost; her heart was his.

"Anything in my power to give you is yours, you need only ask."

"I can now live my life as I wish to, and you helped make that happen. It is a gift I can never repay."

"There is no need, such is the nature of a gift. And you are mine." His hand came to her cheek, thumb rubbing against her lips as he watched the movement. His voice cracked with the weight of emotion. "You have captured me body and soul. I fear you only need to say a word, and I will make it a command. Such exquisite surrender for a god to embrace."

Cupping the sides of his chiseled face, she drew him down and tasted the salt of his lips. They had shared experiences in her dreams, kissed more times than she could count, but this was different. The silk of him against her, the rasp of his sigh, the smoky musk of his skin converged into a singular spark that ignited her. The dreams had allowed her to focus on one facet of him at a time, but being with him in real life, she admired the entire gem. The dreams alone would never be enough for her again.

They relearned their bodies in the reality of their moment, taking pleasure in the sights and sounds that made the experience unique compared to that which they had shared in her dream state. And when they found their release, the pulses of ecstasy that they each bore witness to, the joy that filled them, provided a sense of calm that not even the poppies could duplicate.

There was no sense of time in Morpheus's arms. Each hour blended into the next until they had succumbed to his crafted slumber. Arachne woke before he did and spent some time watching emotions play against his timeless face. As she watched him in respite, she wondered what the Lord of Dreams dreamt of. She rather hoped it was her.

13

Slipping away from the bed they shared, Arachne walked the hall outside Morpheus's room as to not wake him. He looked so peaceful, and she had the impression he wasn't able to sleep much with all the demands on his time. She found that transforming in and out of spider form wasn't hard once she used the symbol as her focus. Placing her hand on the red hourglass and closing her eyes, she connected with the artist inside and thought of the things she wanted to create, urging the creature forward. Within a few hours, she had transformed countless times in various sizes and created several intricate webs in the corners of his enormous halls.

Peeking through the doorway and seeing Morpheus still asleep, she snicked the door shut. Keeping her tread light, she retraced her steps in the direction that she remembered coming from the night before. The space in the throne room was lighter now, as if his palace was on the same solar schedule as the Earth realm. Much like the place she called home, there were all manner of creature bustling about. They hardly gave her a second glance as she made her way to the place where Morpheus's throne was centered. Awed by the enormity of his importance, her feet padded gingerly up the steps toward his seat. After a quick glance, assuring that the creatures weren't paying her any mind, she sat on the intricately carved seat on a padded cushion covered in midnight fabric.

The obsidian throne faced the entrance they had come through the night before as well as the tapestries, the detail of which went unnoticed by her until now. There was a prickling in her shoulders and a slight sinking in her stomach as she recognized scenes. Confusion clouded her mind as she spied the tapestry that she had sold to Cassandra which detailed the experiences she had with Morpheus in his true form. Next to it hung the waterfall scene that she had sold to a young man as a gift for his wife. Also, a landscape purchased by an old woman with a thick accent not weeks before.

Every tapestry created from a dream with him hung in mid-air on either side of his throne. It made her wonder how many other forms he had approached her in, with or without a purchase. The sinking had turned into a churning as she realized, once again, he had lied to her about who he really was.

His footsteps, then the weight of his hands on her shoulder, startled her from her thoughts.

"About those…"

She tipped her head and shrugged her shoulder toward her ear, as if to shake off his touch. The warmth of his hand paused then slid away. He cleared his throat then made his way to the side of the throne. His tone was questioning.

"I thought you would be happy that I had these on display?" Her lack of response caused him to step back. The creatures who had once filled the room had disappeared. Hesitation now flavored his tone. "Touched that I always had them visible in a reality I was forced to endure without you. I love you, Arachne, with every fiber of who I am. No matter the form you take or the form I shift into. Since my creation, I have never felt this way for another."

He was scrambling, but she kept her response cool. "I'm not sure there is much you can say about them or this situation that will make me feel secure."

"Meaning?"

She turned in the seat and looked up at him with irritation. She couldn't believe after all they had been through, after all she had explained about her own journey, that she needed to explain this topic once more. "Meaning, Morpheus, that you lied to me more than once about who you are."

"And what I am," he added. His tone had a bite, which surprised her. "I had to. I don't have the luxury of living as a human or loving one for that matter. I did everything within my power to give you what you dreamed of and supported your creativity in a way that no one ever did. That was how I showed you love."

"You speak of love as if you understand it," she snapped. "Showing love is so much more than supporting someone's dreams. It's about honesty and sharing experiences. Of walking life's paths together in harmony."

"I gave that to you, each moment we spent together."

"No, Morpheus. What you gave me was a beautiful illusion. A version of yourself that you believed would make me happy. And perhaps it did for a time, but I need more than that. I need to know the person I give my heart to, inside and out, flaws as well as perfection."

"You know me better than anyone."

Arachne looked into his eyes, seeing the truth of his words in their depths. Even with that, she needed more than what he was offering.

"I'm sure you believe that to be true. But I've grown tired of allowing others to manipulate my heart, only to obligate me to forgive them for breaking it. Knowing and accepting someone is no longer enough for me. The price for my love is untainted truth and honesty, and I can no longer trust those who lie to me."

"They aren't lies, merely truths with partial information." He tried his best to make light of the situation, and if she wasn't so angry, that admission would have made her laugh.

"See that's the thing, I need truths with all the information. I must weigh them on their own merit then make a decision on who I give my heart to. Trust is a huge part of love for me, and it was broken too many times by people who were supposed to love me, no matter what happened in the world around us."

Sighing, he knelt by her side and placed his hand on the arm of the chair. It was as close as he could get to touching her without laying a finger on her. "I agree trust is important, and I apologize for making light of that." He sounded sincere, but was he only saying what she wanted to hear? "I struggle with my purpose, with the way I was created, and I was trying to protect you the best I knew how."

She knew she needed to get her point across. Her life would never be her own until she did. "You just took someone to the ferry who let me down centuries ago. I was born into that family and felt obligated to love my sister long after she had broken my heart. But love shouldn't be based on obligation or a warped sense of loyalty. Love is a choice, and I can choose to love you or leave you based on what I need in my life at this moment. And if we don't have trust between us, you make that decision for me easy."

"Don't loose your venom on me, I wasn't the one who caused you to be condemned to the life you are now living. That was entirely your sister's fault. And against my better judgement, when you wanted to seek change to what had been done to you, I came to your aid."

His statement caused her to stand. Shocked by her abrupt movement, he followed suit. His stance screamed defiance, but his eyes told another story. She had surprised him.

"First of all, I forgave my sister in order to heal myself. I did it for me, for my journey. I happen to love my life and who I am as well as the art I create. The repercussions of the curse were unexpected, yes, but I learned to live within its parameters." Her voice cracked as she continued. "I built a life worth living with what I had to work with. But then I met you, which caused me to want more than I could dare hope for. The moment I realized it might be possible, I sought it out without fear. I knew what I wanted, and I went for it, even when I feared there was a chance that I could lose it all."

She straightened her spine, and her hands gravitated to her hips. "You said you helped me against your better judgement, so my question to you is what do you really want? And what's holding you back from seeking it out? What is it you fear, Morpheus?"

Confused by her question, he shook his head. "Nothing, I'm a god. Fear is a human emotion, which I create for those who seek it. It's also used by the gods and goddesses as a way to control..."

"Control?"

"That isn't what I meant..."

"There are other words for it, Morpheus. Guide. Sway. Restrain."

Arachne pulled in a breath and centered herself. He wasn't picking up on her point, and it was frustrating her. Much as she wished she could pull back the sands in the hourglass, it was too late. For the first time in her existence, she needed to stand up for herself. "Morpheus, my fear is that you will never truly understand what it means to love someone. To realize the compromises that must be made to earn their devotion every day. To trust them body and soul, without hesitation and to feel in your heart that they will always be there for you."

"You are life to me, Arachne. The air that I breathe. Everything I've done for you must show you that."

"It's not enough." The look on his face was that of shock, but he was listening. She continued. "I have everything to lose by staying with you—the world I'm a part of, the business I run, the friends I have. I was willing to choose that, but trust is the line in the sand that I must make, especially with the King of Dreams who can manipulate others with a thought. Manipulate… Another word for control."

"I wouldn't do that to you."

"How do I know? Never truly knowing whether I'm being controlled is something I can no longer do. It's perhaps what I fear the most." She left him standing near the throne as she descended the steps. His voice was soft, barely perceived over the haunting echo of her footsteps on the marble as she walked away from him.

"Losing my heart to you is mine."

Arachne stopped her movement and lowered her eyes. Those words from him would have been like water in the desert to her a few months ago, but now they were a mirage. A reality which evaded her. She needed more than his offered illusion. More than dreams. She turned and raised her gaze to him straightening her back as she spoke.

"I need more," she stated flatly. "Most importantly, I need time to think, and I can't do it with you around. I need to finish what I started and go home."

Morpheus's shoulders slumped, and his head fell forward with its weight as he filled his lungs with a calming breath. She could sense the change between lover and god within seconds. He tipped his head back up, their gaze locking. "As you wish. We will leave as soon as you are ready." Her lover was gone. Lord Morpheus was back.

Irritated, she responded without hesitation. "I'm ready now," Arachne said. "If you let me know where to go, I can find Epimetheus myself."

The breath he took in through his nostrils was telling. An attempt to regain his patience. She was glad to see the rise in him. It gave her hope he would think about what she had said. "Don't be ridiculous. I wouldn't allow anyone to wander around alone in my domain, it is much too dangerous. Give me a few minutes."

The thought was not lost on Arachne that she could use the coin in her possession to get out of the Underworld on her own, however, she had made a promise to Pandora that she would take it to her husband, Epimetheus. Knowing that Pandora was counting on her to relay the message, which started "one day closer, my love" after dropping the coin off with him, had her agreeing to whatever Morpheus suggested. It was his world after all. She was merely a visitor. The thought that her visit was coming to an end, never to return, almost brought her to her knees.

As irritated as she was with him, she had to admit that it felt good to be back in his arms during the flight. No words were spoken as he lifted her, and she placed her hand on his chest. As they flew, and with her cheek cradled against his chest, she had a hard time seeing his expression and took a moment to enjoy the touch of his lips on her head as well as the almost imperceivable intake of his breath as he pulled in her scent.

Hope was not lost, it seemed, but she needed some space to make sense of it all. Her feelings for him couldn't cloud her decision to think about what they each needed from their relationship.

It was a much quicker journey to the place where Pandora's husband awaited his destiny. It was a cave, much like the one where Pandora lived, but less in the way of accommodations or luxuries. Once she saw him, she understood why. He had no need for it.

Morpheus walked up to the prone man, holding his hand out to Arachne to guide her to his side. "I should like you to meet my…" he paused then and looked at her, clearing his throat before continuing. "My friend, Arachne. She has a message from your wife." Morpheus nodded then took a step back to give them privacy. He knew she had a message but hadn't been part of knowing what it was. That he was giving the couple a little privacy during such a difficult time was something she knew Pandora would appreciate.

Arachne whispered Pandora's message precisely as she was asked, tears coming to her eyes as she witnessed the dazzling smile on the man's face that was born from it. To know the couple had waited so long broke her heart. Looking around the room and seeing the lack of carved symbols as compared to Pandora's space crushed her. There were way more in Pandora's realm than there were here. It must be that most of the people Pandora helped didn't follow through. Perhaps like Arachne, they, too, used their coins for beloved people they wanted to help along their journey.

She stood before his jar and paused. Dropping the coin in would seal her reliance on Morpheus to leave the Underworld. So many unknowns. The least of which was whether she would be able to retain her spider form long enough to make it home, the greatest involved trusting the man who stood beside her to follow through on getting her there. She looked over to him once more, and he nodded.

"I'll get you home if it's the last thing I do. Trust me."

She lifted the flat lid and held her hand over the opening. Releasing her fingers, she dropped the coin into the earthen container and heard it tink far below the lip on the other coins present inside. The scratching on the surface of the pot took her notice, and she watched as the same shape she had on her abdomen scratched along the surface and became part of the design on the jar. A beautiful poppy red was added, and her's was one of the only colored symbols on the jar. Her part of the deal was complete. Now to see if Morpheus would follow through with his.

Morpheus held out his hand to help her down the step. "Pandora will receive an identical symbol in her realm, so she will know you kept your promise."

"I wondered," she said honestly. "So how much longer for them?"

"When the last evil she is obligated to collect is gathered, she will be reunited with him. Her pregnancy will only end when all ills are collected, and loops are completed only if the person brings their coin here to do so."

"It could be centuries."

"It already has been," he whispered. They walked out of Epimetheus's chamber and into the small entranceway. "But time is irrelevant in the dream world. He's well taken care of, as is she. I can't help but parallel our relationship to theirs. One lives in the dream world, and the other in reality."

Arachne swallowed her response as they moved through the corridor. It wouldn't do any good to dredge up anything more. She had already said her piece. He was onto his next thought.

"We should probably get you back to my palace. I will need to see what I can do about getting another coin from Hades, and it would be more comfortable for you to wait there. I should be able to negotiate with him, but it could take some time."

Arachne shook her head. She was glad she had an alternate plan; it would get her home more quickly. He paused and watched with surprise as she turned into a small spider, scurried around, then popped back into shape.

"I've been practicing off and on all night, and I believe I can hold this smaller form for the time it will take for you to fly me back home as a bat. If you can do me this one last favor, I would appreciate it, Lord Morpheus."

"So, it's Lord Morpheus now?" He shook his head and pinched between his eyes. After a sigh and a shrug of his shoulders, he agreed. "It seems I have no choice."

14

Her plan worked, and their goodbyes were quick. Before she knew it, Arachne had been back at the shop for over a month, and there was still no sign of the bat or any of the customers she now knew were him. While she couldn't be sure that Morpheus hadn't visited in other forms, she hoped that he hadn't gone back on the word he had given when they parted ways. His last words to her were delivered with such longing and despair, it caused her the agony of more sleepless nights. She had been successful in keeping her tears from view until he left her that night but not on any night since. Her only reprieve from them was to be in the form of her creature as she created her art. She had gotten the space she had asked for, but whether it was truly what she wanted was now up for debate.

As her emotions flowed so did her creativity. There had been no end to it since her return to the shop. The number of tapestries created from her memories of him were piled in the corner, and she was starting to run out of excuses as to why they weren't adequate to sell. She couldn't stand the thought of them hanging anywhere but his throne room, and she couldn't be sure it was him purchasing them until they talked.

Thyia worried, as she always did, but kept her opinions to herself. She understood the moodiness of being a creative. They both did. It was one of the reasons they got along so well. But the showroom looked a little sparse, and Thyia was just looking out for their business. Arachne made an effort on some smaller pieces to fill the gap, but they didn't hold her same passion.

The tapestries she poured herself into featured her handsome obsession, in some cases winged but in most presenting as a man. Over time, her anger with him had turned to acceptance with her realization that she also had broken a trust. She had poured her past experiences into a decision that should have been based on his actions alone. He was a god, yes, but like all creatures, he had limitations. In that case, she should have been more understanding, especially considering he never truly lived within humanity like she had. She had condemned him for not being honest about who he really was but never gave him the opportunity to show her. They needed to spend time together in reality to truly know if they were compatible with one another. She knew that now.

There was the added realization that her creativity was fed by her experiences with him, so how could he ever trust she wasn't using him for her art? It seemed to her that the web of lies, both the ones they told each other and themselves, had ensnared them both. Because he was honoring her wishes and staying from her side, she was the only one who could untangle the threads and rework the image. Although he was limited in what he could do in her world, she no longer was. Since the removal of the curse, she was able to change at will and already knew that she was able to live in both realms. It would be her responsibility to bridge the divide and make the connection. It had been what he alluded to in his goodbye.

It would be the first piece created from that thought. Unlike the dreamscapes that she had created before, this scene would be one she wished for, not one she had experienced with him. It took her three straight days and nights to complete the scene depicting both sides of their truth living in harmony with the other. Two worlds blended; two hearts melded.

Putting her faith in Hermes, she hoped that her message would be received with an open heart and mind. She didn't have to wait long to find out. The morning after her delivery was made, in the middle of the first restful sleep she experienced since Morpheus left her side, he flew into her dream with his midnight wings and commanding presence.

After landing steps away from her in the poppy field where she stood, he bowed and then closed the distance. His hands were at his sides, fingers twitching, as if he longed to reach out. The muscles in his jaw clenched as he calmed himself to address her. "I received your gift." His voice crackled with hope that touched her soul. "I came as soon as I could."

"Morpheus, I…"

"You were right. Without trust, how could you ever believe anything I ever said to you?" He took the final step toward her that brought them inches apart. Her arms gravitated toward him as if led by a string, and her hands splayed on his firm chest which nearly caused her to weep with relief. When she looked into his eyes, they were brimming with tears. He cupped her face, his thumbs caressing her jawline as he finished his thought. "Without trust, how could you be certain that my love for you was real? If I didn't assure you that you were the only creature on Earth I opened my heart to, how could you feel confident in our relationship? And as I looked up synonyms for trust, this other one jumped out at me… Hope. Please tell me it isn't lost."

Arachne smiled and pulled his hands from her shoulders, grasping them at her chest and pulling him closer. "It's not, for either of us."

He lifted their clasped hands to his lips and kissed the back of her hand, before drawing them tight to his chest. "I'm so sorry I caused you to question me. It wasn't until I got back home that I realized what you were trying to say."

"I was emotional at the time and wasn't thinking straight, so the time apart did help clarify some things for me as well. I believe I understand you more now than I did."

"You understood me more than you realized," Morpheus said. "No one in this realm has ever seen or spoken to the being I truly am, other than you. Not only did I fall in love with your spirit, but also the way you made me feel when we were together. It was as if every other version of myself was a lie except the one that I was when I was with you."

"I was more myself with you than any other as well. I think what made me uncomfortable was feeling that it had been one-sided, that you had seen the ugliest part of me and heard my most excruciating truths. Somehow, I felt I didn't get the same from you, and I was embarrassed, but I see now that you inviting me into your world and showing me the inner workings of your purpose was just that."

"It was, but it was also in a lot of ways my way of getting you to stay in my world. You asked me what I feared, and I wasn't honest with you. When I told you I helped you against my better judgment, it was because I feared the removal of the curse would change you to the point where we could never be together again. That you would become human and die a mortal death. That somehow, we would change what we had together."

Arachne allowed the tears to fall, the vision of her beautiful Morpheus blurring as he shared his truth.

"But what I realized was that I could never live with myself knowing I didn't do everything within my power to help you achieve whatever you wanted. Even if it meant that you would be taken from my reality."

"You never manipulated anything, only enhanced what I had already been pursuing. That the control I imagined was created by the past experiences I unfairly brought into our relationship. I was allowing fear to hold me back from getting to know you better, for giving us time to truly know if we were compatible."

"I'm pretty sure that we are very compatible."

She slipped her hands from his and put her arms around his shoulders, drawing him in for a kiss. "Not what I meant," she laughed. "But I agree."

He crushed her against him, his body humming with desperation. Her hands smoothed over the terrain of his body, and knowing she was in a dream state was the only thing preventing her from suggesting they take their desires further.

"I never want to be away from you again. Please tell me I still have a place in your life."

"You are my everything, Morpheus. I can't imagine spending eternity with anyone else but you."

"So, does that mean I can pick you up and take you back to my place? As amazing as you feel in the dream world, I long to make love to you in reality. The things I've been dreaming of, the experiences I want to share with you…"

"Like what?"

"Things you could only ever imagine."

"That sounds intriguing, especially since I have a pretty good imagination."

"Precisely what I'm counting on, my bloom."

"Come get me."

"Already on my way."

EPILOGUE

Dreams were forever changed when Arachne came into Morpheus's life. Creatively, one picked up where the other left off. The illusions they created together gifted the dreamer with something they had never had before… A bridge to forgiveness and hope. Each scene the dreamer walked through, each experience they drew to them, held the opportunity to find meaning and resolution for decisions made in their reality. Dreams became a way for humans to make sense of their emotions and to face their daily fears through faith in themselves and those who loved them.

Time split between the Earth realm and the land of the dead. Arachne made deliveries of woven fabrics and tapestries to the shop on a regular basis. From Thyia's viewpoint, not much had changed since Arachne had slept through most of the hours the shop was open before Morpheus had come into her life anyway. While they had never met, a dream planted firmly into Thyia's mind had taken root and was now a memory. She was ecstatic for her friend who spent the majority of her time traveling the world and experiencing new cultures with the love of her life. The shop was busier than ever and was one of the only places in the area to carry exotic fabrics from other lands.

Arachne often joined Morpheus while he worked, something he had learned to rely on since she was able to pick up on the reasons for the dreams much easier than he could. They would spend hours researching and talking about the best resolution for a particular situation, then she would weave the dream and he would deliver it. Her ability to bridge the gap between immortal and human was an invaluable tool, and the souls receptive to receiving the messages she provided were forever changed. Forgiveness was a common theme they helped with.

In some ways, it allowed them to plant seeds of change in those open to it, and in others, they pulled the fears like poison from a wound. When those who had spent their lives dispelling evil finally came to the Underworld, they were received with open arms by Pandora. After drawing the world's ills from the souls of saints, heroes, and spiritual guides, Pandora was closer to seeing her husband than she had been in a millennium. Athena had just finished escorting one such visitor.

"I really like her," Pandora said with a smile.

"I thought you would," Athena agreed. "She lived her life with such grace and strength of character. She reminds me a lot of you."

Pandora watched as the newest etched symbol was filled in with a stunning blue hue. The color was identical to the robes the woman had worn. The circle was complete. "One step closer, my love." She closed her eyes and drew in a breath, before turning to her guest. "You honor me, my goddess. I am merely fulfilling my purpose, completing the tasks I was designed for."

Athena looked at her with pity. Pandora was aware of the thoughts Athena had about the purposes they all served. "And in your case, it's been particularly cruel. Curse the Titans."

Pandora laughed. "Better not let them hear you, the walls have ears. Especially in this place." She gave a wink as she rubbed her back and sat down. "Sorry, I need to sit. She's getting larger by the day now."

"Of course," Athena said as she sat across from her.

"What I meant was that there are some humans that are designed for one thing but embrace a chosen role for the betterment of others. They enrich the lives of strangers then provide a sense of solace to all they meet. That is a true gift to our world."

"Like I said, she reminds me a lot of you. I feel better every time I visit you and your little one. The day is drawing near I see. Soon this will all be behind you, and your story can be told."

"Yes, much closer now that things are moving along. The dreams that Arachne and Morpheus are weaving together have been helping immensely."

"They are good together," Athena agreed. "It's nice to see him so happy. The alternative made for some dark times in humanity."

"Especially with his ability to shapeshift. The messages from the divine had some devastating interpretations in his wild days. I'm glad that he has Arachne in his life to keep the story threads organized."

"Me too. Now if we could just get Ares to keep his bloodlust in check, we would all be better off. It's part of the reason I'm here, by the way. There is another battle underway, in Thermopylae, the Spartans and Persians won't let it go. There will be 300 men who won't be making it."

"I'll be ready for them," Pandora nodded. "Even in the worst of humanity, I've managed to find promise for our future through the eyes of those who stand for it."

"Which is by far the most noble of pursuits. You are a gift, Pandora."

Pandora rested her hands on her belly, one on the underside and one cradling it from the top. She looked down as if speaking to her unborn daughter, her soft melodious voice soothing Athena's irritation with her brother.

"I'm only the vessel, the true gift grows inside of me. Isn't that right, Hope?"

AUTHOR'S NOTE

I have a very distinct memory of borrowing the same small teal hardcover book from my local library growing up. I believe I borrowed it so many times that at some point I may or may not have kept it for much longer than the allotted 2-week period. I would bet money that I had overdue fees on it when I moved away years later since I can't be 100% sure I ever returned it. The book was a collection of Greek mythology tales, and from the first time I read these stories, I was hooked.

It isn't a surprise that when I decided to write shorter works as a palate cleanser between my fantasy novels, my thoughts turned to these stories. What is also not surprising was that I gave the characters a happily-ever-after, even though the stories didn't always end that way in the myths. I couldn't help myself; I am a romance writer after all. But I also try to stay true to the core of the story and include recognizable elements from the myths, like Medusa's snake hair, and Athena's "creation" of the olive. I had a great deal of fun turning the myths on their head and letting my Muse lead the way. She always knows the best places to go!

The first book was a nod to a little talked about Titan, Hekate, the Goddess of Witchcraft. I struggled to find stories about her so decided to remove the darker bits of the Hades/Persephone pairing and have them truly fall for one another. For Hecate's love interest, I've always liked tricksters (think Loki) so Hermes was a perfect fit for her. The idea that they helped the couple go on a blind date while falling in love themselves was just too good to pass on.

Medusa was another challenging character, well, because… the whole head thing. Pairing her with the very man who kills her was something I knew I was going to do from the start, but I also wanted to stay as true as I could to the original story. I knew the couple would be going through some stuff, but how it ended up was all my Muse.

Athena was a challenging character from the start. She is headstrong, stubborn, yet one of the most accepting characters I have ever written. When I asked my readers who should get a happily-ever-after next, she won by a landslide. So, there was another challenge… how would I stay true to the myth, but give a goddess who never had a partner a romance? When Tiresias entered into my mind, I knew his story would be tied with Athena's, but the how is always the issue as I noodle on a story. It took me a while to figure it out, and I am so happy with the result.

And finally, Arachne and Morpheus. To be honest, this was one of the most difficult books for me to write to date. My intimate circle of loved ones has suffered profound loss, as has the world in the circles they belong to. It's been a lot. It was thinking about loss, regret, and death, that changed the direction of this story, but it was the realization that the world moved on through hope and love that had me adding Pandora's character. I have to say, she got me through some stuff.

And while it isn't out at the time I write this; I just finished the first draft of Pandora's origin story. Like her beginning, the story is still being molded and formed, but I'm excited to announce it should be out soon. Like many of the women in mythology, Pandora became so much more than what happened to her. And like many of the women I know in real life, she took a bad experience and turned it into something positive and inspiring. I'm proud of the end result and I hope you will check it out when it is released.

As always, thank you dear reader for following my journey and for supporting my dreams by reading my words. I am truly grateful and appreciative you have spent time in the worlds of my creation, and hope that you keep coming back to visit when I head to a new location. I never know where the Muse will lead me… but I can promise you, it will always be an amazing journey!

Much Love and Happy Reading!
D.A.

ACKNOWLEDGEMENTS

These acknowledgements span over a 2-year period, and 4 books, and first I foremost I would like to thank GDRW for supporting me as a writer, a leader, and as a friend. Your network of support has been the thing that has kept my butt in the chair.

A big thank you to the Muse Crew, who let me chat through the beginning stages of my mind map for this story. Your "what ifs" were instrumental in bringing this story to life. You were the first to meet Tiresias and they will never forget that.

To my amazing editor, Alexa Nussio, thank you for guiding me through the wilderness once again. Your insight makes me a better writer. So glad you are on my journey with me.

Thank you to Jen at Sumo Design for another meaningful and artistic cover. I love how you take my ideas and bring them to life. The symbolism for every book just keeps getting better!

To Celia Mulder, thank you so much for taking the time to provide your input and ideas on *Athena's Challenge*, and in particular Reese's character. Your insight was just what this story needed.

To my family who continue to support my creative journey by giving me the space and support I need to bring these stories to life. I adore the office we have created together that my Muse now calls home. The bookcase is like a dream come true! I love you all.

To my friends, especially Barb and Nettie, who continue to read everything I send their way. You are the best cheerleaders a girl could ever ask for. I'm forever grateful the Universe brought us together. BFFs forever!

To my beautiful ʻohana on the island of Maui, mahalo for welcoming me during my stay there and for healing the part of my soul I needed to complete *Web Of Lies*. Your pain is mine, my strength is yours. A hui hou kākou.

Most of all, to my readers. It was because of you that these stories come to life. Thank you for your continued faith in me. If you keep reading them, I'll keep writing them. XO

Lastly, my acknowledgment wouldn't be complete without thanking those who were part of my life and who are no longer with us. My hope is that you all know how much I love you. Thank you for your continued light and inspiration, I feel it every day.

While it hasn't always been part of her occupation, writing has always been part of D.A. Henneman's life—poetry and song lyrics through teenage angst (no, you won't get to read any of them), short stories in college classes (perhaps you will get to read some of them), and random marketing materials during her stint as a flower shop owner. Even with all of that writing in her life, ten chapters of a book stayed buried in her file cabinet until she closed her flower shop. The timing was finally right, and the Power of Four series was born.

Most days she can be found on her blog posting about her writing journey. You can find her at **dahenneman.com**. You can also follow her on multiple social media plaforms.

Amazon author page: amazon.com/author/dahenneman

Facebook: dahenneman

Pinterest: pinterest.com/daauthor

Instagram: dahenneman

Goodreads: goodreads.com/dahenneman

BookBub: bookbub.com/profile/d-a-henneman

Universal Book Links: books2read.com/ap/xXG1QX/
DA-Henneman

DAHENNEMAN.COM

The best place to find other books by D.A. Henneman is by checking out her Universal Book Links! You can link to these through her website at DAHenneman.com.

Download a free bonus story by subscribing to the author's newsletter! Head to dahenneman.com for details.

Created as a curse... she is now our only Hope.